Stalker: The Search for the Truth

Stalker

The Search for the Truth

Peter Taylor

faber and faber
LONDON · BOSTON

333114

First published in 1987
by Faber and Faber Limited
3 Queen Square London WC1N 3AU
Reprinted 1987

Photoset by Parker Typesetting Service Leicester
Printed in Great Britain by
Richard Clay Ltd Bungay Suffolk

British Library Cataloguing in Publication Data

Taylor, Peter, 1942–
  Stalker: the search for the truth.
  1. Stalker, John   2. Royal Ulster
  Constabulary   3. Police shootings—
  Northern Ireland—Investigation
  I. Title
  363.2'09416   HV8197.5.A2

  ISBN 0-571-14836-0
  ISBN 0-571-14899-9 Pbk

For Susan, Ben and Sam

Contents

Acknowledgements

Writing a book of this nature, it is impossible to thank by name many of those who have made it possible – some at meetings which never took place. They know who they are and they have my thanks. Without their assistance, it could not have been written. My endeavour has been to make this book the most detailed and accurate account possible of these remarkable events and I am most grateful to all those in Britain and Ireland who have tried to help me do it. If I have failed, the fault is mine.

There are those, however, whom I can and must thank. My BBC colleagues at *Panorama*: David Wickham who pursued the original investigation with me and produced pictures to which my words seldom did justice; Peter Ibbotson, who allowed us to keep the story alive by accepting a hole in his *Panorama* budget that enabled us to build haysheds in fields; David Dickinson, *Panorama*'s current editor, for his tenacity, political skill and constant support; and Peter Pagnamenta, for providing the climate in which this book could be written. I am also grateful to BBC colleagues elsewhere: to Chris Moore, for his persistence along the shores of Loch Neagh and elsewhere, and to his colleagues at BBC Northern Ireland for their political support; and to Colin Cameron and those at BBC North West who bore so understandingly the intrusions into *Brass Tacks*. I am grateful also to Nigel Bowden for his excavations along the Costa del Sol. I must also thank Will Sulkin, my editor at Faber and Faber, whose enthusiasm and patience have always driven me on; Jane Robertson, who co-ordinated the production operation and all her colleagues at Faber and Faber who met the demands of a near impossible schedule; Brian Raymond for his painstaking legal advice; Heather Laughton, who for the third time has suffered draft and redraft before transforming my variable dictation into an illuminated manuscript; and lastly, Susan, Ben and Sam, for the 'J.P.s', for their unending support and tolerance of my ups and downs, and for handling the builders while I tried to handle the words.

A Day in May

On Friday, 30 May 1986, I was in Belfast researching a controversial 'supergrass' case. At noon I had an appointment to see an official who was familiar with the case and the issues involved. I hadn't gone into any detail over the telephone and the person concerned, whom I knew, had no idea what I wanted to talk about. When I walked into his office, he said 'I know why you're here. You've come about Stalker.' I looked surprised. 'You mean you haven't heard? It looks like he's off the inquiry.' I was poleaxed. At that stage nobody outside the tightest of inner circles knew what was going on. For a fortnight it had been one of Britain's best-kept secrets. The news didn't break until 2.27 p.m. that afternoon, when Councillor Norman Briggs, Chairman of the Greater Manchester Police Authority, told the astonished members that John Stalker was being investigated for an alleged disciplinary offence. I couldn't believe it.

I had been following the Stalker story for BBC Television's *Panorama* for over eighteen months, since I'd made a programme in November 1984 called 'Justice Under Fire', that examined two of the incidents John Stalker was investigating. I had kept a close watch on developments throughout 1985 and was aware of the sensitive nerves Stalker and his team were touching as they dug deeper. In the summer of 1985, producer David Wickham and I had tried to put together a follow-up programme, but the legal obstacles at the time proved too great. We did, however, film reconstructions of the three shooting incidents Stalker was investigating – which included building a replica Hayshed in a Buckinghamshire field. We thought we knew quite a bit at the time: but we didn't know the shed was bugged. We kept the sequences in the can, anticipating that at some stage the story would break. We never suspected it would break as it did. I dashed round to the BBC in Belfast to break the news to the Controller Northern Ireland. No sooner had I done so than an executive rushed in and said 'Stalker's off.' It was a front-page story anyway, but to those who knew anything about the shadowy world that Stalker had entered – of under-cover agents and covert operations – the news was a bombshell. Stalker, it seemed, had been 'got'.

At 5 p.m. I had a meeting already arranged at Royal Ulster Constabulary (RUC) headquarters to discuss the supergrass case; but that story was abandoned. I asked what had happened; they said they didn't know, it was nothing to do with them. Whether that was so or not, I suggested, people would assume it was a set-up. They were furious and one senior officer walked out of the room. I stayed up all that night until five the following morning, talking and trying to find out what had happened. I was awakened at 8.30 a.m. by a phone call from my wife. She was worried. Where was I? What had happened? While I was checking out of my hotel, there was a tap on my shoulder. It was a close friend, Peter Bluff, a producer for CBS News who was in Belfast doing an item on Lambeg Drums. He said I looked dreadful, and offered to run me to the airport. In the car I told him some of what I knew. He couldn't believe it either. It all felt unreal: fiction become fact. I caught the next flight to Manchester. That was the beginning of my search for the truth. This book is the result.

Chapter 1

A Policeman's Progress

John Stalker never wanted to be a policeman. Policemen, he thought, assumed their authority from the uniform they wore. Authority, he believed, should come from within. That was the view of John Stalker, the schoolboy. One day his teacher asked the class what their ambitions were when they left school. Two boys said they wanted to be policemen. John Stalker was surprised and amused. To him, they were 'wimps' – albeit tall ones – who wanted to achieve stature by wearing a uniform. Young Stalker, the school's star athlete, form captain and prefect, had no need of a uniform. By general agreement, he exuded a natural authority. As a schoolboy in the mid-1950s, he had no real idea, or particular concern, about what a policeman should be. He never dreamt *he* would be one.

His father, Jack Stalker, was a skilled engineer, acknowledged to be the best of his time, who'd worked all his life for Metro Vickers – the heavy engineering company which in the heady postwar years of full employment provided work for 25,000 people in Trafford Park. Thirty years ago it was natural for son to follow father into the firm, where a job and a pension seemed secure for life. Encouraged by his father, John Stalker was no exception. He put on a new suit, polished his shoes, brushed his hair and set off for an interview for an office job at 'Metro Vicks'. The journey across town involved changing buses at Stevenson Square. It was the kind of day that made Manchester notorious: the rain was coming down in buckets. For all his fleetness of foot over 400 yards, not even John Stalker could dash through the sheeting rain, leap on to his next bus and arrive for a job interview as his mother had turned him out. Stalker, who has always had a disconcertingly healthy habit of arriving early for appointments, was running well ahead of time, and sought refuge from the rain in a bus shelter. It was there, a few weeks earlier, that he'd seen one of the 'wimps' from his class, now proudly wearing the cadet's uniform of the Manchester City Police. The vision niggled Stalker. Across the road, through the puddles, was Newton Street Police Station. He'd never been in a police station before. On instinct he abandoned the shelter, ran across the road, walked in and said he wanted to join. On 2 May 1956 John Stalker became a police cadet. Thirty years later to the month, as Deputy Chief Constable of the Greater Manchester Police, John Stalker was suspended from duty. His police career, which seemed destined for a chief constable's office once his Northern Ireland inquiry was successfully completed, vanished as suddenly and seemingly as inexplicably as it had begun.

John Stalker was eminently suited for the Northern Ireland inquiry. Not only did he have the reputation of being a first-class detective, but his family's roots lay in Ireland, one branch on either side of the religious divide. Manchester and Liverpool had long been the historical magnet for Irish men and women, both Orange and Green, fleeing poverty, hunger and the Troubles – roughly in that order. In those days, Liverpool was the nearest gateway to prosperity, and Manchester was the first stop. John's mother, Theresa, came from a Catholic family in County Westmeath. Her father was a stationmaster who emigrated to England around 1910. John's father, Jack Stalker, was the last in a line of Orangemen transplanted to Liverpool. The bigotry of this side of the family became a legend. Jack Stalker remembers being taught to hate Catholics at the knee of his father, James Denton Stalker. 'If I had a rope I'd hang the Pope,' he used to say. And there was doggerel to go with the one-liners:

> When William came to England, the king of it to be,
> He brought with him a plant which they called the Orange
>   Tree.
> He rooted it and tended it and nursed it carefully.
> We, the sons of William, cry 'Down with Popery.'

Such gems were invariably linked with stories of how the young James Denton Stalker and his Orange friends used to ambush the local Catholics as they marched through Liverpool on St Patrick's Day around the turn of the century, pelting them with slates from the roofs; and of how the Catholics got their own back when Orangemen marched on the Twelfth.* But such lessons were lost on Jack Stalker. To him, Orangemen were right-wing Conservatives and his own political leanings were already well set in the opposite direction. James Denton Stalker knew he'd lost the battle and an Orange son when, on leaving school at fourteen, Jack took out a subscription to the *Daily Herald* – Labour's flagship in the old days of Fleet Street. The incentive to do so was a complete set of Dickens, at a bargain price. His father went 'absolutely crazy' when he discovered the family betrayal. In 1930 Jack Stalker joined the Young Socialist League. His political allegiance was sealed.

Theresa Stalker shared her husband's political philosophy. Nye Bevan was their hero. When the great man came to Manchester and electrified Belle Vue the Stalkers were there – part of the overflow crowd on the speedway track. (Toddler John was raised on his father's shoulders and dropped ice-cream down the neck of the man in front.) Because of the poverty they saw all around them, it was unthinkable that his parents should vote anything other than Labour. 'A blanket was a luxury,' they recall. 'It wasn't a question of passing the knives and forks. Just the knives. We didn't have forks.' When John was born in 1939, six months before the Second World War broke out, the family lived in a tiny two-up and two-down terraced house in Ash Street, north Manchester, which they rented for nine shillings a week. When John was two and a half, they moved to a slightly larger rented house to accommodate John and his three brothers, Michael, Tony and Paul, over the next twelve years. But the Stalkers still had no bathroom. As for many in those days, bathtime was a ritual – pouring hot water from a kettle and pans into a tin bath in front of the fire, with the attendant

---

*12 July. The anniversary of the Battle of the Boyne (1960) – the most important date in the Orangeman's calendar – when the Protestant champion King William of Orange defeated the Catholic King James.

risks of being scalded by the water or scorched by hot metal. But the lack of a bathroom eventually got the Stalkers a council house in Failsworth. John passed his eleven-plus, went to Chadderton Grammar School, and became the school's star athlete. He boxed for the county, played football and cricket and was victor ludorum more than once. But it was running he excelled at. In 1952 John Stalker was 'Sportsman of the week' in the *Rover* comic; his prize, a £2 postal order, a week's wages at the time. John sent it back, afraid it might jeopardize his amateur status. The *Rover* took the point and sent him a watch, which was stolen during a race after he had asked someone to look after it. In 1953 the Stalkers got their council house with indoor bathroom and lavatory. They'd been on the waiting list for some time when the Foreman of the council told them that Failsworth couldn't have its future Olympic athlete soothing his aching muscles in a tin bath.

Although John was baptized a Catholic, his Catholic education was short-lived in his pre-grammar school days, being rapidly terminated after Jack Stalker had an altercation with a less than liberal priest. In the confession at 10 a.m. one Sunday, the priest asked why the ten-year-old John Stalker hadn't been to the 9 a.m. children's mass. He accused him of being a bad Catholic and staying in bed. As a punishment, he dismissed him from the church band in which he played flute. John came home in tears. His parents couldn't believe what he told them. Furious – the priest had also asked John's name and address in the sanctity of the confessional – his father went to the church and confronted the priest. The priest was unrepentant and added insult to injury by remarking that he didn't see much of the boy's father either – presumably unaware of his Orange ancestors. The priest was informed that from that moment his school was minus one Catholic. The following day John came home from school and said that in assembly the priest had asked the school to pray for the soul of John Stalker, 'whose father is taking him into eternal purgatory'. From that point on the Stalker education followed a secular path.

At school John Stalker excelled at English language and literature and his ambition was to be a journalist. His parents

4

thought it a proper career for their son to pursue and Mrs Stalker wrote to Nye Bevan, asking how John should go about it. Bevan passed the letter to Michael Foot, then editor of *Tribune*. Foot wrote back, saying he should do A-levels, go to university and then get in touch with *Tribune* again. But for working class families in the mid-1950s, university was seldom an option. The Stalkers were no exception; they simply couldn't afford it. With regret, the young John took *Tribune*'s point and abandoned the idea. He'd also tried for a job on the *Oldham Chronicle* and saw it go to someone from the same school who was twelve months his senior. By this time Stalker was impatient to get out in the world and get on. He applied for a job with an insurance company. He had a tidy mind, and was good with files and at keeping control of paperwork. He got the job. But life at the British Engine, Boiler and Electrical Insurance Company wasn't brimful of excitement; it didn't even have a football team. After nine months of looking at the grey faces of his older colleagues John Stalker decided insurance wasn't for him and baled out. That was how he came to be sheltering from the rain in the bus shelter in Stevenson Square.

From the very beginning, John Stalker felt comfortable in the police force. As a seventeen-year-old cadet – interviewed by Robert Mark,* then a superintendent in Manchester City Police – he had no grand view of policing, no great visions of serving society or the community. To him, communities for the most part settled their own problems but occasionally needed recourse to an outside agency, be it the council to see to the drains or the water board to fix a burst main. The police, he believed, came into the same category. When they intervened they, like the other agencies, had to be seen to be effective, but they also had to be seen to be fair. John Stalker's yardstick at the time was 'Would I like anyone to do that to any member of my family: and if I didn't, would I expect a policeman to do something about it?' The yardstick never changed. 'Always remember,' Jack Stalker told his son when he joined the force,

*Robert Mark was later to become Commissioner of the Metropolitan Police.

'however poor the house you enter, the people in it aren't rubbish.' Stalker never lived in an ivory tower. Years later, when he went to Northern Ireland, he visited the bereaved families of the six men shot dead by the RUC and expressed surprise that they'd never been visited by the police. In particular, his friends say, it was the death of seventeen-year-old Michael Tighe in the Hayshed at Ballynerry that affected him most and fuelled his determination to get to the bottom of what happened there.

From the beginning of his police career, John Stalker was fortunate. Cadets started off by doing the rounds of the different departments, 'seeing a lot, saying nowt, brewing up and running errands'. John was attached to the Chief Constable's office, and the officers in it applied for an extension to keep him there. The office was a nursery for future chief constables. One of the officers John Stalker worked for was Constable James Anderton (later Chief Constable of Greater Manchester). Others included Constable David Graham (later Chief Constable of Cheshire), Constable Peter Wright (later Chief Constable of South Yorkshire) and Constable 'Bert' Laugharne (later Chief Constable of Warwickshire and Deputy Commissioner of the Metropolitan Police). It was not long before Stalker was confronted with death. On 14 August 1957 a BEA Viscount crashed during its approach to Manchester Airport. Five crew members and fifteen passengers were killed. Stalker was on patrol with a police car, sitting in the back of the black Wolseley – cadets weren't 'allowed' to sit in the front – when the call came over the radio. Four nurses were walking down the road. The experienced sergeant squeezed them into the car and sped to the scene of the crash. Soon Stalker was picking his way through the bodies, tray in hand, collecting jewellery and other bits and pieces which might help identify the charred remains. The smell of burning flesh never left him. He watched good policemen at work and felt part of the team. For the first time he felt proud to be a policeman; that day he felt he grew up. His grounding continued for the next three years, taught by men of great experience who'd been prisoners of war, built the Burma Railway and fought in Korea. But he didn't always parade his credentials outside the force. Manchester City Police didn't have its own sporting facilities, so cadets were made members of the YMCA. The 'Y' had dances on a Saturday night. It was here that John first met his wife Stella. He caught sight of her and thought how pretty she was. He asked her to dance. The band was playing 'Blue Moon'. 'He sang to me,' remembers Stella, 'he was a right smoothie. He didn't tell me he was a policeman.'

But it was the detectives that Stalker most admired; they were 'God'. He watched them in the canteen and playing snooker at lunchtime. He wanted to be one of them. The height of his ambition was to be a detective sergeant. They were 'super-God'. In 1961 he joined the Criminal Investigation Department (CID). He loved the freedom of movement and opportunity the plain-clothes branch offered and relished throwing away the rigid patterns of uniform work. Within a few days he was assigned to his first case, 'the Red Rose Murder', involving the death of Veronica Bondi, an ageing prostitute and former show-girl who'd turned to the game rather late in the day. She always wore a red rose. She'd been battered to death, strangled, and her body dumped in a back entry in Moss Side. Stalker remembers her face still covered in rouge and lipstick, her dress still that of a show-girl. A man was arrested. Once again Stalker watched good detectives at work, trusting their instincts but making sure they were never carried away by them. In 1964 he was promoted to Detective Sergeant – the youngest in the history of Manchester City Police. Normally such promotion came only after fifteen years' experience. For John Stalker it came in three. It was then he received his first taste of a 'political' inquiry. Manchester City Police was asked to investigate allegations that Stockport Borough Police had been rough during Sir Alec Douglas Home's election rally at the Bull Ring during the 1964 General Election campaign. Manchester totally exonerated their colleagues in Stockport. Stalker was also involved in the Moors Murders investigation – the case which ironically resurfaced twenty-one years later in December 1986 and was instrumental in finally triggering his decision to resign from the force. In 1965 Detective Sergeant Stalker was one of six members of the CID's Missing Child

Squad which was attached to the Hindley–Brady murder inquiry, in the hope of tracing other children who had disappeared – among them nine-year-old Keith Bennett, who had gone missing in a street market which Ian Brady and Myra Hindley were thought to have frequented that day. Keith was never found. (It was his mother's letter to Myra Hindley – who has since admitted the killing – in Holloway Prison in 1986 that led to her much-publicized return to Saddleworth Moor in the cold of that December.) This was also the point in John Stalker's career, working as a detective sergeant in the city centre's 'A' Division, when he first came into contact with men who became known as the 'Quality Street Gang' and whose associations with his friend Kevin Taylor were to haunt him twenty years later.

In 1968 Detective Sergeant Stalker became a Detective Inspector and was posted to Salford, following the amalgamation of the Salford and Manchester forces. He spent six months on a course for middle-ranking officers at the police training college at Bramshill and, on his return to Manchester, was asked by the head of the CID, Douglas Nimmo, to take over the operational side of the Drugs Squad. Manchester's drug problem in the late 1960s was popping pills, not shooting heroin or snorting cocaine. Manchester was the mecca of the North. Thousands of youngsters flocked to its nightclubs and dosed themselves with amphetamines and 'sleepers' to keep them going from one night to the next. It was around this time, when John Stalker was a Detective Inspector in the early 1970s, that he first met Kevin Taylor, who was then selling used vans in the Ancoats district of Manchester.

After his time with the Drugs Squad, Stalker was asked to form a small unit to monitor IRA (Irish Republican Army) activity in the city. Manchester had already experienced the Angry Brigade – a British (not Irish) terrorist cell responsible for several bombings. The police wanted to be ready should the IRA also choose to direct its attention to Manchester, as it had to other English cities. Detective Inspector Stalker was transferred to the Special Branch for service on the Bomb Squad. In 1973 he was positively vetted for the first time – a screening process designed to ensure that those involved in countering subversion are not suspect themselves.

In 1974 John Stalker was promoted to Detective Chief Inspector. The IRA struck. The Bomb Squad was ready. Manchester's law courts and a number of government buildings were hit. Bombs were also left in stores. Two illustrations show that luck as well as skill played its part in cracking the IRA cells. A group of Irishmen was having a meal in an Indian restaurant in the Wilmslow Road when one of them asked for a bottle of wine to take out. The waiter refused. The man pulled out a gun and shot him and then shot the policeman who came to the scene. There was a 'Wild West' chase through the streets and the man was arrested. On another occasion, an astute fireman called the police after an explosion and the Bomb Squad caught an active service unit in its bomb factory. Stalker's work in the Bomb Squad was highly regarded by his superiors. The former head of the CID, Charles Horam, remembers, 'He wasn't one of these airy-fairy Special Branch men. He was a sharp-end lad and he knew a lot about the IRA. His knowledge and his work there were absolutely invaluable in bringing those people to justice. I think everybody had a great regard and respect for him. He didn't suffer fools gladly but got stuck into the job. You could trust him with any inquiry you gave him.'[1]

By now, with experience in the Drugs Squad and the Bomb Squad, Stalker was anxious to get back into the mainstream. In June 1976, now thirty-seven years old, he was promoted to Detective Superintendent and asked to beef up the complaints and discipline department. He wasn't over-enthusiastic at the prospect of having to investigate his colleagues, but he was being told, not asked, and had no choice. He did it for nearly two years. By then it was time for a career move, away from Manchester. No ambitious police officer could hope to make it to the top – or would be permitted to do so – if his experience was restricted to one force. So on 13 March 1978 Stalker moved to Warwickshire on promotion as Detective Chief Superintendent in charge of the CID. Stalker was positively vetted for the second time. On his first night he was called out on a murder hunt. A man had shot three of his neighbours dead in the adjacent West Midlands area. He'd stolen a car and driven across the border into Stalker's patch. There he'd killed again, murdering an Italian and his wife who ran a filling station just outside Nuneaton. Stalker used the media to catch the killer. In the middle of the night he telephoned the Birmingham local radio station, spoke on air, and warned of a murderer in a Ford Capri who had killed five people, had a tankful of petrol and could be anywhere inside a 300-mile radius, from the south coast to Scotland. The man was spotted in a Derbyshire garage, and gave himself up without resistance.

A year later, the Chief Constable put John Stalker's name forward for the élite Senior Command Course, which trains and equips selected officers for the highest ranks of the police service. After a three-day grilling at an Eastbourne hotel, Stalker was accepted. One of his colleagues on the course was Trevor Forbes, then a Chief Superintendent in the RUC, who later, as Assistant Chief Constable in charge of the Special Branch, met Stalker under very different circumstances in the course of his Northern Ireland inquiry.

Stalker and his family were happy in Warwickshire. Only Manchester could lure them back. On 1 April 1980 he returned to his home town as Assistant Chief Constable in the now reconstituted Greater Manchester Police under Chief Constable James Anderton. For the first time in nearly twenty years, he moved away from the CID and assumed what was essentially a management job, administering a budget of nearly £200 million and overseeing the installation of the force's new office computers.

In 1982, ACC Stalker was given the ultimate accolade: he was asked to spend a year at the Royal College of Defence Studies. Students don't apply; they are invited. The College was set up on the recommendation of a Cabinet committee in 1922, presided over by Winston Churchill, then Secretary of State for the Colonies. It was originally known as the Imperial Defence College and in those early days its work was chiefly concerned with the defence of the Empire. It is now concerned with the defence of the West. Its purpose is:

To give selected senior officers and officials of the United
Kingdom the opportunity to study, with representatives of
the Commonwealth and NATO and certain other nations,
defence issues affecting the Western democracies and other
countries with similar interests and the strategic, political,
economic and social factors that bear upon these issues.[2]

In 1983 seventy-six senior officers, civil servants and dip-
lomats took part in the course. Two were police officers; John
Stalker was one of them. His fellow students were all of
brigadier rank or equivalent in their respective services. There
were thirty officers from the British armed forces – army, navy
and air force – nine senior officials from the Foreign Office,
Department of Industry and Ministry of Defence, and thirty-
five senior officers from Australia, Brazil, Canada, Egypt,
France, Germany, India, Israel, Italy, Jordan, Malaysia, New
Zealand, Nigeria, Pakistan, Portugal, Saudi Arabia, Spain,
Sudan, Sweden, Turkey and the USA. There was no longer any
doubt that John Stalker was a high-flyer. Now he was not just a
Manchester policeman but one of those chosen to be the ideological and institutional defenders of Western democracy, as
the curriculum makes clear:

The focal issue is . . . defence in the military sense against the
threat of external aggression, both in the NATO context and
in the setting of global power relationships . . . The central
theme of the course is the challenge of managing change
while preserving stability and the relevance of political,
economic and military power in this context, and conversely
of deterring and if necessary frustrating attempts by others to
promote instability and violent change through the threat of
use of military power.[3]

The course is divided into groups, each of which chooses a
particular field of study. Stalker chose Latin America. As part
of the round, his group visited the White House and the Pen-
tagon – although they weren't able to see President Reagan and
Secretary of Defense Weinberger, who were preoccupied at the
time with the crisis over the shooting down by the Russians of

the Korean Airlines jumbo jet, KAL 007, over sixty of whose passengers were American. They went on to South America, where they were hosted by the presidents of Colombia and Brazil, and President Pinochet of Chile. The prestige of the course was such that heads of state were as honoured to receive the students as the students were to be their guests. As his project, Stalker chose to study the relationship between urban problems and crime, with particular reference to the *favellas* and shanty towns of South America.

The course also concentrated on matters closer to home: the threat of *internal* subversion. One of the course headings in the first term is 'Protest and conflict in developed societies':

> The social fabric and cohesion of Western democracies, which affect their willingness and ability to defend themselves, are at risk when protest, the causes of which are legion, escalates to violence. In addition, support of the civil power in the control of violence represents a potential call on a nation's military resources. Accordingly a study is made of the progression from protest to violence, of the part played by subversion in fermenting the progression (including the extent to which this is encouraged and exploited by external sources) and of the remedies. *Northern Ireland is examined as a case study* [my emphasis].[4]

It was his experience and performance on the RCDS course that made John Stalker a natural candidate for the RUC inquiry. Any officer singled out for the course and who emerged from it with credit was bound to have the qualities required for such a sensitive undertaking. His year away from Manchester lifted Stalker on to a different plane, that of national security and the defence of the realm. That, in a nutshell, was the significance of that year in his life. The thought that anyone with a skeleton in his cupboard would be selected for grooming at this rarefied level was either inconceivable or a serious oversight on the part of 'the Box' (the name given by the police to MI5 after its box number address in central London). On a course of this sensitivity, whose fees alone (without accommodation) cost £15,000, there was no room for error. In 1982, the year John Stalker was selected for the course, his friendship with Kevin Taylor was well known. Taylor had already been his guest at several Mess dinners at Chester House, the head-quarters of Greater Manchester Police (GMP), and there was no secret about the holiday he'd spent in Miami on board Kevin Taylor's yacht, the *Diogenes*, the year before.

The course over, Stalker's rise continued. In 1984 he returned to Manchester and on 1 March became James Ander-ton's Deputy Chief Constable. Two months later Anderton asked him if he would lead a GMP team to do a job in Northern Ireland. Stalker agreed. No one suspected that John Stalker had a potential Achilles heel: his millionaire friend, Kevin Taylor.

Chapter 2

A Gambling Man

Kevin Taylor has been a gambler since his days in short trousers. He used to come home from St Wilfred's Junior School in Hume, to the consternation of his mother, with his pockets bulging with pennies and threepenny bits, won from his less artful friends in the privacy of the classroom or the school playground. While other children were playing more conventional games, the young Kevin was becoming master of the 'five-knuckle nudge'. He'd hold five halfpennies in one hand and spin them one at a time into the other. Odds were laid on the number of heads facing upwards when the coins had landed. Five heads – or none at all – was eight to one: one head or four heads, four to one; and two or three heads, two to one. Taylor would run a book and invariably cleaned up. 'Of course I was good at it,' he smiles, 'it's like everything else in life. If you don't do it well, there's no point in doing it.' Did he play fair? 'You learn to give yourself an edge,' he smiles again. But his mother wasn't too happy about the first signs of her son's youthful ability to make money; she felt he was doing something dishonest. A good Catholic, she sought guidance from her priest, a man of more liberal spirit than the Stalkers'. 'Don't worry, Mrs Taylor,' he said, 'I likes a flutter myself.'

Kevin Taylor and John Stalker both came from the same working class Manchester background. But the Taylors found life in those early days even more of a struggle than the Stalkers – not least because his father left home when Kevin was three and a half, never to be seen again. His mother subsequently remarried, but life didn't get any easier. Kevin inherited his instinct for survival from his mother. He lost count of the number of 'two-up and two-downs' he lived in. His mother would go to the estate agents, get the keys to view a house, have a duplicate set made and move in the next day. When the agents finally rumbled the new sitting tenants, the Taylors would move on, visit another estate agent, borrow the keys and start all over again. The average stay was two months. In the process, which inevitably meant ranging far and wide over the city, Kevin Taylor calculates that he must have attended every Catholic school in Manchester and Salford.

Kevin left school at fourteen just after the Second World War, when there was an acute shortage of men to work on the railways. He started as an engine cleaner at £2 a week and within six weeks passed out as a fireman with a man's rate of pay. For two years he knew nothing but the railways, earning good money, working seven days a week and often seventeen or eighteen hours a day. He wasn't sorry when National Service called and he went to the 17–21st Lancers at Catterick to train as a signals gunner. His wages dropped to twenty-eight shillings a week. He sent seven shillings home and spent the rest at the NAAFI, on egg and chips. But even eggs and chips lose their attraction, so he joined the boxing team for a more varied diet and bigger portions. When he'd worked on the railways he'd done a first-aid course, and on being posted to Germany soon found himself in charge of the medical centre. He got his mother to send him small tins of Nescafé, which he could sell on postwar Germany's flourishing black market at twelve marks a time. He spent most of the proceeds on food, 'eating horsemeat in restaurants. I didn't know it was horsemeat, but it was delicious. I'd never had a steak before in my life.'

When the regiment was posted to Korea, he could have waved goodbye, his National Service over, but he signed on for another three years, having tasted life beyond the streets of Salford. His only previous experience of the world outside had been two and a half days in Blackpool. He enjoyed army life and recognized the potential for a man with initiative and enterprise. He arrived at Pusan on the southernmost tip of Korea after the city had suffered heavy aerial bombardment.

A great black pall of smoke hung over the ruins: it seemed there wasn't a building left standing. It was the middle of winter, with temperatures down to minus thirty. The regiment was loaded on to a train with open billets and sent north to Seoul. The wind never stopped blowing. Half a dozen men had to sleep huddled together to keep warm. The landscape was as bleak as the weather, flattened as one army advanced and the other retreated, before turning round and pushing the advancing army back again. What stuck in Kevin Taylor's mind, as did the air crash in John Stalker's, was the terrible plight of the children. 'They were maimed and starving and frostbitten. Hundreds and hundreds of thousands of them. They had no parents, there was not a building in sight. And all these kiddies were dying.'

The regiment encamped near the lines where the 'glorious' Gloucesters had been wiped out. To combat the Korean cold they devised their own heating system and burned diesel oil in the bottom of empty shell cases until the metal glowed white-hot. But DIY heating along the 38th Parallel was a risky business. Glowing shell cases and canvas thrashing in the wind soon reduced the number of tents available. 'Then we had to start digging holes in the ground. They also kept us away from the rats. The Koreans buried their dead in shallow graves and the whole place was overrun with rats. We used to put loaves out to feed them so they wouldn't get into the sleeping bag with you.' Corporal Taylor put his initiative to work. On a trip to Seoul he increased his cash flow by organizing the collection of empty Coke bottles which the Americans had left behind. There were ten cents back on each bottle. But his real entrepreneurial skills were best displayed along the front lines where the British fought alongside their American allies. Being a medic, Taylor had freedom of movement to maximize the business potential. The American lines were dry; the British lines were not. Taylor was ready to rectify the imbalance. He took over Scotch for the officers and the sergeants' mess and beer for the GIs; and came back with American equipment. His going rate for half a dozen bottles of Scotch (at 6s. 6d. a bottle) was a Jeep. 'I had the best-equipped squadron in Korea. We had the most beautiful tents and cooking equipment and every one of the junior officers and sergeants had his own Jeep.' Kevin Taylor had a good war. 'It put some drive into me. I now knew there was more to life than shovelling coal into an engine.' None the less, home again in Manchester, fireman Taylor returned to the railways. 'What, you back already!' they said as they gave him his uniform. But he soon received a letter from the Chief Superintendent of the area, saying that he couldn't be reinstated in his old grade; and he'd have to start again at the bottom. Taylor slammed the letter on the table and said good-bye to the railways. But with the average rate of pay around £10 a week, few jobs offered the money he'd expected to earn back in his old job again. Better money was there to be earned, provided you didn't mind the risks to life, limb and lungs. Forty-two pounds a week plus bonuses was on offer from a battery manufacturer, working on the 'lead pot'. Taylor stuck it for a year, shovelling old batteries into a furnace a hundred feet high. 'If you got a whiff of the air, you were on your back.' By this time, Kevin's mother had remarried – a miner who had spent all his life 'working on an eighteen-inch coal seam in the worst colliery in Lancashire.' At forty-five he was worn out, his body covered in blue scars. He tried to persuade his stepson to follow him down the pits. He was wasting his time.

Taylor decided to try his hand at selling. He saw an advertisement in the paper seeking reps to sell sewing machines. After a week's training in Lancaster Gate, London, he was given an Austin A35 van, a load of machines and sent on the road. The technique was known as 'switch' selling. The customer saw a newspaper advertisement for the machine; the salesman arrived and showed her the model. She would express surprise that it wasn't quite what she'd expected from the advertisement. He would then point out that this was the small model, but if she wanted something better there was always the de-luxe version for fifty-two guineas, which did everything and came with a twenty-five-year guarantee. (In those days sewing machines never went wrong.) Thus the 'switch' was made. Stage two of the operation was to persuade the customer to buy it. This was done by the 'chop and close' technique: the salesman 'chops' down each argument and then 'closes' the deal. 'They'd only have a dozen arguments why they wouldn't have it,' explains Taylor. 'You have a counter-argument to each one. Eventually you'd get to the stage where they hadn't got any arguments left. They'd then have two options. Throw you out of the house, or buy the machine.' Faced with the master salesman, they usually bought the machine. His first week on the road, Kevin Taylor was put into Liverpool – the 'salesman's graveyard'. He broke the company's record. He then moved on from sewing machines to refrigerators. By the mid-1950s, frozen foods were just catching on, but in the pre-supermarket days Bird's Eye and Findus didn't have that many outlets. Taylor would drive round, walk into a shop where he did *not* see the Bird's Eye sign, and ask why they weren't into frozen foods. He'd produce a brochure and run through the enormous profits fish fingers could bring. He'd then point out that they'd need a fridge, but he could oblige with that too. Kevin Taylor sold a lot of fridges.

Taylor thrived on the one-to-one encounter, especially at cards. By the early 1960s, he'd become expert at a game called Kalooki, a form of thirteen-card rummy which first became popular in the gambling schools and casinos of north-west England and soon swept London as the gambling boom of the 1960s exploded. Taylor relished the 'head-on situation', the test of nerve, stamina and skill that came from facing down your opponent in a card game that could last, without interruption, for up to forty-eight hours. The winner was usually the one who was most awake and alert in the last four hours. Taylor never fell asleep. He moved to London to taste the life of a professional gambler. 'The money in those days in gambling circles was beyond belief.' He used to frequent a casino in Bayswater called the Olympic. It was the haunt of Greek shipowners and it wasn't unknown for them to lose a tanker or two in a night. Taylor never went home with a tanker. 'I just wasn't in that league.' In his three years at the tables in London, Taylor says he made hundreds of thousands of pounds. 'Don't forget, there were 10,000 people in London who were bent on learning Kalooki. They thought they knew how to play but they just didn't have a clue. They played for astronomical figures compared to what we used to play for in the North.' But the money didn't seem to go far. 'The lifestyle was crazy in those days. If you won a thousand pounds, you'd spent £950 of it in clubs and restaurants.' Taylor loved every minute. 'I'd no responsibilities: it was pure enjoyment. I was introduced to the kind of life in the West End of London I'd never even dreamed about. And I used to play a fantastic game. People used to come from all over the place, just to play me.' But the fastest hand in town didn't always win. On one occasion he gambled his BMW and lost – a piece of information that emerged only during a casual conversation with his wife, Beryl, in 1986.

Kevin Taylor had met Beryl in Manchester and taken her to London to share his gambling days. There wasn't much sharing about it. Beryl was very unhappy. 'I never saw him,' she says. 'He was in bed late into the afternoon. We didn't have any friends as such because he was working all the time. I was alone in a flat with only the porter to talk to.' In the end Taylor got the message. He wasn't prepared to gamble his wife as well. 'If we'd stayed there, we wouldn't have had a marriage.'

In the mid-1960s, Taylor returned to Manchester and went into the motor trade in Great Ancoats Street, the used-car district of the city. He's adamant he was never a used-car salesman; vans and commercial vehicles were his business. He built Vanland with girders he bought cheaply for £500 and filled his premises with vehicles he purchased from the rental companies with 18,000 miles on the clock. 'They were a bit battered but they were better than used cars that had done 100,000 miles.' He added a body and paint shop to knock out the dents and did most of the work himself – without protective clothing. He ended up with a prosperous little business, a collapsed lung and pneumonia.

It was after his return to Manchester in the 1960s that he made two different sets of friendships, which were to connect with such dramatic effect years later. The first set, which he made in the late 1960s, was with a group of motor traders who operated from neighbouring patches in Great Ancoats Street and who became known as the Quality Street Gang. 'They were local boys from poor backgrounds who tried to make money the best way they could.' The other friendship, made in the early

1970s, was with John Stalker, then a detective inspector in Manchester City Police.

John Stalker lived 400 yards round the corner from Taylor in a modest, small three-bedroomed house on a new estate in Failsworth. Stalker drove a smart Ford Corsair. Taylor drove a clapped-out Humber Hawk. On the face of it, the Stalkers were better off than the Taylors. The two couples met one evening at a parents meeting called to raise funds for Werneth Covent in Oldham, the school attended by the young Kate and Emma Taylor and Colette and Francine Stalker. The convent was poor and run by nuns who were ignorant of such worldly matters as raising money. John Stalker was a great organizer and Kevin Taylor could sell fridges to Eskimos. Their combined talents were a timely asset to the school. The friendship between the two families developed and the mothers shared running the children to school. When Stalker was promoted to Detective Chief Inspector in 1974, he thought it advisable to remind Taylor of the ground rules: that he'd always enjoy having a drink with him, but he should never expect any favours. Both their careers developed apace. In 1972 Taylor had acquired a short-term lease on a plot of land in Moulton Street, a few hundred yards up the road from Strangeways Prison. Through his company, MBE Properties, he built over eighty warehouses and small units on the site and rented them, predominantly to Asian traders seeking refuge in Manchester from Amin's Uganda. He wanted to call it the Khyber Pass but wasn't allowed to. Although Taylor makes no secret about being a right-wing Tory or of his adherence to the 'hang 'em and flog 'em' brigade, he's not a racist. Today his former tenants greet him with genuine affection as he wanders round the precinct lined with shops selling 'perfect seconds – socks and underwear' and 'radios, watches and high-class fancy goods'. It was this leap from selling vans to developing property that set Taylor on the road to becoming a millionaire. In 1984 he sold the precinct to a company within the Virani Group for a considerable but unspecified sum.

Taylor's lifestyle flourished accordingly. Over the years John Stalker was an increasing part of it. His friendship with the rising policeman and the invitations he received to dinners in the officers' Mess at police headquarters helped confer on the former motor trader and professional gambler a social respectability and credibility he needed with the financial institutions, as he climbed higher in the business and political world of Manchester. The higher John Stalker rose, the more valuable the friendship became. To drop his name in conversation or add him to a guest list didn't do Kevin Taylor any harm in the circles in which he now moved. But it would be wrong to give the impression that Taylor's friendship with Stalker was based purely on self-interest. Although Taylor undoubtedly benefited from it, the relationship was close and each enjoyed the other's company. Stalker found it useful too; he felt it kept him in touch with some of the realities of life beyond the police service. But Stalker wasn't naïve. He knew his friend's history and the reputation of his former associates in the motor trade. Early on, he'd advised Taylor to smile, be sociable, but to keep certain people at arm's length. John Stalker also took the precaution of making his own inquiries: he asked someone to make a quiet check against Kevin Taylor's name on the police files. (There were no computers in those days.) Taylor was found to have no criminal record, the only blemish being a fine of £2 for obstructing the pavement, 'smudging', taking photos in Blackpool when he was nineteen. So the friendship continued through the 1970s on the ground rules Stalker laid down: no favours asked and none given.

In 1972, Taylor obtained a pilot's licence and started to take his friends flying in the light planes which he hired from Westair Flying Services in Blackpool. John Stalker appears to have made about four trips with him. On 7 April 1973 Taylor piloted him to the Isle of Man. 'One of the joys of flying a light plane is that you can just pop over to the Isle of Man to have a nice plate of oysters while you're there.' The purpose of taking John Stalker for a spin on that particular occasion was kippers, not oysters. The weather wasn't perfect to start with. There was light drizzle on the windscreen which turned to sleet and then snow, 'with a million white arrows darting straight at you. I remember looking at John, who didn't look concerned at all.'

Afterwards he told Taylor he'd made his mind up they were finished, so there was no use worrying about it. They got to the Isle of Man and back again – with the kippers.

By the late 1970s Kevin Taylor had made his money through a variety of property deals involving a handful of limited liability companies, of which he and his wife were the directors and shareholders. His overseas ventures were less successful. He was on the brink of making another small fortune by exporting second-hand earth-moving equipment to Zambia – a deal which sprang from a chance encounter with an Asian trader on a plane between Nairobi and Malawi – when the operation collapsed. As invoices were being prepared for the foreign exchange, Frelimo guerrillas closed the Mozambique border, landlocking Zambia and freezing out the hard currency. He also tried a similar venture in North Africa, after he caught wind of the World Bank's plans for the Sudan. He planned to tender for the first hard-topped road from Port Sudan to Khartoum, but that too never materialized. 'These are things you dream about. If one of them happens in a man's life, that's sufficient.' Taylor had no reason to complain.

By the time John Stalker returned from his two years in Warwickshire, to become an Assistant Chief Constable in the Greater Manchester Police, Taylor had bought and converted an early nineteenth-century mill at Summerseat near Bury which had once been used to make blankets for Wellington's armies. Set in an acre of ground beside the river Irwell, it was a house for the man with everything – from an indoor swimming pool and jacuzzi, to bathroom scales that speak your weight. The seal was set on the millionaire lifestyle in early 1981 when he bought a yacht called *Diogenes* at the Miami boat show. He'd been introduced to yachting by an experienced sailor called Arthur Bowen-Gotham, who'd taken him across the Channel from Poole to Cherbourg in a gale. They returned in even worse weather, having been stormbound in Cherbourg for two days. Far from putting him off, the experience whetted his appetite for a yacht. 'The two happiest moments in a sailor's life', he reflects, 'are when he buys the boat and when he sells it.' Those early days were happy. In November 1981 he invited

John Stalker to spend a week with him, cruising around the Bahamas. On 29 November they flew to Miami where *Diogenes* was moored. But things didn't go according to plan. Stalker was seasick and the engine broke down just off Cat Key, the southernmost part of the islands south of Bimini. Taylor went below, leaving his friend on deck ill and past caring. He wrapped his arm in a large bath towel, lifted the engine cover, released the cap and was blown down the cabin. Taylor's arm was badly scalded and *Diogenes* was immobilized in a one-mile-an-hour wind. Flares were sent up but no one responded – perhaps fearing a pirate trap, which was not uncommon in those waters. Eventually they were rescued by a braver powerboat and towed into Bimini, where they rested up in a bar reputed to be Hemingway's old house. They drank beer, ate barbecued fish and the local delicacies, until an American sailor finally appeared with a spare part for the engine. Because of his injury, Taylor couldn't sail *Diogenes* and entrusted another skipper with its return to Miami, while he and John Stalker flew back to Florida and then home to Manchester. A month later, on 2 January 1982, the Stalkers were among the guests at the lavish party Kevin Taylor gave at his Summerseat home, to celebrate his fiftieth birthday.

Kevin Taylor was generous to friends and good causes alike, a prominent figure in the city's 'Charity Commandos', a Mancunian business version of the Variety Club of Great Britain. At fund-raising events like the one I attended with him at St Bernadette's Social Club in Bury, he was the first to peel off a £20 note for the raffle in aid of handicapped children; and, with uncanny coincidence, was the first to win one of the prizes – a luminous orange designer bag by 'Giovanni'. Kevin is invariably lucky in raffles. He has a cupboard full of prizes at home, which he raids from time to time to give back to other charities or to auction again. He sometimes brings them home again.

Taylor's apparent readiness to give his money away, coupled with his right-wing political views, made him a natural target for Manchester's Conservative Association. The Association was desperately in need of money and an enthusiastic fund-raiser like Kevin Taylor. 'God sent us this millionaire to solve all our problems,' one of them said. As Tory supporters fled to the suburbs and the left became more dominant in the city, many businessmen became increasingly reluctant to nail their colours publicly to the Conservative mast, lest they jeopardized their prospects and their local authority contracts. Taylor believed that Conservatives had to stand up and be counted and was prepared to put his money on the table to prove it. His introduction to the Association came in the form of an invitation to sponsor the annual ball. He obliged and, the commitment sealed, was then asked to stand as a candidate in the safe Labour seat of Cheetham in local elections of 1979. He canvassed hard and increased the Conservative vote by 50 per cent. But because of the attention his campaign attracted – Kevin Taylor is no shrinking violet – he also increased the Labour vote by 50 per cent. In the Manchester City Council elections of 1982, he was selected as a candidate for the Fallowfield ward, but withdrew and never stood. In 1983 he was elected chairman of the Manchester City Conservative Association, but by this time he'd made bitter political enemies within the party. Bluntly, they feared that his lifestyle, flamboyance and friends would give Conservatism a bad name. His fiercest critic was Anne Carroll, a former ward chairman and a Conservative party worker of the more traditional kind. 'The question is,' she says, 'was he a suitable person to be chairman of the Manchester Conservative Association? My answer is no.' The image that sticks in her mind is of the evening she was elected ward chairman in Lloyd Street Conservative Club. 'The door opened and four people walked in. Taylor was wearing a long black overcoat with a velvet collar. "My God, this looks like a B-movie," I thought. I shall never forget that moment. It took me about six months to 'sus' out Taylor. John Stalker knew him for seventeen years.'

Anne Carroll wasn't alone in her views; they were shared by a small group within the Association who feared the effect the increasingly ambitious Taylor would have on their party. They were worried, for example, by the plans he announced at a meeting at the Piccadilly Hotel to raise money and recruit members by sending out 'dolly birds' to identify Conservative supporters and then have their calls followed up by a team collecting money. They feared he was using the Association to further his own ends as he planned and hosted functions whose guests included Tory luminaries like Linda Chalker and David Trippier, as well as the Deputy Chief Constable of Greater Manchester. 'Taylor shouldn't be running functions; he should be doing the pools,' sniped one of his political enemies. Concern increased at some of the company he kept. Anne Carroll was horrified when one of the men she met with Kevin Taylor told her in the course of a conversation about law and order of the long periods he'd spent in gaol. To the police, he was a member of the Quality Street Gang. She spoke of her anxieties to members of the Management Committee in a move to ensure he was not elected Chairman. Certain members of the Committee conducted a company search of Taylor's business interests and concluded that he seemed to be living beyond his means, given the salaries he seemed to be paying to himself and his wife, the sole directors of the companies. In August 1984, as moves were made to oust Taylor from the Chairmanship, Anne Carroll says she started to receive anonymous threats. One of her colleagues, she says, was openly intimidated. Kim Berry had worked as one of the Association's fund-raisers, and in Kevin Taylor's office for six months in 1983. Miss Berry says Taylor spent a lot of his time drinking, smoking and playing cards in his office (overlooked by a portrait of Winston Churchill) with characters who were 'obviously unsavoury'. She wasn't happy at the way she saw the Association being run and left, although she was owed a considerable sum in wages. Her solicitor advised her to hold on to the car that had come with the job until her wages were paid. Shortly afterwards the car was repossessed, allegedly with some violence, by a former policeman with a criminal record, and another man. Taylor denies there was any intimidation and says the girl went wild and the man and his colleague had to protect themselves. But Taylor had more friends and supporters in the Association than Anne Carroll. He dismisses her attitude as the bitterness of a political rival.

The last function John Stalker attended with Kevin Taylor was the Conservative Association's autumn ball on 23 November

1985. On 15 January 1986 John Stalker told Chief Constable James Anderton that he was distancing himself from his friend. Six months later he was suspended from duty. Taylor said he was convinced his friend was a victim of a conspiracy emanating from Northern Ireland.

Chapter 3

Shooting to Kill

In May 1984 James Anderton called his new Deputy Chief Constable, John Stalker, into his office. He asked him if he'd be prepared to take a team of GMP detectives to Northern Ireland to do a very delicate and difficult job. He said Sir Philip Myers, HM Inspector of Constabulary for the North West (which administratively includes Northern Ireland) had asked him to make the approach. Stalker said he would. But Anderton didn't want an instant answer; he suggested he go away and think about it as the team could be in Northern Ireland for some time. He didn't elaborate on the details, beyond saying that there were some cases that needed looking into. Stalker said he didn't need time to consider, he'd do it. He was flattered that Sir Philip and his superior in the Home Office, Sir Lawrence Byford, HM Chief Inspector of Constabulary, had thought him capable of doing the job. Stalker was proud that GMP had been asked because of the reputation of its CID, in which he'd grown up. On a personal level, he thought that if a job needed to be done properly, he might as well be the one to do it. Although he wasn't directly familiar with Northern Ireland, his experience the year before on the RCDS course had made him aware of the political and security sensitivities of the situation there. When there'd been discussions at the Home Office and in Belfast about Stalker taking on the assignment, there'd never been any hesitation expressed about his rank or insistence that a *Chief* Constable should be appointed. A *Deputy* Chief Constable seemed an appropriate ranking for a job which, it was anticipated, would not involve interviewing under caution any officer above the rank of Chief Superintendent.

Nationalists in Northern Ireland (those who want to achieve a United Ireland through constitutional means) greeted Stalker's appointment with no great enthusiasm; here was an obscure Manchester policeman being sent to Northern Ireland to investigate the RUC and he wasn't even a Chief Constable. Republicans (many of whom support the use of violence to achieve unity) saw it as yet another attempt by the British establishment to whitewash the excesses of the security forces. Since the present round of 'Troubles' began in 1969, there have been four major, official inquiries into alleged abuses by the police and army in Northern Ireland. In 1970 an inquiry by Scotland Yard under Commander Kenneth Drury into the death of Samuel Devenny, who had allegedly died after being beaten by the police at his home in the Bogside during rioting in Derry, was unable to make headway because of an alleged 'conspiracy of silence' within the RUC. There were no prosecutions. In 1971 an inquiry by the Ombudsman, Sir Edward Compton, into alleged brutality by the security forces on the day of internment, concluded that there had been no 'physical brutality as we understand the term'.[1] There were no prosecutions. In 1972 a tribunal under Lord Widgery largely exonerated the paratroopers who had shot dead thirteen civilians on 'Bloody Sunday'. Again there were no prosecutions. Finally, in 1979 an inquiry under Mr Justice Bennett arising out of allegations of ill-treatment at Castlereagh and other RUC interrogation centres concluded '. . . if, as we have found on the basis of the medical evidence, ill-treatment causing injury could occur, so could ill-treatment which leaves no marks.'[2] Nevertheless the Secretary of State, Roy Mason, was adamant: 'The Bennett Report has not said that ill-treatment has taken place.'[3] There were no prosecutions. Without doubt, the inquiry Stalker was asked to undertake was the most sensitive and politically explosive in fifteen years of violence in Northern Ireland. Inevitably it became known as the 'shoot to kill' inquiry, although that is not what it was.

John Stalker was *not* asked to report (as is often believed) on whether there was a 'shoot to kill' policy but on the circumstances which had allegedly led police to fabricate cover stories in three incidents where six men had been shot dead by the RUC's anti-terrorist unit in the autumn of 1982. All three incidents happened in County Armagh at the end of a black year for the security forces. Twenty-one soldiers, seven members of the Ulster Defence Regiment (the UDR – a territorial regiment of the British Army) and twelve policemen were killed by the Provisional IRA (PIRA) and the Irish National Liberation Army (INLA). Fifty-seven civilians also died.[4] The two groups did not co-ordinate their attacks but there was sufficient liaison between them to ensure they didn't get in each other's way.

It is important to place these events in their political and military context. The year 1982 saw the rise of the Provisional IRA's political wing, Provisional Sinn Fein, in the wake of the hunger strike of the previous year. The leadership of the Republican Movement (the umbrella term for the IRA and Sinn Fein) was committed to a strategy of using 'the Armalite and the ballot box' to get the British out of Northern Ireland. Both were used to devastating effect that year – although the British didn't budge. In the elections on 20 October 1982 for the new Northern Ireland Assembly, Provisional Sinn Fein took five of the seventy-eight seats with more than 10 per cent of the first preference votes.[5] (Northern Ireland has proportional representation.) Tactically, the IRA had to reassure the harder men on its ruling Army Council as well as its traditional supporters on the ground that it hadn't gone 'soft'. The campaign in the autumn of 1982 left no one in any doubt.

As far as the general pattern is concerned, the death toll for 1982 is distorted because eleven of the twenty-one soldiers died in one incident – the INLA bombing of the Droppin' Well pub in Ballykelly on 6 December. The main targets of the Provisional IRA were the locally recruited members of the RUC and UDR. Government policy since 1976, when 'police primacy'* was announced, was that Ulster should be defended by its own

*This was Labour government policy based on a document called *The Way Ahead*: the RUC was to take over the army's security role as troops were gradually withdrawn.

citizens. In practical terms this meant that the price was to be paid in *Protestant* blood as nearly 100 per cent of those who joined the police and UDR were unionists. This suited the British government since (with occasional, dramatic exceptions) fewer soldiers were carried back to Britain in coffins, and suited the IRA because its enemy was more vulnerable. Off-duty policemen, RUC reservists, and full- and part-time members of the UDR were soft targets once they left their uniforms and guns at home and went about their normal business. The IRA's tactic was to hit them as hard and as often as possible, to weaken their will to resist and deter others from joining. That, the IRA reasoned, would leave the province defenceless and the British, reluctant to reverse policy and commit more troops, with no alternative but to negotiate withdrawal. This was the context of the IRA's 1982 autumn offensive in County Armagh.

On 27 August, Wilfred McIlveen, who'd left the UDR the previous year, was killed by a car bomb. A *former* member of the UDR (or police), according to the IRA's rationale, still constituted a 'legitimate' target. The thirty-seven-year-old barman left the Milford Everton Football Club shortly after midnight, got into his Ford Fiesta and, as he was driving off, was killed instantly by a bomb which had been placed under his car. On 7 October, a serving UDR officer, Pte Frederick Williamson (33), was ambushed by gunmen who fired about twenty shots at his Ford Escort. Out of control, his car crashed into a Ford Fiesta coming the other way. Both drivers were killed in the crash. The driver of the Fiesta was a twenty-seven-year-old prison officer called Elizabeth Chambers. On 16 November, two Reserve Constables, Ronald Irwin (24) and Samuel Corkey (41) were shot dead in a burst of automatic fire from a moving car while they were manning security barriers in Newry Street, Markethill. And on 27 November, John Martin, a thirty-four-year-old shopkeeper and garage proprietor from Armagh was gunned down. A man walked into his shop, fired a single shot into his head and a further two shots into his body as he fell. He was killed instantly. John Martin had been a member of the part-time RUC Reserve but had left in about 1976.

But there were two attacks in late 1982 which shook the

community even more. One was not in County Armagh, but its impact was felt throughout the province and nationally. On 6 December the INLA planted a bomb in the Droppin' Well pub in Ballykelly, County Londonderry – a favourite haunt of off-duty soldiers. Monday night was disco night. Shortly before the last few records, there was a huge explosion and the roof caved in.[6] The bomb had been carefully planted under a wall which supported the pre-stressed concrete roof. Eleven soldiers and six civilians died in the blast and the rubble, and seventy people were injured. After the explosion, the British Prime Minister, Mrs Thatcher, told the House of Commons:

> The slaughter of innocent people is the product of evil and depraved minds, the act of callous and brutal men. No words can express our revulsion and complete condemnation. However, nothing will deflect the government from its resolve to free Ulster of terrorism and to restore peace to Northern Ireland.[7]

The other attack did take place in County Armagh. On 27 October 1982 three police officers, Sergeant Sean Quinn and Constables Alan McCloy and Paul Hamilton were investigating a report of a theft. They were driving along the Kinnego embankment just outside Lurgan in their armour-plated Ford Cortina when the IRA detonated a 1,000-lb. landmine hidden in a culvert. The explosion hurled the car sixty-nine feet into a field and left behind a huge crater forty feet wide and fifteen feet deep.[8] Politicians and the public were outraged at the slaughter and there was terrific pressure on the RUC to act. The force was under great strain and still adjusting to the increase of a thousand extra men the Prime Minister had sanctioned following the assassination of Lord Mountbatten and the deaths of eighteen soldiers at Warrenpoint on 27 August 1979.[9] 'They'd broken every rule in the terrorist's book,' one senior police officer told me. 'In the run-up to the Assembly election, it changed from minimum risk to cavalier killings. It was a debonair, flamboyant approach to murder. It raised the temperature. We had to put in all our resources. We had to stabilize the community with high-profile policing. We had to get out on the ground.' The Secretary of State for Northern Ireland, James Prior, sensed the effect on the police. 'In the circumstances, the province gets very tense,' he told me, 'and particularly the police get very hyped up, which is perfectly understandable, and of course very angry as well.' The areas where the IRA had been most active were saturated with police, many of them under-cover, and covert surveillance operations were increased. Most important of all, the Headquarters Mobile Support Unit – the RUC's anti-terrorist squad – was sent in. In the space of a month, between 11 November and 12 December 1982, HMSU officers killed three IRA volunteers, two senior members of the INLA and a seventeen-year-old youth with, apparently, no para-military connections. On 11 November 1982 Eugene Toman, Sean Burns and Gervaise McKerr were shot dead after a car chase along Tullygally Road East, just outside Lurgan. On 24 November seventeen-year-old Michael Tighe was killed and Martin McCauley was seriously wounded in a Hayshed in Bal-lynerry Road North, again just outside Lurgan. And on 12 December Seamus Grew and Roddy Carroll died near the Mullacreevie Park housing estate just outside Armagh city. The three shooting incidents were apparently unrelated. Five of the six dead men were believed to be active members of the Pro-visional IRA and INLA. None of them was armed at the time. John Stalker had to unravel what happened. How he did so and what he found are the subject of later chapters. These are the bare facts of each case.

Eugene Toman, Sean Burns and Gervaise McKerr were three known IRA men who were driving along Tullygally Road East in a green Ford Escort. Toman and Burns were on the run; McKerr was their driver. Toman and Burns were suspected of involve-ment in the Kinnego landmine explosion a fortnight earlier in which the three policemen had been killed. The police tried to intercept them but they roared off. There was a car chase and Toman, Burns and McKerr were shot dead. The police had fired 109 bullets at their car. The Northern Ireland Director of Public Prosecutions, Sir Barry Shaw, consulted the Attorney-General, Sir Michael Havers, and charged three police officers – Sergeant William James Montgomery and Constables David Brannigan and Frederick Nigel Robinson – with the murder of Eugene Toman. The three policemen were acquitted. In his judgment on 5 June 1984, Lord Justice Gibson said the three police officers were 'absolutely blameless' and commended them 'for their courage and determination in bringing the three deceased men to justice, to the final court of justice'. His remarks caused an uproar. Those who wanted to believe that there was a 'shoot to kill' policy were now convinced it was sanctioned at the highest level. Lord Justice Gibson tried to still the controversy by making a rare statement from the Bench in which he clarified his remarks, and said they had been misinterpreted (see Appendix 1). He stressed:

> I would wish most emphatically to repudiate any idea that I would approve or that the law would countenance what has been described as a shoot-to-kill policy on the part of the police.[10]

But whatever Lord Justice Gibson's reassurance, the damage had been done. The words 'shoot-to-kill policy' stuck.

The second shooting took place a fortnight later at a Hayshed in Ballynerry Road North, in the country outside Lurgan. Inside the Hayshed were two youths, seventeen-year-old Michael Tighe and twenty-year-old Martin McCauley. Also in the Hayshed were three Mauser rifles of pre-Second World War vintage. The police fired forty-four shots. Tighe was killed and McCauley seriously wounded. No police officer was charged, but McCauley was prosecuted for possession of the rifles. On 16 February 1985 Lord Justice Kelly gave McCauley a two-year sentence suspended for three years.

The third incident occurred nearly three weeks later, on 12 December 1982, at the Mullacreevie Park housing estate just outside the city of Armagh. There was a car chase involving two high-ranking members of the INLA, Seamus Grew and Roddy Carroll, in a yellow Allegro, and an unmarked police car. Grew and Carroll were shot dead by Constable John Robinson, a member of the HMSU, as they were about to enter the estate, where they lived. Neither was armed. Constable Robinson was charged with murder and was acquitted by Mr Justice MacDermott on 3 April 1984. The judge concluded:

. . . while policemen are required to act within the law, they are not required to be 'supermen'.

Nearly five years later the inquests on the six dead men have still to be held. At the time of writing (spring 1987) the coroners are still waiting the DPP's decision on the Northern Ireland inquiry.

At this stage it is relevant to examine the regulations governing the use of firearms by the security forces in Northern Ireland and the law by which they are bound. The police and army are tied by strict rules. Their enemy is not. Soldiers carry the famous 'Yellow Card' (see Appendix 2) which lays down the precise conditions under which they may open fire. Police are bound by similar constraints. The card states that in all situations only *minimum force* is to be used and (in capital letters) 'FIREARMS MUST ONLY BE USED AS A LAST RESORT': a challenge *must* be given before opening fire and fire may be directed only if the person 'is committing or is about to commit an act *likely to endanger life and there is no other way to prevent the danger*'.[11] On several occasions the Northern Ireland judiciary has expressed its view of the Yellow Card. The Lord Chief Justice, Lord Lowry, said it was:

. . . intended to lay down guidelines for the security forces but [did] not define the legal rights and obligations of members of the security forces under statute or common law . . .
However, on reading the Yellow Card one may say that in some ways [the security forces] are intended . . . to be more tightly restricted by the instructions they are given than by the ordinary law.[12]

The army's Yellow Card and the RUC's force equivalent have no standing in law. Soldiers and policemen are citizens in uniform and as such are bound by the common law of the land which states:

A person may only use *such force as is reasonable in the circumstances* in the prevention of crime or in effecting or assisting in the lawful arrest of offenders or suspected offenders or persons unlawfully at large.[13]

In addition, in both jurisdictions common law permits a person to use reasonable force in self-defence and, in certain circumstances, in defence of someone else. This means that if any member of the security forces is brought to trial as a result of a shooting incident, the court has to decide whether the force used was 'reasonable under the circumstances'. Theoretically the same test applies whether a policeman is tried in London or Belfast, the only difference being that in Belfast he wouldn't face a jury but a single judge sitting in a Diplock court. But, as we shall see, case law in Northern Ireland has placed a wider interpretation upon the 'circumstances', which critics allege has given the security forces more latitude. In both the shootings John Stalker investigated, where police officers were charged with murder, the judge reached his verdict having considered whether the force used was 'reasonable'. In the case of the three officers charged with the murder of Eugene Toman (who was in the car with Sean Burns and Gervaise McKerr) at Tullygally Road East, Lord Justice Gibson observed:

> As seen and understood by the accused the car still contained three . . . murderous gunmen who not merely had given no indication of submission but seemed prepared to shoot it out or at best to escape into the dark. In those circumstances to open fire was to my mind the most obvious and only means of self-defence and the only step consistent with their duty . . . It was in my view the use by them of *such force as was reasonable in the circumstances* as appreciated by them . . . to effect the arrests . . . Their use of gunfire into the car was, therefore, plainly lawful . . . as well as being the use of appropriate and commensurate force in their own self-defence.[14] [My emphasis.]

On this assessment of 'reasonable force', the three officers were found not guilty. In the case of Constable John Robinson, who was charged with the murder of Seamus Grew, Mr Justice MacDermott concluded:

> I am satisfied that the accused honestly believed that he had been fired at and that his life was in danger . . . both in

relation to [the law] and to self-defence, the fundamental issue is one of *reasonableness*. That depends upon a consideration of all the circumstances and while policemen are required to act within the law they are not required to be 'supermen' and one does not use a jeweller's scale to measure what is *reasonable in the circumstances*.[15] [My emphasis.]

Constable Robinson was acquitted.

The concept of 'reasonable force' is ill-defined and that of the 'circumstances' even more so. They are essentially subjective definitions which depend upon the judge's interpretation. He not only makes his own assessment of the situation but consults case law on the subject which, in this instance, is considerable. The landmark case which examined in extensive detail the 'circumstances' which existed in Northern Ireland (as opposed to the rest of the United Kingdom) involved the shooting of a young farmer called Patrick McElhone by a British soldier in 1974.

McElhone lived with his parents on a farm near the village of Pomeroy in County Tyrone. He had never been involved with the IRA. On 7 August 1974 an army patrol came to search the farm after there had been IRA activity in the neighbourhood. They were looking for IRA suspects and carried photographs of the men they were after. In the course of their search two soldiers brought Patrick McElhone to their sergeant for questioning. They had difficulty in understanding him because of his rich country accent. A lorry arrived, diverting the soldiers' attention. They told McElhone to 'clear off' while they went to talk to the driver. The soldiers were nervous as they'd just arrived and this was their first operation in Northern Ireland. One suddenly thought that McElhone might have been on the list of suspects and went back to his sergeant to check. McElhone had gone, as he'd been told. The soldier was ordered to go after him. He caught McElhone up as he was crossing a field a few hundred yards down the road. The soldier was about eight yards behind when he called upon McElhone to halt. McElhone broke into a run. The soldier, Corporal Jones, brought him down with a single shot. He was charged with murder. The community was shocked and television film of his ageing parents, both simple and uncomprehending country folk, remains a moving image. They were awarded a £3,000 *ex gratia* payment (no liability accepted) and were commended by the judge for their lack of hostility towards the soldiers who had killed their son.[16] The judge who heard the case was the same Mr Justice MacDermott who later acquitted Constable John Robinson for the murder of Seamus Grew. In a famous and controversial judgment delivered on 27 March 1975, he made it clear that McElhone was 'an entirely innocent person in no way involved in terrorist activity', but said he had to decide whether the force used by Corporal Jones was reasonable under the circumstances. In a twenty-four-page judgment he concluded that, because Northern Ireland was a 'war or quasi-war situation' and because the soldier honestly believed at the time that McElhone was a terrorist who was seeking to escape, the force used was reasonable under the circumstances. Corporal Jones was found not guilty of murder.[17]

The Attorney-General, Sam Silkin, was not happy with the judge's broad interpretation of 'reasonable under the circumstances' and exercised his rarely used power to seek an opinion on the point of law from the Northern Ireland Court of Appeal.[18] But the Lord Justices did not reach a unanimous verdict. The Lord Chief Justice, Lord Lowry, and Lord Justice Jones agreed with Mr Justice MacDermott's interpretation. Lord Justice McGonigal did not. The Attorney-General then referred the case to the House of Lords. In his leading judgment, Lord Diplock made it abundantly clear that in Northern Ireland the 'circumstances' were very different from those existing in the rest of the United Kingdom, and the view that the security forces were 'citizens in uniform' was misleading in the context of Northern Ireland because:

> In some parts of the province there has existed for some
> years now a state of armed and clandestinely organized
> insurrection against the lawful government of Her Majesty by
> persons seeking to gain political ends by violent means – that
> is, by committing murder and other crimes of violence against

persons and property. Due to the efforts of the army and
police to suppress it, the insurrection has been sporadic in its
manifestations but, as events have repeatedly shown, if
vigilance is relaxed the violence erupts again.[19]

In conclusion Lord Diplock said that the court had to balance
the harm that might be done to McElhone (by the soldier
opening fire) against the harm which might have been caused by
his escape. This he specified to be:

The killing or wounding of members of the patrol by
terrorists in ambush and the effect of this success by members
of the Provisional IRA in encouraging the continuance of the
armed insurrection and all the misery and destruction of life
and property that terrorist activity in Northern Ireland has
entailed.[20]

Lord Diplock's critics feared that his judgment so widened
the interpretation of what was 'reasonable under the circumstances' that it would render the successful prosecution of members of the security forces increasingly difficult as well as
deterring the prosecuting authorities from bringing charges in
the first place. Some of these fears may have been justified.
Since 1969 over 1,300 civilians have been killed in Northern
Ireland. It is estimated that loyalist paramilitaries have been
responsible for over 560 of those deaths, Republican para-
militaries (IRA and INLA) for over 490 and the security forces
(British Army, UDR and RUC) for 160.[21] As of October 1986
eight regular soldiers, six members of the UDR and five RUC
officers have been prosecuted for murder or manslaughter in
connection with incidents involving the lethal use of firearms
while on duty. Two soldiers were convicted (one for murder
and one for manslaughter); all four UDR members were convicted of murder; and all four RUC officers were acquitted.[22]
Three of them had been charged with the murder of Eugene
Toman at Tullygally Road East, and the fourth with the murder
of Seamus Grew at Mullacreevie Park.

On the face of it, these four police officers were more than
just 'citizens in uniform'. They were members of the RUC's

anti-terrorist flying squad, the Headquarters Mobile Support Unit that had been set up within the RUC under the control and direction of the Special Branch. The Special Branch had been set up in England in the nineteenth century to counter Irish terrorism. This group of specially selected officers was trained by the Special Air Service (SAS) and other army units to operate at close quarters. In 1982, the average age of the officers in the HMSU was twenty-eight and the average length of police service nine years. A handful of them were former British soldiers.[23] There are two HMSUs, each with around two dozen officers. A Special Branch inspector is in charge of each unit. The unit is broken down into smaller groups of three or four Special Branch officers, each with a sergeant in charge. They operate in unmarked vehicles, known as 'Q' cars. Overall command of the HMSUs rests with a Special Branch superintendent who is answerable to the Assistant Chief Constable at police headquarters who is head of the Special Branch.

The origin of these units goes back to the 'AA' (anti-assassination) squads of the early 1970s, but their equipment, training and tactics evolved over the years to respond to the changing threat posed by the Republican and Loyalist para-militaries. If police officers were met with maximum force, it was argued, they had to be in a position to respond accordingly. As a senior officer told me, 'We tended to be a little behind on the ball. We had to carry on with normal policing duties whilst gearing up to face a full-scale terrorist threat.' By 1982 the HMSU was on the ball, although many of its successes went unrecorded as they were seldom publicly attributed to it. The key to its operations was intelligence provided by one of the RUC's most secret Special Branch departments, E4A, often supplemented by information from Army Intelligence and the Security Service, MI5. It's impossible to say with precision how the RUC Special Branch is structured, but there is reason to believe it is along the following lines. 'E' is the RUC code for the Special Branch. E Department has five sections: Administration (E1); Legal Services (E2); Intelligence (E3); Operations (E4); and E5, which involves the Special Military Intelligence Unit (SMIU).[24] The Special Branch works closely with the

Security Service (MI5) and Army Intelligence. The Security Service has a presence in Northern Ireland in the person of the Director and Co-ordinator of Intelligence (DCI) who works from the Northern Ireland Office at Stormont Castle. MI5 is also represented at RUC headquarters in the form of a Security Liaison Office, staffed by MI5 field officers who liaise directly with Special Branch Intelligence (E3) and Operations (E4). E4A, the undercover surveillance unit involved in the area Stalker investigated, is the sub-section of E4 (Operations) responsible for carrying out physical and technical surveillance. The HMSU is usually mobilized by E4 on the basis of intelligence fed back by E4A. A rare public glimpse of the training and operation of the HMSU was given in court by the RUC's Deputy Chief Constable, Michael McAtamney, at the trials of the officers charged with two of the shootings. At the trial of Constable John Robinson, who was charged with the murder of Seamus Grew, McAtamney explained the training of the unit to which Robinson belonged:

> *Michael Lavery QC*: And did they receive training that other members of the police force did not?
>
> *Michael McAtamney*: They did. They received it by a selection process first and then a two-week assessment in which they would assess aptitude, mental ability, fitness, endurance under pressure. And then a four-week course of training – and a week of that would be taken up with firearms . . . The type of firearms training was quite extensive in that they spent a number of hours in what they called dry-range tactics – that is, static, seated and walking – and they were trained to anticipate being attacked in any of those positions. This is particularly [the case] with a hand weapon and they had to produce a very high response without a weapon and then they would do that with weapons for longer periods . . .
>
> *Judge*: And the second phase was?
>
> *McA*: The second phase would be using live ammunition. The whole idea was to produce a very quick response. In other words, he would know exactly what he had to do when

attacked. They would add to that then, people firing beside him with live ammunition and that would be done under different conditions – under stress, under oppressive conditions and in conditions in which they would have to identify a target from amongst people not involved – in other words a gunman and innocent bystanders. They would be expected to identify that and respond quickly and their performance under these conditions would be assessed afterwards . . .

Lavery: And once a dangerous target was identified, it is their training and duty to neutralize that as effectively as they can?

McA: Yes, that is their training.

Lavery: And the key words in training are I think 'firepower, speed and aggression'?

McA: That is the terminology, yes . . . if they wait too long they may be dead, but if they react too quickly . . .

Lavery: An innocent person may suffer?

McA: Yes.

Lavery: But the duties these men are selected for are possibly the most dangerous duties on the police force?

McA: They would be at the forefront, yes.

Lavery: And their whole work really is the apprehension and confrontation with dangerous men?

McA: That and the protection of certain targets . . .

Lavery: And notwithstanding the situation in Northern Ireland, police officers are not really like soldiers in a trench. They are not under fire every day?

McA: No, a great deal of the work is normal police work.

Lavery: So they do not have an opportunity to acquire a great deal of experience of battle conditions?

McA: Well, the great majority of the force would not be

trained to anything like these standards.

Lavery: So once an officer then takes the decision to open fire, there is no question in those circumstances of his simply firing to wound or disable or to fire warning shots?

McA: There would be no warning shots. And certainly it would be governed by the qualification that minimum force should be used, but at the same time the objective of this training is to eliminate the threat.

Lavery: And the only way to do that is by bringing to bear as much firepower as you have in the time possible?

McA: Yes, the necessary firepower. [25]

Two months later, at the trial of Sergeant William James Montgomery and Constables David Brannigan and Frederick Nigel Robinson (not to be confused with Constable John Robinson), who were accused of the murder of Eugene Toman, McAtamney was in the witness box again. This time he gave evidence about shooting to kill.

McA: Their training is on the basis that once they have decided they are entitled to open fire, that they should fire, in order to put their assailant out of action as quickly as possible.

QC: Would that involve the application of a considerable degree of firepower on any given occasion?

McA: Well, the necessary amount.

QC: Does that mean that, like the army, they are trained to fire at a part which would be fatal rather than shoot at the legs?

McA: That's right, actually to aim at the largest target.

QC: The largest target?

McA: Yes, which is in fact the trunk.

QC: When you say 'Put them out of action' – do you mean permanently out of action?

McA: Yes, in that situation.

QC: And is that because experience shows that unless you do that, unless you take those steps, there is a potential risk from the target to the various police?

McA: There is . . . if the person is armed and one is shooting at the legs. Their training is based on shooting at the largest target.[26]

There was no doubt that the instructions given to members of these units were that once they had decided to open fire, they should shoot to kill. But it does not follow that there was a shoot to kill policy in the sense that they were under orders by their superiors, acting with or without the tacit approval of government, to eliminate known members of the IRA – like the INLA leader, Dominic McGlinchey, 'the most wanted man in Ulster'. James Prior, Secretary of State at the time of the shootings, remains adamant that there was no shoot-to-kill policy. I asked him whether there was ever any feeling at the time that suspected 'hit men' like Dominic McGlinchey should be 'taken out' or 'got'. 'I never heard it expressed like that,' he replied. 'I don't think any of us would have minded particularly if McGlinchey had been "got" – but that wasn't the way we ever talked – and we were very careful not to talk in that way. I'm absolutely emphatic that as far as I was personally concerned, and as far as my office was concerned, there was absolutely no change of policy. There never has been a shoot-to-kill policy emanating from the Secretary of State's office at any level. Never.' But what made many nationalists incredulous, in particular politicians like Seamus Mallon of the Social Democratic and Labour Party (SDLP), was not only the fact that five of the six dead men were known IRA activists and were unarmed when they were killed, but that when the cases came to court it was revealed that the police officers involved in the shootings had taken part in an elaborate cover-up, designed to hide the true facts of what happened in each instance. This is where John Stalker began his search for the truth. It led him into the dark world of intelligence, covert operations and informers.

Chapter 4

A Very Dangerous Game

Intelligence is the key to winning or containing a guerrilla war. Through its experience in postwar counter-insurgency operations – from fighting the Mau Mau in Kenya, EOKA in Cyprus and FLOSY (Front for the Liberation of South Yemen) in Aden to countering the IRA and other paramilitaries in Northern Ireland – the British Army has probably acquired more experience and knowledge of counter-insurgency techniques than any other army in the world. Brigadier General Sir Frank Kitson, the acknowledged authority in this field, who first used converted terrorists to defeat the Mau Mau in Kenya, observes:

> Two separate functions are . . . involved in putting troops
> into contact with insurgents. The first one consists of
> collecting background information, and the second involves
> developing it into contact information.[1]

The first function is the responsibility of the intelligence organizations – be they Military Intelligence, MI5, MI6 or the Special Branch. The second is the responsibility of operational commanders, be they in charge of 'special forces' (SAS or otherwise) or, as in the three cases investigated by John Stalker, the Special Branch officers who directed the HMSUs. The information which feeds the intelligence services comes from a variety of sources ranging from the careful observations of soldiers and policemen on the ground to covert observation posts (OPs), telephone tapping and sophisticated electronic surveillance. But the most important and sensitive source of intelligence is provided by informers – or 'touts', one of the most despised words in the Republican vocabulary. Penalties for 'touting' range from tarring and feathering and kneecapping to a bullet in the back of the head, depending on the severity of the offence. Informers may be agents infiltrated by the intelligence services into the IRA under 'deep cover' or converted terrorists (CTs) who have changed sides for financial, ideological or personal reasons and who continue to provide information from within the ranks of the organization itself. More than anything else, the informant or agent is the instrument by which the enemy can be demoralized or destroyed. 'They're national assets,' a senior officer told me, 'it's impossible to quantify their value.' The essence of a clandestine organization is its secrecy. Once that is breached, its organization is penetrated, its operations jeopardized and its personnel put at risk. That is why the IRA shows no mercy.

This chapter traces the development of the use of informers and intelligence to the point where John Stalker was called in. In the early days, operations were often unco-ordinated, *ad hoc*, and hampered by the internal rivalries of the different intelligence services. By 1982 old differences had been buried and the intelligence systems, now strictly controlled and often devastatingly effective, were in place.

When the army came to the aid of the civil power in 1969 and subsequently found itself under attack from the IRA, the RUC's intelligence apparatus was not equipped to cope; Special Branch records were out of date, based as they were on the previous IRA campaign of 1956–62, which was largely fought in the rural areas. The 'new' IRA was born on the streets of Belfast and Derry, not in the hills of South Tyrone and County Armagh. The intelligence available did not cover the new phenomenon of an urban guerrilla campaign. After the introduction of direct rule in 1972, when Northern Ireland's own Parliament at Stormont was abolished and the government of the province was assumed by Westminster, an intelligence 'supremo' from MI6, the Secret Intelligence Service which deals with overseas intelligence, was seconded to the new Northern Ireland Office; his deputy was an officer from MI5, the Security Service which deals with internal subversion. From the start there were rivalries and problems between the two branches of the British Secret Service. Traditionally, Ireland had been regarded as the preserve of MI6, as the IRA had its origin and base of operations in the Irish Republic, but its grip on Northern Ireland intelligence was loosened following, among other things, the scandal over the Littlejohn brothers. These men were arrested in Britain in connection with a £67,000 armed robbery at the Allied Irish Bank in Dublin in October 1972. The Irish government sought their extradition. The proceedings were held in secret in February 1973, with the Attorney-General referring to 'matters which might imperil national security'.[2] Kenneth and Keith Littlejohn claimed they had been employed by MI6 to rob banks and carry out assassinations in the Irish Republic; they alleged the purpose was to bring about anti-IRA legislation in the South. The scandal broke over the head of the newly appointed head of MI6, Maurice Oldfield, who succeeded Sir John Rennie as 'C' – the Director of the Secret Intelligence Service. Oldfield is said to have called his troops to a meeting in the canteen at the top of Century House (MI6's headquarters in south London) and assured them there was no truth in the allegations that the brothers had been operating at MI6's request.[3] They had, however, been interviewed by an MI6 officer after they'd volunteered to help against the IRA, and the Ministry of Defence had admitted that Kenneth Littlejohn had been 'put in touch with the appropriate authorities'. As Rennie's deputy, Oldfield was said to have expressed doubts about the control that the Director had over the innumerable sub-agents or 'cut-out' men employed by his field officers.[4] Neither was Oldfield reported to have been happy about the role of MI6 in Northern Ireland; he felt it was more desirable and constitutionally appropriate that MI5 (the domestic intelligence service) should do the job. By the end of 1973 the intelligence services in Northern Ireland had been reshuffled and improved much more to Oldfield's liking. The MI6 officer stationed in the Northern Ireland Office at Stormont Castle was relieved by a senior MI5 officer who became Director and Co-ordinator of Intelligence (DCI), and the MI6 Intelligence Controller at army headquarters at Lisburn was replaced by another MI5 man. Co-ordination between the intelligence services was said to have improved accordingly.

Despite the improvements, the wheels didn't always run smoothly and co-ordination often left much to be desired; it was not unknown for the police and army to be running the same informant unbeknown to each other. The beneficiary was the informant, who picked up money from both. The relationship between a source and his 'handler' is inevitably close as each depends on the other for survival. There were invariably two handlers to each informant as an insurance policy, lest one be killed and the source lost. A rare glimpse into this shadowy world was afforded in March 1982 at the trial of Charles McCormick, a former detective sergeant in the RUC Special Branch, who was charged with bank robbery and murder. The principal witness against him was the informer he'd handled in the 1970s, Anthony O'Doherty – known to the RUC as Agent 294. O'Doherty was one of the first 'supergrasses' and, at the time of McCormick's trial, was already serving an eighteen-year prison sentence for the forty-seven scheduled (terrorist) offences to which he'd confessed: they included bank robbery, attacks on the security forces, hijacking, firearms and explosive offences. O'Doherty alleged that McCormick had been his accomplice in twenty-seven of them, committed between 1973 and 1977. Additionally, however, McCormick was charged with the murder of a police officer, Sergeant Joseph Campbell of Cushendall. He pleaded not guilty and strenuously denied every single one of the allegations. Ultimately, McCormick was acquitted on all the charges on the grounds that there was insufficient corroboration of O'Doherty's testimony. The judge, Mr Justice Murray, accepted O'Doherty's credentials as a Special Branch agent:

> There is no doubt that in the years 1972–74, O'Doherty was regularly every week in contact with the accused and through the accused was passing extremely valuable information to Special Branch about the IRA and other Republican terrorist organizations, information which he had gleaned from associating with terrorists and frequenting their haunts.[5]

In the course of the trial, a senior Special Branch officer had vouched for O'Doherty's reliability and said that his information 'had saved many lives'. The story of the relationship between agent and handler emerged at the trial.

The two first met in 1969 when O'Doherty was selling a Republican newspaper, the *United Irishman*, at a Roger Casement memorial rally in Ballycastle. O'Doherty was one of those arrested in the internment operation of 9 August 1971 and was interviewed by McCormick before being released the next day. Six months later he was arrested again in connection with an armed robbery. Again he was interviewed by McCormick and this time started to give information. He was detained on the *Maidstone* (a thirty-four-year-old vessel moored in Belfast docks to hold detainees)[6] for four or five months, and then spent about two months in Long Kesh (now called the Maze Prison). On the day of his release McCormick was waiting and asked him 'to get into the Provo scene', keep his eyes open and report back. O'Doherty became an informer and provided McCormick with information about the position of between eight and ten Provisional IRA landmines which were then defused by the army. In court O'Doherty never admitted to being a member of the IRA. 'I do not know if I was in the IRA or not,' he told the judge. He said he met his 'handler', McCormick, around three times a week. 'If . . . there was going to be an attack on a member of the security forces or a landmine, I would ring him and we had pre-arranged meeting places.' The meeting place was often in the back of a blacked-out Volkswagen or Ford Transit van with a grille through which agent and handler communicated. McCormick gave O'Doherty a number of guns for his own protection. 'I was sitting on a knife edge,' he told the court. 'I was playing up to a point a double game and it is a dangerous game . . . a very dangerous game.' To enhance his credibility with the IRA, O'Doherty staged attacks on the security forces – one, he alleged, after consultation with McCormick, with a sten gun which he fired at a UDR patrol. 'I just fired in the air because it was immaterial,' he said. 'I was maybe sixty or seventy yards short of my target.' He got over a hundred rounds back in return. On another occasion he opened fire on an RUC Land Rover with the sten gun (allegedly supplied by McCormick) and a .45

revolver (supplied by his other handler). He also alleged that, with McCormick's connivance, he attacked a reserve constable's home. 'A gun and bomb attack on a reserve man's house was going to give me a bit of a boost up in and around Republican circles.' He also opened fire on a police station. Throughout the trial, McCormick maintained his innocence of these and all other allegations, insisting that his relationship with his informant was entirely proper.

The IRA grew suspicious, however, and those suspicions were confirmed after it had seized and interrogated a former Special Branch officer, Ivan Johnson. Johnson had left the RUC and started up in the cross-border haulage business. The IRA seized him one day when he was crossing the border. Johnson knew that O'Doherty was working as an informer for his Special Branch colleagues. He was held by the IRA for two or three days, allegedly tortured and shot. It was thought he'd given the IRA thirty-five names, including O'Doherty's. On 15 December 1973 Ivan Johnson's body was found dumped by a roadside near the border. The IRA lured O'Doherty to the Four Seasons Hotel in Monaghan. 'I walked in and I bought a drink and I noticed everything was not right – intuition,' he said. O'Doherty made a run for it, fought his way out of the car park and escaped. The IRA also made an attempt to seize him in Northern Ireland. 'They stuck a gun on me. They were taking me away to an interrogation and, I would say, probably to shoot me.' But the resourceful and lucky O'Doherty had a gun concealed in his 'cowboy boots', turned the tables and escaped again. He then went on the run, living rough and depending on McCormick for survival. 'We were like brothers at that stage, because I was dependent on Charlie and up to a point he was dependent on me.' O'Doherty was told by his brother that he'd been 'court martialled' by the IRA and sentenced to death. 'The party is over once they pass the death sentence on you. It stands for evermore, so long as they are in existence.' An IRA 'death squad' was sent after him to carry out the sentence. O'Doherty was in luck again; most of the hit squad ended up in gaol. 'There is plenty of "Provie" volunteers, but not many good hitmen,' he told the court. 'There are not many prepared to travel over 300 square miles looking for you.' Then he went on to describe how, in late 1974, he'd been trained in surveillance, camouflage and unarmed combat by undercover soldiers whom he'd met in McCormick's house. He ended up working for them too, without McCormick's knowledge. The first the Special Branch heard of it was through a phone call from the officer in charge of the soldiers, simply known as 'John'. 'I hadn't a clue,' McCormick said in court.

Although the relationship between Agent 294 and his handler may have started and developed in a routine manner, it ended in a most untypical way. The Crown case was that McCormick had not only been involved in bank robberies with O'Doherty but, on 25 February 1977, had murdered a policeman, Sergeant Joseph Campbell of Cushendall. It was alleged that McCormick had carried out the killing after he'd believed Campbell had become suspicious of their freelance operations. Shortly afterwards, according to the Crown, McCormick and O'Doherty decided to plant a bomb under McCormick's car to divert growing suspicion from their activities. 'A series of crimes had been committed and we were suspected . . . and this was to give the impression that there was . . . an active service unit of Provies operating in and around that area.' The plan was carried out and O'Doherty planted the bomb.

McCormick denied all the charges against him, and his counsel, Desmond Boal QC, maintained that his client was the victim of a Provisional IRA plot to bring down a Special Branch man and so discredit the force. He denounced O'Doherty as 'a killer, a liar, a hypocrite, a play-actor, a devious and plausible villain and a maker of bargains with police'. He also described him as 'a person of considerable intellectual dexterity, which he frequently used to attribute to other people crimes which he himself committed, or in which he was involved'.

On 2 April 1982, Mr Justice Murray delivered a judgment which was of added significance, given the other 'supergrass' trials which were to follow. He said:

It will be highly dangerous and wrong to convict on any of the evidence of O'Doherty unless there is clear and compelling corroboration.[7]

On twenty-three of the twenty-seven charges McCormick faced, including the murder charge, the judge was not prepared to convict on the basis of O'Doherty's evidence alone. But on the four remaining charges, he said there *was* corroboration and sentenced McCormick to twenty years for the armed robbery of the Northern Bank in Cushendall, with concurrent five-year terms for possessing a rifle and hijacking cars. McCormick appealed and on 12 January 1984 the Appeal Court quashed his sentence on the grounds that the crucial corroborating evidence was not compelling enough and that the judge had run the risk of disregarding O'Doherty's character in assessing the evidence. Eighteen months later, the former agent became, like his former handler, a free man. On 7 August 1985 Anthony O'Doherty was released from gaol after the Royal Prerogative had been exercised, following a recommendation from the Secretary of State, James Prior, that his sentence be reduced. O'Doherty walked free, having served only three and a half years of his eighteen-year sentence. Critics of the 'supergrass' system saw O'Doherty's release as a cynical exercise *pour encourager les autres*.

O'Doherty's involvement with Army Intelligence was only a brief flirtation and is mentioned only to illustrate that on the ground one intelligence arm was not necessarily aware of what the other was doing. The army had always run covert operations in Northern Ireland since the early 1970s, but these were stepped up and widened following the operational introduction of the SAS in 1976. The army didn't mince its words in giving instructions: 'It must be made quite clear to each soldier that the worst crime he can commit – worse than buggery, rape or shooting another soldier – is to compromise a source.'[8] The tip of these covert operations was seldom revealed. The 'execution' of Captain Robert Nairac in May 1977 was one of the rare occasions when it was. Nairac, a Grenadier Guard who'd served with the SAS, was 'liaison officer' between the army, police and a squadron of SAS (about sixty) who were based in South Armagh. Much of his work was, necessarily, under cover. Posthumously, his activities became a legend. Nairac blended into the human landscape of South Armagh so effectively that he could sing 'Danny Boy' in pubs and get away with it. (The Londonderry Air was played at his funeral.) One senior officer told me of how military eyebrows were raised on one occasion, when Nairac walked into a reception for visiting top brass from England, 'as if he'd walked straight off a building site'. Nairac's chances of surviving his year's tour of duty were rated as 50/50. He survived, but chose to return to carry on his work, despite advice to the contrary. He never came back. Late on Saturday night, 15 May 1977, at the Three Steps pub at Drumintree, where he'd been singing Republican songs, he was overpowered by half a dozen men, who suspected him of being 'a stickie' – a member of the Official IRA, with whom the Provisionals had tended to feud. Nairac was taken across the border a few miles away, to Ravensdale Forest just outside Dundalk, severely beaten and shot through the head. Most of those responsible were finally brought to justice – on both sides of the border. On 9 November 1977, in Dublin's Special Criminal Court, Liam Townson, aged thirty-seven, was sentenced to life imprisonment for the murder of Captain Nairac. In his confession, Townson is alleged to have said, 'I hit him with my fist on the head and with the butt of my gun. He said "You are going to kill me. Can I have a priest?" He was in a bad state. I aimed at his head. I only put one in him. The gun misfired a few times . . . He never told us anything. He was a great soldier.'[9] A year later, on 15 December 1978, Lord Justice Gibson gaoled five men from South Armagh for involvement in his kidnapping and murder. It was the first time a murder trial had been held in Northern Ireland without a body. It was thought to have been ground up and fed to the pigs. Captain Nairac was posthumously awarded the George Cross. One of the officers involved in writing the citation said 'Before we made the award, we just had to know whether he had given away any information when he was tortured. We found he had not.'[10] Captain Nairac's activities in Northern Ireland still remain unclear.* One of

---

*According to Fred Holroyd, a former Army Intelligence officer who served in Northern Ireland in 1974–75, Captain Nairac was involved in much more than 'liaison' activities. Holroyd alleged that Nairac had been trained by MI6 for work in Ireland and had been part of an assassination squad involved in the killing of John Francis Green, a senior IRA commander from Lurgan, North Armagh. When he was shot, he was staying across the border at a farm in County Monaghan. According to Holroyd, Nairac produced a Polaroid photograph of the bloodstained body. Holroyd claims

A Very Dangerous Game

Captain Nairac's former commanding officers told me that some of the operations he set in motion were still ongoing and that was why the matter was so delicate. I've always assumed, given that it is virtually impossible to get confirmation of such sensitive material, that the ongoing 'operations' were in connection with intelligence contacts he had made and which are still bearing fruit. Whether these would be informers he 'turned' or agents he helped infiltrate can only be a matter for speculation.

The Nairac story also illustrates another important aspect of intelligence operations. The five men from South Armagh who were gaoled for their part in his murder had, like hundreds of IRA suspects, been interrogated by the RUC at Castlereagh in 1977. The purpose of these interrogations was not just to obtain statements which could be used in court, but to gather intelligence. One of them, Thomas Morgan, like many others at that period, claimed that he'd been ill-treated.[11] Interrogation by the police and Special Branch that year came close to breaking the IRA, not just because it resulted in the conviction of many of its activists, but because it swelled the files of the Special Branch. A jubilant Secretary of State, Roy Mason, said:

We are squeezing the terrorists like rolling up a toothpaste tube. We are squeezing them out of their safe havens. We are squeezing them away from their money supplies. We are squeezing them out of society and into prison.[12]

The IRA had to reorganize or face defeat. It abandoned the traditional military structure it had embraced for nearly sixty years – with brigades, battalions and companies along British Army lines – in which, rhetorically speaking, everyone knew everyone else – and regrouped into 'cells' which were far less vulnerable to penetration. The IRA's reorganization Order, drawn up in the autumn of 1977, outlines this new structure and the need for it:

---

he handed it to Superintendent George Caskey of the RUC, who investigated his allegations. A file was sent to the DPP, but no prosecutions were directed. In February 1987 the allegations of 'dirty tricks' arose again, revived by Holroyd and another former Army Intelligence officer, Colin Wallace, who had just been released from prison after serving a sentence for manslaughter.

The three-day and seven-day detention orders [the emergency powers governing the periods for which terrorist suspects could be held for questioning] are breaking volunteers, and it is the Republican Army's fault for not indoctrinating volunteers with the psychological strength to resist interrogation. Coupled with this factor, which is contributing to our defeat, we are burdened with an inefficient infrastructure of commands, brigades, battalions and companies. This old system with which Brits and Branch are familiar has to be changed. We recommend reorganization and remotivation, the building of a new Irish Republican Army. We emphasize a return to secrecy and strict discipline.

We must gear ourselves towards long-term armed struggle based on putting unknown men and new recruits into a new structure. This new structure shall be a cell system. Ideally a cell should consist of four people . . . cells must be specialized into IC cells, sniping cells, execution, bombings, robberies, etc. . . . cells should operate as often as possible outside of their own areas both to confuse Brit Intelligence (which would thus increase our security) and to expand our operational areas.[13]

'Brit' Intelligence responded accordingly. A study was commissioned to examine the future organization of Military Intelligence in Northern Ireland. One of its recommendations was for a further study of future trends in terrorist tactics and weaponry. The recommendation was carried out by the Defence Intelligence Staff at the Ministry of Defence, and two years later became a secret document entitled 'Future terrorist trends'. It assessed the likely threat from the IRA and INLA over the ensuing five-year period, 1979–83.* The document had been prepared in consultation with MI5's Director and Co-ordinator of Intelligence (DCI) at Stormont Castle. It's an

*Much of this document was reproduced in the Provisional's weekly newspaper, *An Phoblacht/RN*, 12 May 1979. A year later, it was reproduced in full in Sean Cronin's *Irish Nationalism. A History of its Roots and Ideology*, The Academy Press, Dublin, 1980, p.339.

invaluable assessment, made at the highest level of military intelligence, of the IRA's strength, capability and vulnerability to informers in the period covered by Stalker's investigation:

Terrorist resources:
The Provisionals cannot attract the large numbers of active terrorists they had in 1972–73. But they no longer need them. PIRA's organization is now such that a small number of activists can maintain a disproportionate level of violence. There is a substantial pool of young Fianna [junior IRA] aspirants, nurtured in a climate of violence, eagerly seeking promotion to full gun-carrying terrorist status and there is a steady release from the prisons of embittered and dedicated terrorists. Thus, though PIRA may be hard hit by Security Force attrition from time to time, they will probably continue to have the manpower they need to sustain violence during the next five years.

Calibre of terrorist:
. . . there is a strata of intelligent, astute and experienced terrorists who provide the backbone of the organization.

Technical expertise:
PIRA has an adequate supply of members who are skilled in the production of explosive devices. They have the tools and equipment and they have the use of small workshops and laboratories.

Rank and file terrorists:
Our evidence of the calibre of rank and file terrorists does not support the view that they are merely mindless hooligans drawn from the unemployed and unemployable. PIRA now trains and uses its members with some care. The Active Service Units (ASUs) are for the most part manned by terrorists tempered by up to ten years of operational experience.

Trend in calibre:
The mature terrorists, including for instance the leading bomb-makers, are usually sufficiently cunning to avoid

arrest. They are continually learning from mistakes and developing their expertise. We can therefore expect to see increased professionalism and the greater exploitation of modern technology for terrorist purposes . . . The expertise of the ASUs will grow and they will continue to be PIRA's prime offensive arm.

Popular support:
. . . by reorganizing on cellular lines PIRA has become less dependent on public support than in the past and is *less vulernable to penetration by informers* . . . [my emphasis]
There are still areas within the province, both rural and urban, where the terrorists can base themselves with little risk of betrayal and can count on active support in an emergency.

The report acknowledged the increasing penetration of the IRA by security force informers and agents:

Collectors of intelligence:
The terrorists are already aware of their own *vulnerability to security force intelligence operators and will increasingly seek to eliminate those involved.* [my emphasis]

The assessment also covered the IRA's proficiency in the use of explosives:

Ingredients for the manufacture of home-made explosives are simple, plentiful and untraceable. Other bomb-making components will also remain readily available. But the Provisionals have been slow to exploit the effective techniques for explosive attack that we know to be within their knowledge and competence. We believe that, possibly aided by external contacts, their performance will improve. In particular we would expect to see . . . more use of radio-controlled devices . . . [and] more use of long-delay electronic timers.

This observation added to the following remarks on propaganda was a grim forecast:

Propaganda considerations will frequently dictate PIRA strategy both in avoiding action that would alienate public opinion and in mounting spectacular attacks that would capture the Press headlines . . .

Three events in 1979 proved the accuracy of the forecast. Their aftermath set the intelligence scene for 1982. On 30 March the INLA planted a bomb under the car of one of Mrs Thatcher's closest political aides, Airey Neave. As he drove out of the underground car park at the House of Commons, a sophisticated Mercury tilt-switch set off the bomb which had been placed under the driver's seat.[14] The INLA claimed it had killed him because of his 'rabid militant calls for more repression against the Irish people and for the strengthening of SAS murder gangs'.[15] The two other incidents happened on the same day, 27 August 1979. The Provisionals first struck in the Irish Republic. In the small fishing village of Mullaghmore in County Sligo they detonated a remote-controlled bomb which blew apart a small thirty-foot fishing boat, *Shadow V*, as it was putting out to sea on the last fishing trip of a holiday.[16] On board was Earl Mountbatten of Burma, aged seventy-nine, the last Viceroy of India and uncle of Queen Elizabeth II. His fourteen-year-old grandson, Nicholas Knatchbull and a sixteen-year-old boatman, Paul Maxwell, died with him. The Dowager Lady Brabourne, who was also on board with her daughter-in-law, later died in hospital from her injuries. Approximately 50 lb. of explosive had been hidden under the floorboards of the boat and were detonated from the land. Later that afternoon, the Provisionals struck again on the other side of the border and at the opposite side of the country. At 4.30 p.m. an army convoy of paratroopers travelling from Ballykinlar Barracks to Newry passed a trailer loaded with hay parked in a lay-by near Warrenpoint – just across Carlingford Loch from the Irish Republic. As the last truck of the convoy drove past, the hay trailer exploded. Packed into milk churns concealed beneath the straw had been 500 lb. of explosives. They had been detonated, again by remote control, by an IRA unit across the narrow stretch of water in the Irish Republic. Six paratroopers were killed. The platoon rushed to the nearest point which afforded cover, the gate lodge of Narrow Waters Castle. As reinforcements arrived from the Queen's Own Highlanders under their commanding officer, Lieutenant Colonel David Blair, there was a second explosion. A 100lb. bomb had been placed in the lodge gates in anticipation of the soldiers' likely reaction to the first explosion. Twelve more soldiers were killed, among them Lieutenant Colonel Blair. He was standing so close, his remains were never found.[17] It was the worst single disaster the army had suffered in Northern Ireland.

The events of that day shook the British government. The army had warned of IRA 'spectaculars' but two 'hits' on this scale, on one day, had probably never been foreseen. It was an intelligence disaster – a measure of the increasing strains that had been felt between the army and police as the RUC gradually took over the army's security role. The army was resentful since it thought it could do the job much better, particularly in the fields of intelligence gathering and covert operations; that, after all, was what it was trained for. The police were insistent, with government backing, that they were now in overall control of security – and that meant control of intelligence too. Differences of style, personality and perception between RUC Chief Constable Kenneth Newman and the GOC, Lieutenant General Timothy Creasey, did not help. Newman, the professional manager wedded to 'police primacy', believed the IRA would eventually be beaten only by a highly professional police force accepted by both communities. Creasey, the 'action man' and experienced operational commander, wanted to stop 'messing around' and get on with the job of taking on the IRA.[18] Inevitably the divisions at the top filtered down in both organizations and affected the collection and sharing of intelligence. The IRA was the main beneficiary. Mrs Thatcher became personally aware of the differences between her soldiers and her policemen when she visited Northern Ireland in the wake of the disaster of 27 August. Her response was to bring Sir Maurice Oldfield out of his MI6 retirement and appoint him as Security Co-ordinator. His job, as it was perceived at the time, was to 'knock heads together'. But within three months of his appointment the 'heads' at the top went and, therefore, the need to knock them. The next year, 1980, marked a new beginning. There was a new Chief Constable, Jack Hermon, and a new GOC, Lieutenant General Sir Richard Lawson, a carefully chosen 'political' general who accepted 'police primacy' without reservation from the start. 'There was total rapport from day one,' one senior RUC officer told me. 'From then on, Maurice Oldfield became increasingly irrelevant.' What Oldfield did do was straighten out the lines of communication and ensure that intelligence was properly co-ordinated so it could be used to maximum effect. With a new GOC who believed that police primacy meant that the RUC should be in charge of intelligence as well as operations on the ground, the obstacles to co-operation, particularly in the field of intelligence, were removed. An authoritative assessment of the situation at the beginning of 1982 is given in the security report, *Trends in low-intensity conflict*, published in the summer of the previous year. It was compiled by Brigadier Maurice Tugwell, who had served in Northern Ireland, and two academics from Canada's Department of National Defence following a field trip to Northern Ireland:

> Current policy emphasizes 'low profile' and covert intelligence operations – plain-clothes surveillance, camouflaged observation posts, covert photography, fewer foot patrols and more [patrols] in unmarked vehicles. The SAS has been in the vanguard of the change to covert action, but SAS-trained soldiers from conventional units are now carrying out an increasing share of the undercover operations. Regardless of the source by which it is collected, intelligence is now pooled centrally at the RUC Special Branch headquarters at Castlereagh, where army and police decide jointly how to exploit it. As in other aspects of security force operations, police primacy is being emphasized in intelligence work.
>
> *Strengths and weaknesses:*
> The most important asset the security forces have at present is the close co-operation between the army and the police.

This may be attributed to three factors: first, the excellent personal relationship between the current GOC and Chief Constable; secondly, the appointment in 1979 of a security co-ordinator [Maurice Oldfield] who was able to make the security committees effective, balancing off the demands and expectations of the army and the police; and finally, the experience of years of working together – procedures and routines are established, co-operation is not something new which has to be relearned with the arrival of a new unit on rotation . . . Other advantages which currently accrue to the security forces are the increased level of cross-border co-operation, experience and professionalism in all units (especially in the field of covert operations), the steady increase in recruitment for the RUC, and the tendency of the population to tire of the violence.

The report also considered the state of the IRA, in particular in relation to intelligence:

Reorganization has not delivered all that was promised – the tight security required to prevent penetration by British intelligence agents hampers communication between cells and, by implication, planning, direction and actual conduct of terrorist operations. The small, tight structure may be more secure, but it cannot sustain a level of violence high enough to render Northern Ireland ungovernable and thus force the British government to relinquish control of the province.

. . . The new cellular structure of the PIRA hampers intelligence work. Consequently, although the intelligence system is working more smoothly, the PIRA is much harder to crack. This is the principal weakness in the security forces' position and it leaves the initiative for operations very much in the hands of the PIRA. They can still plan and carry out operations in relative secrecy, secure from security force penetration.[19]

There were, however, exceptions which for obvious reasons were not mentioned. As John Stalker was to find out, the intelligence services had penetrated the IRA with two agents

– one in County Armagh and the other along the border. One of them, by far the more crucial and, one assumes, highly placed, epitomizes the post-1980 era of security co-operation and co-ordinated intelligence operations. The agent is thought to have been originally recruited by the army during or before the inception of police primacy, handed over to Special Branch officers who became his 'handlers' and to have been retained on MI5's payroll. He became a 'mole' close to the heart of the IRA – his identity so secret and his services so valuable that police officers were prepared to lie in court to protect it. The 'mole' was, without doubt, a 'national asset'. This is one of the main reasons why John Stalker's investigation proved so sensitive.

Informers are a vital weapon in the security forces' battle against the IRA, INLA and their Loyalist paramilitary counterparts. Their value and importance are incalculable. The way in which intelligence information is used and the responsibilities carried by those who use it became a central feature of the Stalker investigation: tactics which may seem perfectly legitimate when exercised by military forces in wartime take on a very different complexion when used by a civil police force in a time of 'peace'. In describing the Stalker inquiry and the issues which it raises, it is impossible to avoid mention of intelligence and intelligence sources. Every precaution has been taken, however, to avoid the possibility of a source being compromised.

Chapter 5

The Cover-ups

It was the cover stories that were fabricated by RUC Special
Branch officers to protect the involvement and identities of
these informants that brought John Stalker to Northern
Ireland. It has generally been assumed that there were *three*
informants – one for each incident. There were not. The 'mole'
was the informant for two of them, Tullygally Road East and
the Hayshed. That is why his role was doubly important and
doubly sensitive. But the 'mole' was more than just an informer. He was an agent of the state. Informers may be paid by
their Special Branch 'handlers' on an *ad hoc* basis. Agents are
paid a monthly retainer by MI5 from funds specially allocated
by Parliament to the Security Services. Although they are paid
by MI5, they are 'run' by the RUC Special Branch. To Stalker,
these agents were men identified solely by coded numbers who
were paid many thousands of pounds for their services. To
Chief Constable Sir John Hermon, their activities (and those of
others like them) were indispensable to the success of the
RUC's anti-terrorist campaign; to expose its top secret operations to any kind of scrutiny – even John Stalker's – was
unthinkable. It was an area in which no risks could be afforded.
Agents could be lost or eliminated were there any suggestion
that their delicate and highly confidential relationship with their
'handlers' might be compromised. The 'handler' and the Special
Branch units most closely involved – E3 (Intelligence) and E4
(Operations) – know that the first duty is to protect their
charge, almost at all costs, if the agent is to remain effective and
alive. All Special Branch officers involved in this area sign a

62

form based on the Official Secrets Act to ensure this confidentiality. The Official Secrets Act makes it an offence to communicate 'information . . . prejudicial to the safety or interests of the state'.[1] The RUC asked John Stalker to sign the form but he did not on the grounds that it might inhibit revelation of the truth.

It would be wrong to suggest that protecting the agent was a purely self-seeking motive on the part of those involved. Running an agent under deep cover imposes a moral responsibility on the 'handler' which is inseparable from the agent's operational effectiveness. Agents are well paid for their high-wire act. In addition to a regular income from being on MI5's payroll, they received what were known as 'incentive' payments; payment by results. The 'mole' would tip off his 'handler' about the movement of IRA weapons and explosives. His IRA colleagues would then, as if by coincidence, run into a vehicle checkpoint (VCP) manned by one of the Headquarters Mobile Support Units. To onlookers and the IRA, they just looked like ordinary policemen carrying out routine duties, who would then seize the consignment and arrest those involved. The 'mole' would get his money and the IRA would think it'd had a stroke of bad luck (the RUC referred to it as 'the Paddy Factor'). John Stalker discovered the 'mole' made around £30,000 over a relatively short period of time. The figure may seem excessive at first but is not over-generous considering it's probably the most dangerous job in the United Kingdom – and with potentially the shortest life-span. As one official told me, 'I'd want 20,000 quid to be an informer, wouldn't you?' The money to pay these 'national assets' comes from a central fund covered by a House of Commons 'vote', either on General Security or Ways and Means, which allocates a lump sum of around £250,000 a year to cover payment to agents and related matters. (The precise mechanism has been impossible to confirm, given the political sensitivities which surround such matters.)

However, John Stalker was not fighting the IRA and saw the role of informers and agents in a somewhat different light. He did not deny their importance in security terms, but was deeply concerned about the obsessive secrecy which not only led to serious distortions of the truth in legal proceedings but made his own search for it so difficult. He also questioned the reliability of those whose survival depended on deceit. Although police forces throughout the rest of the United Kingdom used informers, Stalker and his team had no experience of the kind of operations in which they were involved in Northern Ireland. As his inquiries progressed, he became increasingly worried that the system was open to corruption; that an informer might become an *agent provocateur* and then end up as a bounty hunter. Part of the problem that lay behind the strained relations which developed between Stalker and the Special Branch was that the RUC saw Stalker and his team as men from a different planet – prepared to push their inquiries to the limit into these most sensitive areas, which risked jeopardizing their anti-terrorist operations. To the RUC, the public interest dictated that, as far as possible, these areas should remain off limits. As the investigation progressed, senior officers became increasingly critical that Stalker and his team had no understanding or fine appreciation of the delicate and carefully protected intelligence systems involved. If police officers had been ordered by their superiors to lie under caution to protect the two agents whose information had led to the three shootings, they were unlikely to give John Stalker what he wanted on a plate. Protection of the source was paramount.

Immediately after the three shootings, several senior Special Branch officers clearly believed that protecting the source was more important than telling the truth. That is why the cover stories were devised and the junior officers involved in the shootings were told to give these false accounts to their colleagues in the CID who were investigating the shootings. To what extent, if at all, the decision to use the cover stories was approved at an even higher level within the RUC was a matter for Stalker to investigate. It was a course of action in clear breach of the Home Office Guidelines on the Use of Informers (agreed by the Central Conference of Chief Constables), which apply to Northern Ireland as they do to the rest of the United Kingdom:

The police must never commit themselves to a course which, whether to protect an informant or otherwise, will constrain them to mislead a court in any subsequent proceedings . . . [if it should prove] impossible to protect [the informant] without subsequently misleading the court, that must be regarded as a decisive reason for his not being so used . . .[2] [See Appendix 3 for full guidelines.]

What is remarkable is that the 'mole' appears to have continued in place and continued to give information for at least a year after the shootings – despite, one assumes, the IRA's own intensive internal investigations. One suspected informer, David McVeigh, an IRA volunteer from Lurgan, was executed by the IRA. In a statement (see Appendix 4), the IRA claimed he'd been passing on information to the Crown forces in the Lurgan area since he'd been recruited by the RUC [Special Branch] following his arrest in connection with an explosion at Lurgan golf club on 2 March 1982. In the three years he'd worked for his 'handlers', codenamed 'George' and 'Jim', he'd 'passed on information which led to the arrest of five Republicans and the seizure of explosives, weapons and ammunition. On this occasion he was given bonus payments of up to £200 each time.' When McVeigh was found 'executed' on 9 September 1986, many assumed he was the 'mole' – an assumption the intelligence agencies were in no hurry to contradict. McVeigh was not the 'mole'. Secretary of State James Prior was aware of the RUC's concern for the safety of one of its most important agents. 'One of the things that was worrying the Chief Constable,' Mr Prior told me, 'and which was brought to my attention because of the impending trials, was the disclosure of evidence which might indicate who an informer was. That would either mean that he had either to be taken out and rehabilitated elsewhere or at best certainly couldn't be used again.'

The nerve centre for these anti-terrorist operations was the RUC's Tasking and Co-ordinating Group (TCG), based at Gough Barracks in Armagh. The TCG was under the operational control of the Special Branch, with a Chief Inspector in charge of the specific operations which were 'tasked'. In overall command was a Special Branch Superintendent who was the operational head for the whole of the RUC's South Region, which included County Armagh. In each of the three cases, the HMSUs were 'tasked' to carry out their operations on the basis of intelligence fed into the TCG from E4A, Special Branch and army undercover surveillance squads and, crucially, on information received directly from the informers. The key steps in an operation were: the transmission of pinpoint intelligence from the informant and Special Branch and/or Army covert operatives; the assessment of its accuracy and the evaluation of its implications; and finally, the direction of the HMSU to the target. The 'co-ordination' was designed to ensure that all three intelligence agencies involved – Special Branch, Military Intelligence and MI5 – knew what the other was doing, so avoiding any duplication or accident. But the details of these covert operations were only available on a 'need to know' basis. They were secret and intended to remain so. An embarrassing court case in which some, if not all, was revealed could blow the operations and those involved in them sky high. That's why the cover stories were invented. They were the result of what were known as 'Chinese Parliaments', meetings of senior officers designed to conceal the true nature of operations. A 'Chinese Parliament' appears to be a gathering where a decision is made in such a way that the authors can never be identified. These cover stories might well never have been unravelled had five of the six dead men not been unarmed.

The first cover story involved the shooting of Eugene Toman, Sean Burns and Gervaise McKerr by members of the HMSU on 11 November 1982. Over the next few days Sergeant William James Montgomery and Constables David Brannigan and Frederick Nigel Robinson were interviewed (with others) by detectives from the RUC's Criminal Investigation Department (CID). On 15 November 1982 Sergeant Montgomery gave the first version of what happened to a Detective Superintendent from the CID. This is the cover story he told.

He said he'd been briefed by his inspector to take charge of one of the HMSU groups and carry out anti-terrorist patrols around Lurgan and Portadown. Two officers were to accompany him in one Ford Cortina and two in a second. They drew their weapons from the armoury: all five were given Smith and Wesson 9 mm semi-automatic pistols; in addition the four constables were each issued with Ruger .223 rifles and the sergeant with a 9 mm Stirling submachine gun. All were standard issue for the HMSUs. They spent the afternoon and early evening patrolling and carrying out vehicle checkpoints. Montgomery told his two colleagues in the other Cortina to carry on with the roadblocks after they'd had their evening break. While Montgomery's crew were having their rest, they received a radio message from their colleagues in the other car that they were planning a VCP at the junction of Old Portadown Road and Tullygally Road East. They drove over to give them cover. By then it was about 9.50 p.m. and dark. They'd just arrived as they saw their colleagues stopping a green Ford Escort. As one of the constables walked towards it in the Escort's headlights, it suddenly drove towards him. The constable jumped, or fell, out of its way, and the car roared off. Montgomery assumed the car had hit him. The Escort swerved right into Tullygally Road East with tyres screeching, accelerating all the time. As it straightened up, Montgomery said he heard shots and 'saw a number of flashes coming from the back of the car'. He said he could see a figure in the back seat, but couldn't make out who it was. He saw the rear window shatter, which made him think the man was shooting out. It all happened in a few seconds. Montgomery assumed the shots were being fired at the crew of the other car. He ordered his driver to give chase to prevent the Escort getting away. He said he saw flashes coming from the car and assumed that they too were being shot at. They all opened fire in response as the car sped along Tullygally Road East. They reloaded and then fired again into the back of the Escort, which swerved into a slip road and crashed on to the verge. They stopped, got out and took cover about ten to fifteen yards away from the crashed car. As they were taking up positions, Montgomery said he heard a metallic sound coming from the car, which he assumed to be a weapon being made ready to fire. He gave the order to open fire again. He aimed his shots at the driver's side and continued firing until his magazine was empty. A number of warnings were then shouted; the men in the car were ordered to throw out their arms and come out, as they were surrounded by armed police. 'There was no response.' Toman, Burns and McKerr were dead. McKerr had been the driver, with Burns in the back seat and Toman the front passenger. Early the following morning, the RUC's press office issued the following statement:

> At approximately 9.50 p.m. uniformed police were operating a road checkpoint at the junction of Tullygally East Road and the Old Portadown Road about two miles outside Lurgan. A vehicle, a green Ford Escort, approached the checkpoint and was signalled to stop. It at first did so, but as an officer approached it, the vehicle accelerated and drove at the officer. As he attempted to throw himself out of its path, he was struck by the car and injured but not seriously. Other police opened fire on the vehicle which drove on in an attempt to escape. In doing so, it careered off the road and down a bank. When police arrived it was found that the three occupants were dead. Pending a post mortem, it is believed all three sustained gunshot wounds. In the light of recent murders and the known serious threat of which we have given warning, police in Lurgan and other areas of Northern Ireland were on a high state of alert and road checks were in operation to prevent, disrupt and detect the movements of terrorist gangs.

This statement from the RUC's press office and the original account given to CID investigating officers gave the impression that the shooting happened after a routine police roadblock. It was not true. Those involved in the shooting did not tell the CID that they were part of a top secret operation, based on intelligence from the 'mole' and E4A, to apprehend Toman and Burns, who were known IRA men on the run and wanted for questioning in connection with the Kinnego landmine explosion. All three cases, Stalker concluded, followed the same pattern. Information from a paid informant; covert surveillance and the tasking of a special operation from the TCG; a confrontation and a shooting with corpses at the end. Were it not for the persistence of the Northern Ireland Director of Public Prosecutions, Sir Barry Shaw, and his law officers, the affair might well have been buried with the bodies.

After the CID had conducted its initial investigation into the shooting of Toman, Burns and McKerr, the evidence was examined by Chief Superintendent (later ACC) David Mellor LL.B., and sent to the DPP with the recommendation that no action should be taken against any of the three police officers. Sir Barry Shaw wasn't happy. In April 1983 he decided there were more questions to be asked and some of the answers he received led him to suspect that what happened at Tullygally Road East was not as described in the file prepared by the CID. Sir John Hermon had also expressed his concern to Sir Barry that the initial CID investigation might have been compromised because the officers involved were not telling the whole truth. The Chief Constable's concern has not always been fully recognized, neither has the fact that he flew off to the United States on 12 November 1982, the day after the shooting of Toman, Burns and McKerr. He is said to have left Belfast early the following morning, convinced that his officers had come under fire and that weapons would be found during the follow-up searches. ACC Trevor Forbes, the newly appointed head of the Special Branch, left with him on the same flight. Trevor Forbes returned from America on 29 November and Sir John on 7 December. Both were therefore out of the country for the Hayshed shooting on 24 November. Both, however, were back in Northern Ireland at the time of the shooting of Grew and Carroll on 12 December. By the early summer of 1983 Sir Barry had received the CID files on all three cases and suggested to Sir John Hermon that the further investigation of them should be taken over by a senior officer. Sir John asked his deputy, Michael McAtamney, to undertake the task. McAtamney enlisted Detective Chief Superintendent David McNeill to assist. Sir Barry also consulted the Attorney-General, Sir Michael Havers, who agreed to remove any constraints the officers were under, and gave an assurance that none would be prosecuted for any breach of the Official Secrets Act. The officers were then reinterviewed and given the opportunity to make revised statements. That is how the cover stories came to be revealed in court. On the basis of this reinvestigation, the DPP directed that Sergeant Montgomery and Constables Brannigan and Robinson should be charged with the murder of Eugene Toman. When the case was heard in May 1984 the judge, Lord Justice Gibson, recognized the unusual circumstances in the case. He said he couldn't understand why, at the preliminary inquiry (at which persons are returned for trial), the Crown had not presented the *revised* statements (which were available) made by the accused, following the lifting of the Official Secrets Act. The result was that:

> The evidence presented by the Crown at the preliminary
> inquiry left one with the clear impression that this was just a
> case of an ordinary vehicle checkpoint through which a car
> had driven . . . the accused . . . had originally no alternative
> but to obscure the whole truth.[3]

Although Sergeant Montgomery admitted he'd disclosed the true nature of the operation only after DCC McAtamney had read a letter informing the three officers that they were no longer bound by the Official Secrets Act, he and his colleagues stood by the original account of the actual shooting which they had given to the CID. The Crown case was that Brannigan 'had approached the car in which Toman was and fired a number of bullets at right-angles into the driver's door, one of which killed Toman, and at a time when no resistance was either offered or threatened'. The judge criticized the Crown for bringing the prosecution 'on such tenuous evidence' and warned of the effect the prosecution was likely to have on the security forces on the ground:

> When a policeman or a soldier is ordered to arrest a
> dangerous criminal, and in substance, as in this case, to bring
> him back dead or alive, how is he to consider his conduct?
> May it not be that some may now ask: am I to risk my life
> carrying out this order, knowing that if I survive my reward
> will be the further risk of life imprisonment as a murderer?

One would hope that they will accept the first risk as part of their duty, but should they not also be entitled to expect that, if they do so, they will have the protection of the law unless it should appear with tolerable plainness that they have overstepped or may have overstepped the bounds of the criminal law?[4]

Lord Justice Gibson went on to acquit the three police officers. That was when he praised their 'courage and determination' for bringing Toman, Burns and McKerr 'to the final court of justice'.

The genesis of the cover story which followed the second shooting a fortnight later at the Hayshed at Ballynerry followed a similar pattern. What was not known – a fact which Stalker's team discovered – was that at least one of the officers present at the Tullygally Road East shooting, who was never called as a witness, was involved in the shooting at the Hayshed. The three officers who shot Michael Tighe and Martin McCauley on 24 November 1982 were never named because they were never charged. They were simply known as Sergeant X, and Constables Y and Z. Again, they were interviewed by the CID the day after the incident. This is the cover story they originally told.

They said they'd been carrying out routine anti-terrorist patrols in three unmarked Cortinas when Sergeant X saw a gunman moving to the Hayshed from the direction of the cottage which stood in the field a few yards away. Sergeant X mentioned 'a gunman' and asked one of the officers from the other cars to give cover. X, Y and Z approached the Hayshed. Sergeant X was carrying a Stirling submachine gun and a Smith and Wesson pistol. Y and Z were carrying Ruger rifles and Smith and Wesson pistols. The diagram overleaf shows the basic positions of Tighe and McCauley and X, Y and Z during the following account, which is based on what was said in court.

The three officers ran to the Hayshed 'at a jog' and took up positions, Sergeant X to the left of the door and Constables Y and Z to the right of it. They said they heard the sound of a rifle

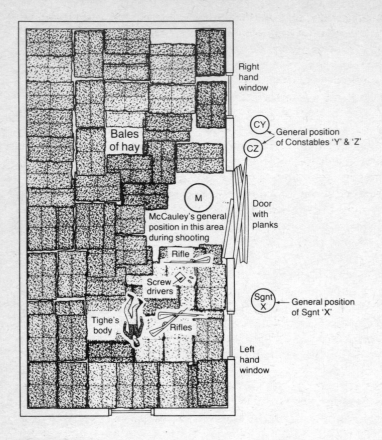

Front of Hayshed, showing position of bullet holes

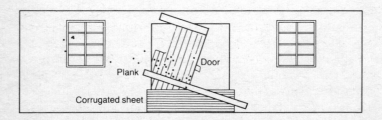

being cocked and 'muffled voices'. Sergeant X said he shouted 'Police. Throw out your weapons.' There was no reply. Sergeant X repeated the warning. Again there was no reply. Constable Z started to pull away the planks across the doorway. Through the gap he saw a man (Martin McCauley) pointing a rifle at him. Z opened fire with two short bursts of three shots. Almost simultaneously, Sergeant X (at the other side of the door) fired two bursts (seven rounds apiece) from his Stirling submachine gun. The man (McCauley) disappeared. There was then 'silence' and 'a few seconds' pause'. Constable Z then stepped back into the cover of the wall and tore away more planks to leave 'reasonable space'. Through the gap he then saw another man (Michael Tighe) standing on hay bales about six feet from the ground, and pointing a rifle. Constable Z stepped back and Constable Y opened fire with single shots from his Ruger rifle. On the other side of the door, Sergeant X saw a 'shadow' through the window. He fired two bursts (of seven shots each) from his Stirling submachine gun and the man (Michael Tighe) disappeared into a 'hole' in the hay bales. Sergeant X then dropped his Stirling, which was empty, took out his Smith and Wesson and fired three rounds at the first man (McCauley), whom he saw reappearing with the rifle. The man (McCauley) fell against the bales but got to his feet and threw the weapon to the other side of the door. Constable Z then bent down to lift the man (McCauley) through the door; as he did so, Constable Y (behind him) saw the second man (Tighe) reappear up on the bales to the left with the rifle. He fired three single shots from his Ruger and the man dropped the weapon and fell backwards. Constable Z pulled the wounded man (McCauley) out through the door while Sergeant X and Constable Y entered the shed. There they found three old Mauser rifles, a sack, a screwdriver kit and the dead body of Michael Tighe in a 'hole' in the hay bales. They found no ammunition. They then radioed for an ambulance. They said there was no conversation with the wounded McCauley. The whole incident was over in about a minute.[5]

Again, after the initial CID investigation, the file was reviewed by Chief Superintendent David Mellor and sent to the

DPP, with a recommendation that McCauley should be prosecuted for possession of the rifles. Again, the DPP was not satisfied that the whole truth had been told about the circumstances of the shooting, or that the incident had been properly investigated: there wasn't, for example, evidence of the briefing the officers and their colleagues in the other two cars had received before the operation. The reason for the cover story, it transpired when McCauley's case came to court, was the same as that given for the cover-up in the earlier shooting of Toman, Burns and McKerr – to protect an informer. The DPP suggested that this case, too, should be placed in the hands of a senior officer – DCC Michael McAtamney (assisted by Detective Chief Superintendent David McNeill) – and that the Official Secrets Act should also be waived in this case, so the truth could be revealed. When X, Y and Z (and their colleagues) were interviewed for the second investigation, they changed their account of the circumstances of the operation, but did not alter their account of the actual shooting. In written statements made to DCS McNeill on 15 August 1983 they removed 'this single untruth and its embellishments'. They said they had not seen a man with a gun making for the Hayshed: that had been a lie. They hadn't arrived at the Hayshed by chance, but had been directed to do so by a radio message received about 4.15 p.m. They said they were taking part in a special operation that involved information supplied by an informant. When Martin McCauley was tried for possession of the rifles in May 1984, his defence counsel, Arthur Harvey QC, elicited the reason for the cover story originally given to the CID about a gunman moving to the Hayshed:

Harvey QC: . . . What was the reason for giving the first account?

Sergeant X: It was stressed to me, my Lord, that under no circumstances to disclose that we were working on Special Branch information, my Lord.

Harvey: That was stressed to you?

Sgt X: That is correct, my Lord.

74

Harvey: Why did you invent – I take it that you did invent it?

Sgt X: I did not, my Lord.

Harvey: Did you not invent the account of seeing the gunman moving from the cottage to the outbuilding?

Sgt X: I did not invent it, my Lord.

Harvey: You did not invent that?

Sgt X: I did not, my Lord.

Harvey: That was invented for you?

Sgt X: That is correct, my Lord.

Harvey: And that was invented for you by senior officers?

Sgt X: That is correct, my Lord.

Harvey: Did they indicate to you or were you given any reason as to why it was necessary to invent an account as to the events leading up to this shooting?

Sgt X: Just as I have stated, my Lord, that it was on Special Branch information.

Harvey: You didn't have to reveal that it was on Special Branch information, isn't that right?

Sgt X: It was to protect the source of that information, my Lord.

. . .

Harvey: Were you not concerned about that [i.e. making an inaccurate statement]?

Sgt X: I was reassured by two senior officers, my Lord.

Harvey: Reassured about what?

Sgt X: That the statement was to be made in the way it was, my Lord.

Harvey: Reassured that it was to be made the way it was, but 'reassured' tends to mean that you had doubts, or tended to suggest that you had doubts, or were concerned about it?

Sgt X: I was naturally concerned, my Lord.

Harvey: And how did they reassure you?

Sgt X: They said it would be covered by the Official Secrets Act, my Lord, and not to disclose the fact that we were working under Special Branch information, my Lord.

Sergeant X said that after the shooting they returned to Gough Barracks and told two senior officers what had happened:

Harvey: And what format did the debriefing take?

Sgt X: One officer chaired and we told him what had happened, my Lord.

Harvey: And was the story told with the three of you really interjecting in each other's conversation?

Sgt X: That would be correct, my Lord.

Harvey: And at the end of the conversation then, was it indicated to the three of you that you should not mention anything that was likely to reveal the identity of the police source?

Sgt X: That is correct, my Lord.

Oarvey: Of the two officers who were there, were they both of the same rank?

Sgt X: They were not, my Lord.

Harvey: Can you say if it was the more senior or the less senior officer who invented the story about seeing the gunman moving from the cottage to the Hayshed?

Sgt X: I can't recall which one it was, my Lord.

In court, X, Y and Z were excluded from each other's cross-examination. Constable Y agreed with Sergeant X's account and confirmed that at Gough Barracks that night it was agreed that Sergeant X should tell the story about the gunman 'probably because he was the senior one there'. Constable Z, however, said that he only saw 'one senior officer' at Gough Barracks and he 'didn't make any comment on anything . . . to the best of my recollection it was a Chief Inspector'.

The day after the shooting, the three officers said that they reported for duty at Lisnasharragh, their base in Belfast. Constable Y said that he'd then seen another senior officer, prior to being interviewed by the CID, a Chief Superintendent who was *not* one of the senior officers they'd seen at Gough Barracks the night before:

Harvey: And what did he tell you to do?

Constable Y: He was more or less getting the story right – the beginning of the statement for the CID that afternoon, the CID didn't know about it, my Lord.

Harvey: Did he really take you over the details that you ought to give to the CID that afternoon?

Con. Y: Yes, my Lord.

Harvey: A 'dress rehearsal' for what was about to happen?

Con. Y: Yes, my Lord.

Constable Z (who said no cover story had been discussed at Gough) told the court it was two senior officers at Lisnasharragh who had directed them what to say in their statements and had told them the reason for it:

Constable Z: My Lord, that morning the reason we were given for the direction [i.e. to tell the false story] was to protect the life of the informant from whom the information had come, and that was the reason given for the direction.

. . .

Harvey: When you went along with the story that had been prepared by these senior officers, were you informed that they were authorized to require you to do what they said under the Official Secrets Act?

Con. Z: Yes, my Lord.

Harvey: Did you give any thought at that time as to whether or not you had any alternative but to go along with these individuals?

Con. Z: Yes, my Lord.

Harvey: And what conclusion did you arrive at?

Con. Z: My Lord, I had been directed that what I was told to say was covered by the Official Secrets Act and the reason was again to protect the life of the informant.

During the trial, McCauley gave a conflicting account of what had happened at the Hayshed. He said he'd driven his Montessa 250 trial bike to the Hayshed with Tighe on the back. He said the owner, an elderly widow called 'Kitty' Cairns, had asked him to keep an eye on her property while she was away. McCauley said he noticed the left window of the shed was open. He looked in and saw 'a metal object rising from the top of the hay'. He climbed up on the sill and saw two rifles. Tighe and McCauley climbed into the shed to take a closer look. McCauley saw a third rifle lower down. While he was looking at it – and Tighe was above him on the bales opposite the window – McCauley heard two shots 'very loud' with a pause between each one. He looked up and Tighe had disappeared from view. He then heard a call, to the effect 'Right, come out!' McCauley turned to the doorway and through a space saw a dark figure moving very fast across it. A burst of gunfire came through the door. McCauley tried to get out of the way and was hit. There was blood coming out of his thigh and dropping off his hand. The shooting stopped. He then heard a call to come out and shouted back 'Right! Right!' There was another burst of gunfire through the door and it was then smashed down, McCauley thought with rifle butts. Badly wounded, he was dragged out on to the grass and asked his name. He was then questioned about the guns and asked 'Where is the explosives at?' He said he didn't know what they were talking about. One officer, he said, held a rifle to his head and suggested finishing him off.

McCauley's defence counsel attacked the credibility of the police evidence, arguing that their untruthfulness was motivated and invented to justify an undisciplined, unwarranted and unlawful shooting. The judge acknowledged that Mr Harvey, 'in a detail that implied "commendable industry and thought"', challenged the police officers' 'integrity, the consistency of their evidence and its improbability in the light of the forensic and medical evidence and otherwise'. In his judgment (which concerned McCauley's guilt) Lord Justice Kelly said:

I have some reservations about the credibility and accuracy of certain parts of their evidence. Unfortunately, they enter the arena of credibility under a cloud; the cloud that initially each of them knowingly made a false allegation in their first written statements to the effect that Sergeant X had seen a man armed with a rifle enter the Hayshed and that on seeing this, had said so to Constables Y and Z. There was not a word of truth in this. It was invented not by them, but regrettably by one or more of their superiors who told them that they were obliged to say it and under orders they did say it. The reason for its invention was that the patrol, in fact, had been directed to the Hayshed on Special Branch information and not on seeing an armed man enter and to disclose this would have put their informant in danger of his life . . .

All three maintain at this trial that save for this single untruth and its embellishment, the remainder of their initial statements [made to the CID the day after the shooting] is a completely true account of what happened after they arrived at the Hayshed, as is their evidence before me.

I have, however, in the light of the forensic evidence, some of the medical evidence and otherwise, doubts as to whether this is so. My two principal areas of reservation about their evidence are in respect of first where they fired their shots from into the barn and second as to whether they did see the accused and Tighe holding and pointing rifles . . . Having regard to my reservations about the weight of the evidence of these police witnesses, I believe the proper course for me at this trial is to exclude their evidence and its implications from my consideration and adjudication of the case.

However, the judge did not believe all of McCauley's evidence either:

Apart from the highly unlikely content of his evidence, the marked unease of his demeanour during cross-examination added to my strong conviction that he was lying in denying possession of the rifle.

McCauley was found guilty and given a two-year sentence suspended for three years.

The way the cover story was fabricated in the third case, the shooting of the INLA activists, Seamus Grew and Roddy Carroll, was almost identical. Constable John Robinson, a former British soldier, who was charged with the murder of Seamus Grew, was interviewed by senior CID officers on 19 December 1982 – a week after the shooting. Robinson told them he'd reported for duty at his base in Belfast at 8 a.m. on Sunday, 12 December. The members of the HMSU, who were to operate in three cars with three men in each vehicle, were briefed by an inspector and told to go to Armagh to receive a further briefing before carrying out anti-terrorist patrols in the area. Robinson said he was a passenger in a silver Cortina. At Gough Barracks they were briefed by an inspector about 'local active terrorists and their associates'. They were shown photographs of them and a list of vehicles they used. Robinson was told that Grew was thought to be involved in a number of recent murders of the security forces in the Armagh area and that Carroll had also been involved in them. During the interview one of the CID officers asked Robinson whether 'there was anything at the briefing you feel you should tell me about'. Robinson said nothing further, except they were to carry out 'snap VCPs' in the Armagh area. This, he said, they did, for example, driving past Seamus Grew's house. At about 8.15 p.m. Robinson said he received a radio message that Seamus Grew's Allegro had broken through a VCP, injuring a man near Paper Mill Bridge on the Keady–Armagh road, about five or six miles outside the city. He said he headed off and intercepted Grew's Allegro at the entrance to Mullacreevie Park, the housing estate where Grew lived. He said he recognized its number, LIA 6399, as it was indicating to turn right into the estate. He wanted to stop the car at that point because 'I understood it to be a strong Republican area and that I knew they must have had a good reason for going through the VCP earlier.' Robinson said he drew level with the Allegro and waved his cap out of the window as a sign for it to stop. He recognized Seamus Grew. His driver forced the Allegro into the verge. Robinson jumped out and rushed round to the passenger side of Grew's car, to avoid offering himself as a target in the glare of the headlights. The Allegro started 'revving'. Robinson shouted to the occupants to halt. The front passenger door was flung open and he noticed a movement behind it. The car broke free from the kerb and the door slammed shut. 'As the door shut, there was a loud bang. I believed I had been shot at. I immediately opened fire with my Smith and Wesson . . . I fired because I believed I had been shot at and my life was in danger.' Robinson emptied his magazine (fourteen shots) into the passenger door. He reloaded and ran round to the other side of the car and fired four rounds at the driver's door. 'I knew the driver was Grew,' Robinson told the CID. 'I knew his capabilities and I still thought someone had arms in the car and they could still be used against us.' Robinson told the CID he fired from a distance of 'about ten feet'. 'I approached the driver's door and opened it with my left hand . . . and the man I knew as Grew fell out on to the road.' Roddy Carroll was also dead. Robinson then said he was debriefed by his inspector at Gough Barracks. 'It was then that I learnt that the constable injured had not been shot, but injured by Grew's car.'

There were several inconsistencies in Robinson's account to the CID, not least the fact that he said he'd fired at the *closed* driver's door after he'd reloaded. The forensic evidence indicated that Robinson's second volley of shots (four rounds) 'were discharged at the driver [Grew] either while he sat in the car – in which case the driver's door was open – or whenever he was outside the car, or a combination of both'. The forensic evidence also indicated that two of the shots that killed Grew were fired from about thirty-six inches away. After interviewing Robinson on 19 December 1982, CID officers returned to interview him again on 9 March 1983 to question him about some of those inconsistencies. Robinson said 'It would seem that my observations at the time were not right. I would like to point out to you that when I opened fire on the *passenger* side [where Carroll was sitting], the door was definitely closed . . . I ran round to that side of the car to terminate any danger that could have come from the driver . . . and thinking about it now, I must have related it [the closed door] to the *passenger* door which was closed . . . The whole thing happened in a matter of seconds and needed a split-second decision . . . I want to emphasize that at all times I believed that my life was in danger . . . Some of the shots could have been fired at a closer range than I believe . . . it is possible that I might have opened the door as I fired my last shot and the body fell out then and not after I had finished firing, as I previously thought.'

As in the previous two cases, Chief Superintendent Mellor reviewed the evidence when the CID had completed its investigation into the shooting of Grew and Carroll. He decided to recommend that Constable Robinson be prosecuted for murder, but his recommendation was overruled by the Chief Constable, who wrote to the DPP advising that there should be *no* criminal proceedings against Constable Robinson. Sir John, it appears, disagreed with CS Mellor's conclusions because he (CS Mellor) was not familiar with the intelligence background. Sir Barry Shaw, as in the other two cases, directed that they should be reviewed at a higher level within the RUC. Again, DCC McAtamney and Chief Superintendent McNeill were given the responsibility. (In all three reinvestigations they worked directly to the DPP's office.) Constable Robinson was seen on 20 July 1983 and informed that the Attorney-General had lifted any constraints imposed by the Official Secrets Act. Again, that was when the true story came out and the cover story was revealed, as the court heard. Constable Robinson and his colleagues had *not* left Belfast for Gough Barracks on Sunday 12 December 1982; they had *not* spent the afternoon doing 'spot VCPs' around Armagh; they had *not* driven past Seamus Grew's house. They had left Belfast twenty-four hours earlier, on the morning of Saturday 11 December, and had stayed overnight at Gough Barracks, where they remained until 8 p.m. on Sunday evening. The circumstances from which the shooting stemmed were no more routine or chance than in the other two cases. Constable Robinson was part of another top secret operation – in terms of the 'target', operationally the most important of all – to capture Dominic McGlinchey. The pressure to do something about McGlinchey, to whom around thirty killings had been attributed (but denied by him), was intense. 'McGlinchey went berserk,' one officer familiar with the operation told me. 'Dedicated terrorists were concentrating on close-quarter murder.'

The operation to intercept McGlinchey was based on intelligence from the second informer, who was not the 'mole'. He was believed to be living across the border in County Monaghan and, unlike the 'mole', was believed to be an IRA supporter, not an activist. There was intelligence that McGlinchey would be coming across the border that weekend (probably on the Saturday) in an Allegro driven by Grew, to carry out an operation against the security forces. Robinson and the other members of the HMSU were to wait at Gough Barracks until there was word that the car had crossed the border, and then they were to intercept it. Grew had driven the Allegro from Armagh into the Irish Republic on the Sunday, to drop off his sister, Irene Leonard, at her home in Monaghan town after attending a family funeral in the North. Unknown to the occupants, the Allegro was under surveillance by Special Branch officers from Armagh (not E4A) who were operating, without authority from Dublin, within the jurisdiction of the Irish Republic. A Special Branch inspector tailed the Allegro back across the border and informed the TCG at Gough Barracks that the car was on its way. At about 8 p.m. on Sunday evening Robinson and two other HMSU car crews were given the word and left Gough Barracks to intercept the Allegro, which they had reason to believe contained Grew and McGlinchey. They also assumed they would be armed and liable to resist arrest. There was a hard frost that night and the roads were bad. As the car Robinson was driving approached the point where they had planned to set up the roadblock to stop the Allegro, Robinson ran into the back of a car which had been involved in a collision with another. The two cars were part of the army's undercover operation, co-ordinated with the police operation through the TCG, to intercept McGlinchey. Robinson's Cortina was put out of action. In the confusion, Grew's Allegro drove by, followed by a silver Peugeot driven by the Armagh Special Branch inspector who was part of the cross-border surveillance operation. The Peugeot stopped, the inspector pointed out that the Allegro had gone by, and Robinson and one of his colleagues jumped into the inspector's silver Peugeot. The rest of the story was as originally told to the CID the day after the shooting. It also explained another discrepancy in Robinson's account. He'd originally told the CID he'd been driving a *silver* police car when he intercepted the Allegro, so the colour was not at variance with the *silver* Peugeot that was involved in the shooting. The Cortina in which Robinson had left Gough Barracks at 8 p.m. that Sunday night, and in which he'd left his headquarters in Belfast the previous day, was *beige*.

During two days of cross-examination, Constable Robinson revealed the extent of the cover-up and wrote down the names of the senior officers involved and handed them, in confidence, to the judge:

Michael Lavery QC: Were you aware that you would be interviewed by the CID?

Robinson: I was indeed, my Lord, yes.

Lavery: And were you given instructions as to how you should deal with this interview?

Robinson: We were indeed, my Lord.

. . .

Lavery: And what officers were involved, without giving names? You could give their ranks.

Robinson: Superintendent, Chief Inspector and others present, my Lord.

. . .

Lavery: Were you given any particular instructions as to how you were to deal with your interview with the CID?

Robinson: We were indeed, my Lord.

Lavery: What was that?

Robinson: To certain facts which weren't to be revealed to the CID.

Lavery: And what were those facts?

Robinson: The involvement of the local Special Branch officer, the fact that we were acting on source information and the fact that the army surveillance unit was involved.

Lavery: Was there any particular suggestion or reason given for not mentioning these?

Robinson: There was indeed, my Lord.

Lavery: What was that?

Robinson: It was to protect the source's life.

Lavery: But was there any legal basis put for this?

Robinson: Official Secrets Act, my Lord, was quoted to us.

. . .

Lavery: Was there any discussion as to what you should tell the CID?

Robinson: There was indeed, my Lord.

Lavery: And what was agreed, if I may call it that?

Robinson: They produced a story, my Lord.

Lavery: What was the story?

Robinson: Basically, my Lord, it removed the accident and replaced it with a VCP.

Lavery: What was the object of doing that then?

Robinson: That was to get rid of the army involvement, my Lord. The accident was all sorted out and there was no source involvement at all.

Lavery: So this was to appear as a chance encounter rather than a planned encounter?

Robinson: That's correct, my Lord.

Lavery: Had this anything to do with the actual circumstances in which you opened fire?

Robinson: No, my Lord.[6]

The Crown prosecuting counsel, Anthony Campbell QC, tried to establish the connection between what Robinson had been told at Gough Barracks immediately after the shooting, and what he'd been told at headquarters in Belfast the following day. It was at this stage that Robinson wrote down the name of a Chief Superintendent:

Anthony Campbell QC: Now on the first occasion that you were interviewed by the CID you have informed the court that you were under instructions from some senior officers as to certain circumstances which you weren't to reveal?

Robinson: That's correct.

Campbell: A position about a roadblock. From what source was that first mentioned to you?

Robinson: That story was first mentioned to me, my Lord, the day after the shooting.

Campbell: If you don't wish to mention in court the name of the officer for some reason, perhaps you'd be good enough to write down the name of the officer who first mentioned it to you. If you would hand it up.

(Witness hands piece of paper to judge.)

Campbell: Would you be good enough to tell us where it was that this person mentioned this to you?

Robinson: That was mentioned to me at my base.

Campbell: In Belfast?

Robinson: That's correct.

Campbell: Perhaps the document should be handed into court. And that was at what time, can you remember?

Robinson: It would have been the next parade for duty.

Campbell: And as far as you were concerned that is the first time any question of the roadblock entered your mind so far as this incident was concerned?

Robinson: No, that was the first time I received *direct instructions* [my emphasis] in relation to that.

Campbell: Would you be good enough to tell his Lordship when this question of a roadblock, issue of a roadblock, first entered your mind following the shooting incident?

Robinson: It didn't enter my mind. I was told about it. That was in Gough Barracks.

Campbell: Was that on the night of the incident?

Robinson: That's correct.

Mr Campbell returned to the cover story in his cross-examination of Constable Robinson the following day:

Campbell: And who was the first person [at Gough Barracks] that told you about that, and if you do not want to name the person you may write down the name?

Robinson: It was a number of people, my Lord. I will give a list of them if you wish. There were other officers there as well but that is the three I specifically remember.

87

Campbell: Just following from there, the next day as I understand it, you were back at your base at Lisnasharragh?

Robinson: Yes, my Lord, I think that is correct.

Campbell: And you there saw a senior officer whose name you wrote down yesterday?

Robinsons: That is correct.

Campbell: First of all, could you say what that senior officer told you?

Robinson: It was in relation to certain matters . . . which we could not mention in relation to the Official Secrets Act.

Campbell: And those items were that you were not to indicate that you had been operating on source intelligence?

Robinson: Yes, that is one of them.

Campbell: And the second?

Robinson: That there was no army surveillance involved . . .

Campbell: And the third?

Robinson: That it was not to be a planned operation. It was just to be a casual thing . . .

. . .

Campbell: I am trying to discover whether the senior officer at Lisnasharragh who spoke to you that day when there was a reference to a roadblock, whether it was he, as it were, merely repeating that there had been a roadblock – which I gather had been discussed the day before – or whether he was, as you understood it, saying 'well, we are going to have a story about a roadblock and we will keep to that'?

Robinson: No, I believe the story had already been given to him by someone else and he was just reiterating it.

Campbell: If I could put it perhaps more crudely, did you understand him to be selling it to you as a story?

Robinson: Not so much selling it. I believed he had been briefed as to what the story was to be himself.

The judge, Mr Justice MacDermott, pointed out that his responsibility was to decide whether Constable Robinson was guilty of murder, not to conduct 'an inquiry into why the officers who advised, instructed or constrained the accused acted as they did'. He found Constable Robinson not guilty, with the observation, as we have seen, that policemen 'are not required to be "supermen" and one does not use jewellers' scales to measure what is reasonable in the circumstances'.

The revelations that emerged at the trial of Constable Robinson caused a storm in the Irish Republic too. The Irish Prime Minister was outraged at the news that the RUC had been carrying out covert operations on its side of the border. The Irish Prime Minister, Dr Garret FitzGerald, summoned the British Ambassador and delivered a formal protest. He said his government viewed the allegation that the RUC had operated outside its jurisdiction:

> with deep concern and as a very serious departure from normal rules of inter-state conduct, harmful to the spirit and the practice of security co-operation and damaging to Anglo-Irish relations.[7]

The Ambassador conveyed the British government's apologies and gave an assurance that it would continue to be RUC policy 'enshrined in explicit instructions' that members of the RUC should not cross the border while on duty. He said the British government was very concerned and regretted that these instructions should apparently have been violated.[8]

The inquests into the deaths of Grew and Carroll, Tighe and Toman, Burns and McKerr were postponed until the conclusion of criminal proceedings which arose from the three cases. As the proceedings in the cases of Grew and Carroll and Toman, Burns and McKerr were over by the early summer of 1984 (McCauley wasn't tried until January the following year), dates were set for the inquests to be held that September. But before they came to court, the Armagh coroner, Mr Gerry Curran, resigned after thirty-three years' experience. In a statement he said:

> Within the past few days I have been engaged in the review of police files in these cases. Certain grave irregularities are documented and recorded on the file. Consequently I am not prepared to preside at the inquest in these cases.[9]

The inquests were again postponed. At the time of writing, almost five years after the six men were killed, the inquests are still to be held. They now await the DPP's decision on the inquiry John Stalker began and Colin Sampson completed.

Chapter 6

In the Jungle

The week after Constable John Robinson was acquitted, the DPP, Sir Barry Shaw, informed Chief Constable Sir John Hermon that he wanted a further investigation carried out. He was exercising a wide power under the Prosecution of Offences (Northern Ireland) Order 1972 whereby:

> It shall be the duty of the Chief Constable, from time to time . . . at the request of the Director, to ascertain and furnish to the Director information which may appear to the Director to require investigation on the ground that it may involve an offence against the law of Northern Ireland . . .[1]

Sir Barry requested Sir John to carry out an investigation into the circumstances in which the Special Branch had lied to the CID, and to ascertain whether any criminal offence had been committed. Although it appears that the DPP had in mind offences relating to perverting the course of justice, it seems he did not rule out consideration of any other criminal offence in connection with the shootings. Although by this time, April 1984, evidence had been revealed in court of only *two* cover stories (which emerged at the trials of Constable John Robinson and the three officers charged with the murder of Eugene Toman), the DPP had in his possession evidence of the third cover story (from the McAtamney–McNeill reinvestigation of the Hayshed shooting) although the case had not yet come to court. So far as the Chief Constable was concerned, he was being given an open-ended request to make further inquiries in the light of disclosures made during the criminal trials; there were, as he saw it, no limitations placed on their scope.

Sir John had little choice other than to look outside his own force for a senior officer to conduct the investigation: he'd already asked his most senior officer, his deputy Michael McAtamney, to reinvestigate the shootings following the DPP's earlier request in June 1983. Under the circumstances, however, Sir John probably felt it appropriate to look outside. Neither did he feel that the outside investigating officer had necessarily to be of Chief Constable rank given that the highest level with which the cover-ups had been associated was Chief Superintendent. Sir John sought advice from HM Inspector of Constabulary for the North West, Sir Philip Myers. Sir Philip, who can go anywhere else in his region uninvited, may only visit Northern Ireland at the express invitation of its authorities. This was such an invitation. Sir Philip took advice on the appointment of the outside officer and, with the agreement of Sir Lawrence Byford, HM Chief Inspector of Constabulary at the Home Office, suggested the new Deputy Chief Constable of Greater Manchester. Sir John Hermon accepted the recommendation though he had never heard of John Stalker.

John Stalker was appointed to head the Northern Ireland inquiry on 24 May 1984. His first port of call had been Colwyn Bay in north Wales, Sir Philip Myers's regional headquarters. Sir Philip outlined what was involved: things had gone wrong; the DPP wasn't happy; there was need for a review. Stalker left Colwyn Bay with the impression that Sir Philip was leaving it to him to decide what should be done. Stalker hand-picked his team. As his number two, he chose Detective Chief Superintendent John Thorburn, a tough, no-nonsense Scot from the 'old' Manchester CID school. Thorburn was a detective of great experience and tenacity; once he'd got his teeth into something, he never let go. Stalker liked Thorburn and trusted him; he was 'sound'. He knew that in strange territory it was good to have friends. The team he assembled was small, on the grounds that fewer detectives doing more work was better than more detectives doing less. For security and personal reasons, too, the smaller and more tightly knit the team, the better. Stalker selected six of his colleagues from the CID – five men and one woman – and split them into teams of two so that each 'team' became familiar with the most minute detail of each of the three incidents.

Stalker's second port of call was Northern Ireland. Thorburn went with him. They met Sir John Hermon in his office at police headquarters in Belfast. 'This is a jungle,' he warned at the outset. Stalker had already been sent a briefing paper by the RUC, which seemed to those who read it to say more about the emotion behind *why* things happened in Northern Ireland than what actually *had* happened. Understandably, Sir John was at pains to point out to strangers in the jungle the vicious nature of the IRA's campaign, the pain and anguish it had inflicted on the community and the dangers to which his men were constantly exposed. (One hundred and ninety-seven policemen had been killed since 1969 and 4672 injured.) The watchword in the jungle was survival. He took Stalker and Thorburn out to dinner at one of Northern Ireland's quieter restaurants, and gave them advice on the difficulties they would face, the prejudices they would encounter, the sensitivity that would be needed and the sensitivities that would be touched. Stalker and Thorburn were assured that no obstacle would be put in their way and that the RUC would afford them all possible help. They discussed the terms of reference for the inquiry, which were based on the directions Sir John had received from the DPP. There were three main areas:

1. To investigate the circumstances in which the three cover stories had been given to the CID and to see whether any criminal offence had been committed. Also to examine the way in which the CID had conducted the three investigations.

2. To discover how RUC officers had entered the Irish Republic whilst on duty on 12 December 1982, the day Grew and Carroll were shot.

3. To examine the problems Special Branch officers face when acting on information which they cannot reveal because of the need to protect an informant.

Stalker was also expected, it seems, to draw lessons from his investigations which would be applicable to the RUC as a whole.

In the course of their meeting, Sir John made it clear that constitutionally Stalker would be reporting to him and not the DPP; when the inquiry was completed, the report was to be sent to the Chief Constable and then he would forward it to the Director. He stressed that he was constitutionally responsible for commissioning the investigation. These constitutional niceties became very important when the going got tough.

In Stalker's eyes, however, the incidents needed *reinvestigating* not reviewing – Thorburn agreed – and that's what he told his team when they returned to Manchester. The RUC had stressed how anxious it was to get it right in the future and how much Manchester's expertise would be appreciated in helping to do so; the assurances were seen as 'bland nonsense'. Although, like the constitutional issue over the commissioning of the inquiry, the interpretation of 'reinvestigation' and 'review' may have seemed like splitting hairs, it was a vital distinction to senior RUC officers, who thought it no part of Stalker's job to dig into dark and sensitive corners. From the beginning, it was Sir John's intention to leave Stalker to get on with the job – as he had done with Sir George Terry, the Chief Constable of Sussex, during his inquiry into allegations of misconduct at the Kincora Boys' Home in Belfast. The Chief Constable never wanted Stalker to feel that he was under constant supervision. The RUC insists that Sir John Hermon never had an argument with John Stalker. But Sir John could not have been deaf to the arguments that raged below – not involving the CID, which was said to be pleased to have Stalker on board – but emanating from the Special Branch, which saw Stalker and his team as bulls in its very delicate china shop.

Stalker was intent on going back to square one and although he never told Sir John Hermon that he planned to conduct a total reinvestigation of the three shootings, his intention soon became clear. When Stalker told Sir Philip Myers of what he intended to do, apparently the HMI agreed; Sir Philip was left in no doubt that the RUC had failed to do the job on two occasions and John Stalker wasn't going to make it a third.

Looking back, some of the team thought they must have hit the RUC like an Exocet. There was to be no cosy relationship with officers of the force they were investigating. The RUC offered to house the team in secure police accommodation. Stalker said no, lest eating, drinking and socializing with officers they might have to interview the next day blunted their appetite. Staying in a police hostel carried all those implications because in Northern Ireland, for security reasons, policemen tend to mix with each other in the evenings and not go out on the town. Stalker insisted his team stay at a hotel out of Belfast. The RUC warned of the risks; Stalker said they were risks he was prepared to take. The hotel was 'RUC approved' but no guards could be provided. Had he been able to, Stalker would have booked separate office accommodation, but the realities of police work in Northern Ireland dictate that renting outside office space is largely out of the question due to the risks involved. So he settled for premises in a former hotel which had been converted to a non-operational police station. The office was set up as if the team were running a murder incident room in Manchester: they used their own stationery with GMP letterheads, their own filing system and they did their own typing – most of that back in Manchester. However, they did use RUC drivers and worked through an RUC liaison officer – a detective sergeant who arranged the internal appointments. The team worked in Northern Ireland from Monday to Friday under the full-time, on-the-spot direction of John Thorburn. Stalker would come over from time to time, as he still had to fulfil his responsibilities as Deputy Chief Constable of Greater Manchester. In the course of their two years with John Stalker in Northern Ireland, the team saw over 500 people and took over 200 statements.

The first thing they had to do was read themselves into what they were there to investigate. They sent for all the files and papers to learn the public face of it. They formed the impression that there was a great deal of material that should have been there that was not. There weren't, for example, any transcripts of the trials – although, technically, there was no reason for there to be; all the officers had been acquitted and therefore there were no transcripts, as they are usually made only on appeal. Nevertheless, the team felt that, having been called in, someone might have had the foresight to have ordered them. Typing hundreds of pages from shorthand notes taken in court during long trials isn't a job done overnight. There was no problem in getting hold of what they called 'the bland stuff', but when they started asking for Special Branch files, the shutters came down. When they asked for the intelligence background on Grew and Carroll and on Toman, Burns and McKerr, they were told the information was classified. The guardian of the files was a senior Special Branch officer whom some of the team came to regard as 'a bloody pain', since getting information and documents out of him was like drawing teeth. They thought he was being deliberately obstructive and wouldn't tell them the day of the week unless he checked with the Chief Constable. No doubt he believed he was doing his job. Everything, the team felt, was delayed. They'd go for a file and they wouldn't get it; it was like constant dripping water. Chief Superintendent Thorburn was Stalker's 'hammer'; the senior Special Branch officer was the anvil. Thorburn, as a matter of pride, was determined to get what he wanted without asking his boss to intervene and, in the end, invariably did. John Thorburn wasn't popular.

The Special Branch was very reluctant to part with its highly sensitive information, which wasn't surprising given that the cover stories had been fabricated in the first place to protect its sources. Eventually the team would get most of what they wanted, but they wouldn't get it all. They felt it was like doing a jigsaw without all the pieces. When Thorburn and the Special Branch officer stood with locked horns over a particular request, Stalker would intervene with ACC Trevor Forbes, the head of the Special Branch, whom he'd met under very different circumstances in 1979 on the Senior Officers Command Course. But the disclosure of some matters was way outside Forbes's authority – and the Chief Constable's too. That's when the Security Service, MI5, became involved.

But the team found the constables and sergeants of the HMSUs which had been involved in the three incidents very co-operative. They got the impression that following the pain of the court cases, in which four of them had been charged with murder, and the embarrassment of having to reveal the cover stories they'd been ordered to tell, morale was poor: the lower ranks felt they were the 'fall guys' and some of them were bitter; they felt they'd been left to their own devices when things had gone wrong. When covert operations went well, for example when the targets *were* armed, cover stories were no problem. Stalker had no difficulty in identifying the senior Special Branch officers whom the junior ranks had implicated in the cover-ups. They were the officers whose names Constable John Robinson had written down on a piece of paper and handed to the judge. Their involvement was confirmed by over a dozen junior officers whom the team had interviewed. One of them was a Superintendent who was operational head of the Special Branch for South Region with responsibility for the TCG at Gough Barracks; another was a Chief Inspector who was attached to the TCG and in charge of 'tasking' the HMSUs. The third senior officer was the Special Branch Chief Superintendent at headquarters, who has since retired. Both the Superintendent and the Chief Inspector (subsequently promoted to Superintendent) were interviewed under caution. The Chief Inspector apparently admitted that he was a member of a 'Chinese Parliament' that would devise a cover story to protect an informant. The Superintendent apparently accepted some responsibility for concealing the involvement of the Special Branch inspector who was involved in the cross-border covert operation and who had picked up Constable Robinson after his collision with the army surveillance cars. It also appears that some of the junior officers participated in manufacturing some aspects of the false accounts. Almost a year into the inquiry, Stalker believed there was *prima facie* evidence that criminal or disciplinary offences might have been committed. This did not necessarily mean that any offence *had* been committed; that was a matter for the DPP to decide or, if it were a disciplinary matter, the RUC. Certainly it could have been argued to both authorities that the cover stories were told to protect the source and were not designed in any way to interfere with the course of justice so far as the actual shootings were concerned. Under the circumstances, Stalker thought it advisable that the Superintendent and Chief Inspector should be suspended from duty in the interests of both the public and his inquiry. In April 1985 Stalker formally requested their suspension. The Chief Constable declined to suspend them, but did remove them from operational duty.

What surprised Stalker and Thorburn, reviewing the way in which the original CID investigations had been conducted, was the apparent lack of co-ordination in approaching three shootings which had happened within weeks of each other, in the same small geographical area of Northern Ireland and, at least in the cases of Toman, Burns and McKerr and Grew and Carroll, in remarkably similar circumstances. Not only were the investigations uncoordinated, the team concluded that the CID officers involved were remiss in gathering the evidence. In all three cases, Stalker's team found forensic and other evidential material which they felt should have been uncovered at the time. Stalker brought in his own forensic and ballistic experts from England, who went over the three incidents in the most minute detail. The team reconstructed the three shootings and reanalysed the evidence the RUC had found and used in the three court cases. Suffice it to say that they did not agree with all the original findings. Stalker also suspected that general intelligence (although not necessarily of a sinister nature) had been added to Michael Tighe's Special Branch file after his death and that Martin McCauley might not have been whiter than white – a fact Special Branch might not have disputed.

Not surprisingly, the area Stalker and his team found most difficult to penetrate was the world of the informers. They pointed out that if they were to fulfil that aspect of their terms of reference, they needed to know their identities and to be given access to all details about them. Even on the Special Branch files, individuals are not named; their identities are only indicated by the word 'agent' followed by a code number. Stalker discovered, contrary to the impression that had been given at the trials, he was dealing with two agents, not three.

Their identities were restricted to their code numbers. One was the 'mole', the other a man from across the border in the Irish Republic. The 'mole' was the source involved in the shooting of Toman, Burns and McKerr, and Tighe and McCauley; the other in the shooting of Grew and Carroll.

Stalker did establish the identity of the cross-border informant – a man called George Poyntz – a fifty-seven-year-old Republican who lived in Castleblaney in County Monaghan. Poyntz was a veteran IRA supporter and a former chairman of Castleblaney Sinn Fein. He also had good contacts with the INLA. After Seamus Grew had dropped off his sister in Monaghan town, he and Roddy Carroll drove to George Poyntz's house in Castleblaney where, it was believed, they'd arranged to meet Dominic McGlinchey. It's thought that the rendezvous did take place, and McGlinchey left the house in the Allegro with Grew and Carroll. They were still being tailed by the Special Branch officers from Armagh. As Grew and Carroll crossed the border, one of the officers rang the TCG at Gough Barracks from Keady (a few miles inside Northern Ireland) and the plan to intercept Dominic McGlinchey and two of his most senior lieutenants was put into operation. Six months later, on 7 May 1983, the body of a man called Eric Dale was found tied in two plastic bags on a lonely border road at Clontygora, near Killeen in South Armagh.[2] He had been shot through the head. A post mortem revealed that he'd been beaten before being killed. Dale had been abducted by six masked gunmen from the farmhouse near the border, where he was living. The INLA said it had 'executed him' because he was a police informer. It claimed he had 'admitted under interrogation' that he'd supplied the security forces with information about the movements of Grew and Carroll. The INLA also said he'd admitted trying to establish the whereabouts of Dominic McGlinchey. A senior Garda detective said 'We believe this man had some links with the INLA, but their claim that he was an informer is utter rubbish.' Dale's family, who lived in Portadown, denied the allegation. His daughter Fiona said 'From what we have learned following the post mortem, my father was beaten and tortured by the INLA.

They say he admitted certain things, but nobody could withstand the terrible torture they inflicted on him.' She said her father had been a 'dedicated Republican for the last eleven years of his life', and 'The people who did this are worse than animals. They cannot call themselves Irishmen. They are nothing but gangsters.'[3] George Poyntz was luckier; it was said that following the shooting of Grew and Carroll, he tipped off the INLA that Dale was an informer, to strengthen his own cover.[4] Constable John Robinson revealed the cover story and its purpose, to protect an informer, on 28 and 29 May 1984. The following day, Poyntz received a mysterious telephone message from 'a woman' in Keady, saying she wanted to see him.[5] Poyntz hired a taxi, went to Keady and was escorted under escort to Gough Barracks. Poyntz was taken into 'protective custody' and subsequently left Northern Ireland to be given a new life and, presumably, a new identity in return for his services. His family was allowed to visit him at Gough Barracks. He told them he was an RUC undercover agent and had no plans to return home.[6]

Stalker never really cracked the precise operational status of the Special Branch officers who crossed the border to watch Grew and Carroll that day. He discovered that it was accepted that both the RUC and Gardai frequently crossed into each other's territory, but that it was done unofficially; if they were apprehended, they could not claim that their presence within a foreign jurisdiction was an operational one, they were to be there as 'private citizens'. Officers involved in this particular cross-border incursion said they were unarmed and were not carrying police radios. In the absence of any evidence to the contrary, Stalker had to accept that they were 'private citizens'.

Eric Dale was dead and George Poyntz had been spirited away, so all Stalker had to rely on was the Special Branch files.

The 'mole' was a different question; he, miraculously, had survived. In February 1985 Stalker formally asked ACC Trevor Forbes, the head of the Special Branch, for access to his file; without it, he is said to have told Forbes, he couldn't carry out the crucial part of his remit, which involved the use and protection of informers. He also asked for access to the register which was kept of payments made to agents. In the end, he finally got what he wanted. The unnamed 'mole' appeared to have few worries about money; over a period of time, he'd earned around £30,000 – presumably tax free as agents don't inform the Inland Revenue. That sum was made up not just of 'incentive' payments for the information that led to the pinpointing of Toman, Burns and McKerr and (as it transpired) the identification of the Hayshed as a place to be watched, but for intelligence that led to explosives seizures both before and, remarkably, *after* the shootings of Toman, Burns and McKerr, and Tighe and McCauley. The register indicated that he'd been paid another substantial amount following the interception by the HMSU of one of the biggest consignments of explosives ever seized in Northern Ireland (see Chapter 7) just outside Banbridge in August 1982 – over two months *before* the shootings. He was also paid around £3,000 *after* the shootings for information which led to another seizure of explosives. Stalker and his team were staggered at the sums involved, coming from a force where informers were lucky to be paid in three figures let alone four. That is why, with such sums on offer, they feared that informers might be tempted to become bounty hunters, perhaps less scrupulous with the truth. They worried too that the quality of the information sold might not always match the quantity paid for it. Who was to know of its accuracy? What was to stop an agent delivering names, true or false, and taking the money? Who was to know the accuracy of the information, apart from the IRA? All these questions, in more public form, were raised at the trials of the 'supergrasses' – the 'converted terrorists' – who decided or had been induced to break their cover. (Some, like John Grimley of the INLA and Raymond Gilmour of the IRA, had been Special Branch informers for some time.) And crucially, if people were killed, as Toman, Burns and McKerr, and Michael Tighe were, in circumstances which stemmed from the 'mole's' information, who was to know, apart from the 'mole' and the IRA, if they were the 'right' people? The team also believed that the 'mole' had been involved in serious criminal offences, in contradiction of the Home Office guidelines on informants who take part in crime (see Appendix 3 for the full guidelines):

Where an informant gives the police information about the intention of others to commit a crime in which they intend that he shall play a part, his participation should be allowed to continue only where (1) he does not actively engage in planning and committing the crime; (2) he is intended to play a minor role; and (3) his participation is essential to enable the police to frustrate the principal criminals and to arrest them (albeit for lesser offences such as attempt or conspiracy to commit the crime, or carrying offensive weapons) before injury is done to any person or serious damage to property.

The informant should always be instructed that he must on no account act as *agent provocateur*, whether by suggesting to others that they should commit offences or encouraging them to do so, and that if he is found to have done so, he will himself be liable to prosecution.[7]

For all these reasons, Stalker felt it was essential that he be allowed to meet the 'mole', whether in Northern Ireland or, by that time, elsewhere. He was particularly anxious to make his own evaluation of the quality of his information. At least, to start with, he wanted to meet his 'handler'. In April 1985, two months after he'd asked ACC Forbes for his file, Stalker made a formal request to Sir John Hermon to meet and interview the 'mole' – wherever he was. Sir John's answer was an unequivocal no; to permit such access – assuming it were possible – would be a dereliction of his public duty and of his responsibilities to the informant. Stalker was touching the very heart of the RUC's anti-terrorist operations, and Sir John was not prepared to be party to any action which might put them at risk. Giving Stalker access to the 'mole' would also create a precedent it would be difficult to defend to any current or potential source (were they ever to hear of it); and such an external meeting would violate the sanctity of the relationship between the agent and his 'handler'. An agent had enough trouble staying in place and staying alive without having to account for his actions, within or without Home Office guidelines, to an outside investigator from England.

Even without access to the 'mole', the team was in a position to record what really happened the day Toman, Burns and McKerr were shot and the circumstances in which the cover story had been told. They had access to the 'mole's' number-coded file and to the E4A officers who were involved in the undercover surveillance operation on 11 November 1982. The origins of the shooting of Toman, Burns and McKerr were traced back to the IRA landmine which killed the three police officers on the Kinnego embankment a fortnight earlier. The same evening it appears the 'mole' was contacted by his two 'handlers' and asked who was responsible. He gave several names – amongst them Eugene Toman and Sean Burns. That's why, when the three police officers were tried for the murder of Eugene Toman, the court was told that Toman and Burns were wanted for questioning in connection with the Kinnego land-mine; and why too, again on information from the 'mole', it was said that Toman and Burns were on their way to murder an RUC reservist. That's why Toman and Burns were kept under surveillance by E4A. On the afternoon of 11 November they were seen in Portadown, checking out the car which they thought belonged to their intended victim who worked at a store in the town. They were then observed going to McKerr's house, where they were joined by another man. McKerr was then seen with this fourth person, fitting a CB radio in a car. There were two cars involved on the night of the shooting: the Escort, driven by McKerr, which was fitted with a CB radio; and another 'scout' car, also fitted with CB, driven by the man who was seen with McKerr fitting the radio earlier that after-noon. The HMSU were ready for the operation – among them, although it was never revealed, at least one of the officers involved in the shooting at the Hayshed. The plan was to set up a VCP and stop the Escort. But later that evening the operation was stood down. The E4A unit had apparently been operating since early that morning and had been 'out in the open' for longer than was usual or advisable. When their 'targets' dis-appeared inside a house, a decision was made to call it a day. It was, I understand, only when one of the unit decided to make a last 'pass' of the house and saw Toman, Burns and McKerr getting into the Escort, that the operation was suddenly called on again. By this time, the HMSU had already started off back to Belfast. They were called back and barely had time to get a car halfway across the road, when the Escort arrived. There wasn't time to get the planned VCP into position. Toman, Burns and McKerr accelerated to their deaths. The 'mole' received around £5,000 for his services. But Tullygally and Kinnego were only two pieces of the jigsaw. Behind the full picture lay the hand of MI5.

Chapter 7

The Riddle of the Hayshed

Stalker, Thorburn and the team found that the thread that led to the killing of Toman, Burns and McKerr went back beyond the Kinnego landmine to the end of August 1982, perhaps even further. Again it led back to the 'mole'. They discovered that he'd provided information that led to the identification of two large consignments of explosives which had come from the South. The first was seized, concealed on the back of a hay lorry, on 20 August 1982, at Lenaderg on the main Banbridge–Guildford road by an apparently 'routine' VCP. The officers manning the checkpoint came from Lisnasharragh, the Belfast base of the HMSUs. Allegedly the police had already noted the 'scout' car and had let it pass. The driver was said to have been Gervaise McKerr. The hay lorry was coming from Dundalk, a few miles across the border in the Irish Republic. Allegedly the police had a reason to stop the vehicle, had they wanted an excuse, since the front number plate (HTK 158P) did not match the rear (HTK 108P). The load, they said, also appeared to be top heavy and leaning to one side. The driver told them he was heading for Lurgan. 'I've nothing to say,' he said, according to the police. Another 'crew' arrived and searched the lorry. On the back, which was piled high with bales of straw, they detected a strong smell of 'marzipan'. The 'marzipan' was the smell of sixty plastic sacks filled with explosives made from chemical fertilizer, concealed under the bales of hay. The police also found detonators and fuse wire. The driver was arrested and taken to Gough Barracks. It was, the RUC said, 'one of the biggest, if not the biggest, explosives finds during thirteen years of violence'.[1]

About a month later, the end of September 1982, the 'mole' gave his 'handlers' what was to prove, in terms of the Stalker inquiry, the most sensitive tip-off of all. He told them about a further consignment of fertilizer explosives coming from across the border and pointed out the location in which they were to be stored – the Hayshed in Ballynerry Road North. This time there was no VCP, no interception and no arrest. That, it appears, was to come later; the plan seems to have been to catch an IRA active service unit with its hands on the explosives. This consignment, too, was concealed in a trailer. The trailer was unhooked and left in the car park of a pub in Derrymacash, a hamlet a couple of miles from Lurgan and a mile from the Hayshed. Its contents were unloaded into a van and driven to Ballynerry Road North, where they were hidden in the Hayshed belonging to the widow of an IRA veteran of the 1920s, Catherine ('Kitty') Cairns. The close surveillance of the whole operation was carried out by E4A. But once the explosives were in place, continuing surveillance was a problem. Mounting a Static Observation Post (SOP) – often literally a hole in the ground manned for days on end with excreta stored in plastic bags – was extremely risky as the Hayshed stood not in the middle of nowhere but in the vicinity of people, houses and dogs. (One SOP, it seems, had already been rumbled by a particularly persistent Republican dog.) Although the location could be – and was – regularly overflown by Army helicopters (crammed, presumably, with high-tech surveillance equipment), they could not provide the round-the-clock surveillance necessary to detect any movement of the explosives.

Under the circumstances, in the interests of effectiveness and security, it was decided that MI5 should plant an electronic listening device in the Hayshed which would monitor the scene twenty-four hours a day without risk to those involved who would be several miles away. There were rumours that some Special Branch officers opposed the solution, arguing that human surveillance was preferable and more reliable – albeit more dangerous. But if there were such differences of opinion, word of them never reached the ears of the policy-makers. It appears that MI5 sought authority from the Home Secretary,

William Whitelaw, to plant the listening device. The Northern Ireland Secretary, James Prior, seems not to have been consulted. MI5's political master is the Home Secretary; he must authorize an electronic surveillance operation, just as he must a telephone tap. How much higher knowledge of the Hayshed 'bug' went, Stalker did not establish; it is possible that the matter was discussed or noted by the Cabinet's Joint Intelligence Committee at which, every Wednesday, the heads of the Secret Services – MI5, MI6, GCHQ and the Defence Intelligence Staff – meet to discuss *operational* priorities with their departmental masters from the Home Office, Foreign Office and Ministry of Defence. The chairman of the Joint Intelligence Committee has direct access to the Prime Minister, as has the head of each individual Secret Service.

In the middle of the night, toward the end of September 1982, an MI5 technical officer was taken into the Hayshed. (This would be known as a 'friendly entry'.) *Two* devices were planted: one in a rafter in the roof; the other under the explosives which would be triggered by any movement. Photographs of the cache were also taken. The explosives stayed in the Hayshed for several weeks. No one volunteered any of this crucial information to Stalker. It was, literally, top secret. All the Chief Constable would tell him was that his men had been directed to the Hayshed on what the Special Branch assessed to be Grade A intelligence. Sir John no doubt knew that the Hayshed was under surveillance at the time, but did not necessarily know that it was being taped. The RUC says the Chief Constable invariably kept himself 'above the battle' and did not necessarily know the fine detail of each operation. Secretary of State James Prior also knew of the 'bug' when it was mentioned to him in the autumn of 1982 by one of his security advisers – almost certainly by MI5's Director and Co-ordinator of Intelligence. But the 'bugs' proved faulty; it appears they may have attracted the attention of birds and vermin in the Hayshed. During this defective period, unknown to those carrying out the surveillance, the explosives were removed from the shed, most probably in the same van that brought them there. At this time the van was also under observation and had been spotted in the vicinity of the Kinnego embankment a couple of miles away. The Tasking and Co-ordinating Group (TCG) at Gough Barracks had issued a warning that this area was a likely location for a terrorist attack. The area was put out of bounds. Entry was only permitted once special permission had been given. On 27 October 1982 the RUC received a call about a theft in the vicinity of the Kinnego embankment. Permission to enter was sought from the appropriate authorities. A check was made and because it was believed that the explosives were still in the Hayshed, three police officers were given the green light to proceed in their armoured Cortina. At 2.30 p.m. Sergeant Sean Quinn and Constables Alan McCloy and Paul Hamilton drove over the landmine along the Kinnego embankment. The explosives from the Hayshed had been used in the bomb. They were detonated from a mound above the embankment. Two men in crash helmets were seen riding way from the scene on a red Honda motorcycle, which was later found abandoned in Lurgan. At the time of the explosion, the Chief Constable was barely a mile away, about to address the audience at a speech day at Lurgan College. He was immediately told the news but stayed for over two hours to fulfil his engagement, not wishing to cause alarm. He then went straight to the scene and met a barrage of pressmen. He knew the explosives had been under surveillance at the Hayshed and wanted to known how they had escaped detection. The RUC says he made no mention of it at the time. MI5's surveillance operation had failed, and three police officers were dead. No Active Service Unit had been caught red-handed. It was that night that the 'mole' was seen by his 'handlers' and asked to name names.

Stalker and his team stumbled upon Kinnego almost by accident. They were going through the files on Toman, Burns and McKerr when they came across additional intelligence linking Toman and Burns (and others as well) with the landmine. The team told Stalker that they believed Kinnego was vital to an understanding of what happened at the Hayshed, but were concerned that Kinnego wasn't in their terms of reference. Stalker told them to push ahead; he wasn't going to ask permission to do so, anticipating more problems. Kinnego became the *fourth* incident in Stalker's investigation. He appointed two of his team to double up on it. Stalker soon learned of the Chief Constable's concern that the team had now extended its inquiry to Kinnego. Sir John never tried to impede them, although he must have known how such revelations might harm the force, damage morale and prove upsetting to the relatives of the three dead policemen. Stalker believed it was impossible *not* to investigate Kinnego.

The team ploughed on and that's how they came to the tape. They had no idea that the Hayshed was bugged. They assumed there must have been some kind of Static Observation Post, but never imagined there was an electronic listening device inside. At first they thought that the reason why the Special Branch remained silent about the surveillance operation was to protect the identities of those involved. The team kept on pushing and, in the end, tucked away in some Special Branch papers, they came across the vital information that the Hayshed had been under 'technical' surveillance. They then found out that the devices had gone wrong. They told Stalker. Stalker told them to go back and find out if they had been replaced. Eventually they established that the devices had been removed and a new, more sensitive and, it was hoped, more reliable device installed. So, was it there at the time of the shooting? Yes. When was it removed? Soon afterwards. (That also explained why it was some time before the RUC's senior CID detectives and scene-of-crime officers were given access to the sealed-off area; they'd had to wait until an MI5 technical officer was called in to remove the bug; he arrived within the hour.) So, if there was a listening device, who listened? Did someone take notes of what was transmitted? Not only did the team find that notes were taken but, to their astonishment, that *tape recordings were made of what the device transmitted*. Hence, the final and one of the most crucial questions of the whole inquiry: *was the tape running when the shooting took place, and if so, was a warning given*? Stalker and his team battled for eighteen months to find out. The tape was so secret that even at the time of the McCauley trial in January and February 1985, the Attorney-General's office did not know of its existence. Law officers knew, although it was not revealed in court, that the Hayshed was under technical surveillance, but they did not know that the surveillance was taped. (It was never considered that the tape might be used as evidence in the case; the rifles were the evidence and McCauley was charged with their possession.)

The team had established the existence of a tape towards the end of 1984 – about six months into their inquiry. Stalker began the tortuous process of trying to gain official access to it in January 1985, the month McCauley's trial began. Stalker sought what became known as the 'product' of the listening device – the tape, transcripts, logs and everything else associated with it. Stalker and the team were initially confident that they would get their hands on the actual tape. John Thorburn asked the senior Special Branch officer at headquarters detailed questions about it. His lips were sealed. Stalker took it up with the Chief Constable, pointing out that the tape was vital to his understanding of what happened at the Hayshed. Sir John said that the 'product' of the tape wasn't his to give; it belonged to MI5 as the owner of the device which had transmitted the 'product'.

At the end of January 1985 Stalker got in touch with Bernard Sheldon, the head of Legal Services at MI5. (Mr Sheldon's name later became public during the government's battle in the Australian courts to prevent publication of the memoirs of the former MI5 officer, Peter Wright.) Stalker went to see Sheldon at MI5's offices in London. He said he knew that the device was being monitored right up to the time of the shooting, and that if there was a tape of the shooting itself, it was vital that he had access to it if he was to establish how Michael Tighe died. Sheldon apparently agreed with Stalker's assessment and promised that MI5 would not stand in his way. He suggested that Stalker should wait until Lord Justice Kelly had delivered his judgment in McCauley's case and then request the head of the Special Branch, ACC Trevor Forbes, to release the *log* of the tape. At this time, there was no suggestion that anything untoward had happened to the tape itself. Shortly afterwards, Stalker talked with Sir Philip Myers, who agreed on the importance of gaining access to the tape. The following month, after

McCauley had been given a suspended sentence (16 February 1985) for possessing the rifles in the Hayshed, Stalker approached ACC Forbes and asked for the logs and the names of all the officers involved in monitoring the listening device. The request went up to the Chief Constable. Sir John refused. The only information he could provide, he told Stalker, was that the Special Branch was acting on intelligence it rated as grade A. Stalker wasn't prepared to let it rest at that, convinced that the tape might indicate whether Sergeant X and Constables Y and Z *had* given a warning before opening fire, as they had said they did in court. At the beginning of April 1985 Stalker saw ACC Forbes again and tried to carry the matter further. By this time Stalker and the team had established the identity of at least one of those monitoring the bug – an RUC constable who was listening with others who were *not* police officers, in a Portakabin a few miles away. Forbes confirmed that the constable was under orders not to divulge anything about his role. Stalker contacted the Chief Constable again and said he couldn't let matters rest as they were; he stressed he had to make progress on this front or the DPP would be unable to issue a proper directive with regard to events at the Hayshed since he would not be in possession of all the available evidence. Stalker still failed to make any headway. By the end of April he felt his position was becoming untenable; he'd been asked by the Chief Constable to conduct an inquiry but he was being denied access to the vital material he needed to do it properly. In frustration he contacted the DPP, Sir Barry Shaw, and asked if he could report directly to him, instead of the Chief Constable, as his remit required. Sir Barry replied that under the circumstances Stalker's remit could not suddenly be changed but, he suggested, if Stalker thought criminal offences might have been committed, he could consider himself a private citizen, furnish evidence to him in that capacity and thereby seek his advice. This the director was empowered to do under section 5 of the Prosecution of Offences (Northern Ireland) Order 1972, which states:

. . . it shall be the function of the Director to consider . . .

with a view to his initiating . . . in Northern Ireland any
criminal proceedings . . . any facts or information brought to
his notice, whether by the Chief Constable . . . or by the
Attorney-General or *by any other authority or person* [my
emphasis].[2]

Stalker was being invited to consider himself 'any other person'. The Chief Constable was adamant that the *status quo* must
be maintained; that constitutionally he had commissioned Stalker to conduct the inquiry and constitutionally Stalker must
remain answerable to him. Stalker insisted that in the light of
his inquiries and his inability to obtain the evidence he
required, that relationship was no longer appropriate. He
threatened to resign and went as far as drafting a press release
which spoke of constitutional differences existing between himself and the Chief Constable: he appreciated that Sir John's
concern was to protect delicate operations in Northern Ireland,
and his men who were involved in them, but that he had a
different responsibility – to conduct a full and exhaustive
inquiry into the activities of certain RUC officers. He concluded
that he couldn't submit a final report as instructed because he
was not in possession of all the evidence; he had therefore
decided to resign. The press release was never issued. It was, at
the very least, a useful lever to help prise out the tape. The
resignation of John Stalker was the last thing the authorities
needed with all the inevitable allegations of 'covering up a
cover-up'.

Around the middle of May 1985 Sir John suggested that he
and Stalker should meet. Meetings between the two men were
rare; not for any suspicious reason but, as Sir John had
indicated at the beginning of the inquiry, he wanted his investigator to be left alone to get on with the job. Stalker met the
Chief Constable at police headquarters. He said he needed
access to the tape and to the RUC constable who was monitoring it; he was determined to succeed. He asked Sir John to
reconsider his decision to deny all access. Sir John said he'd give
it some thought. Stalker repeated his view that it would be more
appropriate for him to report directly to the DPP, as the Chief

Constable had personal knowledge of some of the Special Branch matters he would be reporting on and which had not been fully divulged to the Director's office during the initial investigations. The Chief Constable said that such a change of remit might cause considerable difficulties both for him and the RUC. The meeting was inconclusive.

A few days later they met again. This time there were signs of progress. Sir John said that Stalker must continue to report to him until after his report had finally been delivered to the DPP; that was a most serious constitutional issue on which there could be no compromise. But, having given thought to the matter of the tape, he said he was now prepared to authorize the release of all material the RUC had in relation to the Hayshed. However, he indicated that MI5 had a very considerable interest in it and would require reassurance about the way Stalker proposed to handle the material. Sir John then startled Stalker by indicating that *the tape might not exist.* Stalker felt he was going round in circles. He said he'd already seen Bernard Sheldon at MI5, five months earlier (in January 1985), and he'd assured him that if the RUC was prepared to release the tape, MI5 would not object. Sir John then made a telephone call. About half an hour later the Director and Co-ordinator of Intelligence was shown into the Chief Constable's office. Stalker was asked to leave. Unhappily he agreed. Half an hour later Stalker was shown back in and introduced to the senior MI5 officer. He told Stalker that he would be in touch with London and, subject to unspecified provisos, he would be advising that MI5 should give its full co-operation. Stalker said the matter had been dragging on for nearly six months and his patience was nearly exhausted. MI5's representative said he'd have an answer within a few days and would be in touch through Sir John. It seems there were several contacts over the next few days between Bernard Sheldon of MI5, John Stalker and Sir John Hermon. The upshot was that MI5 agreed to let Stalker have the information he wanted, *but* wished first to review it to see whether it had any objection. Stalker wasn't happy with the qualification but had no option other than to go along with it. An exasperated Stalker was then asked yet again to state precisely what he wanted. He said he wanted to *listen* to the tape at the point at which the police assaulted the Hayshed; if there was a transcript, he'd like a copy; he wanted to interview the RUC constable who was monitoring the device and, without any constraint being placed upon him, to take him beyond the point where the police moved in (the constable had already been interviewed by Stalker's team but he had refused to say anything beyond the point of the assault). Finally, Stalker said he would like to examine the authority for installing and monitoring the device (at this stage, Stalker did not know it was the Home Secretary). Stalker pointed out he was unable to be more specific, as he had no idea what material existed; when he did, he could itemize his request.

In the middle of June 1985 Stalker had his second meeting with MI5 in London. Present were Sir John Hermon, Bernard Sheldon and MI5's senior officer in Northern Ireland. Sheldon made it clear that MI5 was prepared to release any information which Stalker thought might be used as *evidence*, given the seriousness of the matters he was investigating at the Hayshed. (This had apparently been one of the stumbling blocks. The tapes were used for *intelligence* purposes, not evidence.) The Chief Constable was left in no doubt that MI5 was not standing in Stalker's way. But Sheldon said he was not prepared to discuss the authority for installing and monitoring the device unless he were given directions to do so; that was because it was a *political* issue and not because there had been any impropriety or breach of procedure. Stalker was prepared to accept Sheldon's word and agreed not to pursue the 'authority' question any further. He then asked the Chief Constable when he could have the tape and the transcripts. Sir John, presumably to Stalker's stunned surprise, said that *the tape had been destroyed*, but there was a transcript. Stalker asked when it had happened. Sir John couldn't answer. He then, one assumes, surprised and dismayed Stalker even further by telling him that he couldn't hand over the material unless he was directed to do so by a higher authority, namely the DPP or the Attorney-General. He told Stalker he wanted him to complete his report and deliver it to him *without* the evidence from the tape. Stalker could note, he suggested, that the report was incomplete as there was still further evidence to be obtained. Sir John explained that he needed to be instructed that disclosure would be in the public interest (presumably not just because of the secrecy of such surveillance operations, but because of the involvement of the 'mole').

Stalker was furious. A few days later he spoke to the DPP and Sir Philip Myers. He told them both of his frustration and disappointment: he'd considered resignation but decided against it as it was unlikely to help matters; it was better, he thought, to bide his time in the expectation that eventually the DPP would authorize the Chief Constable to release the material; with hindsight, he never would have agreed to terms of reference which bound him to report to the head of the force he had been appointed to investigate. By the end of June 1985 Stalker gave in. He agreed to do what he said he never would – submit an incomplete report. But he felt he had no option. There were no short cuts. But however much he felt the personal slight, Stalker was a professional policeman who appreciated the extreme sensitivity of the Chief Constable's position, and acknowledged his need to seek clarification of 'the public interest'. The authorities faced an awful dilemma: was the public interest best served by disclosure or by continued suppression – to protect top-secret operations which were, it could be argued, above all in the public interest since their supreme object was the public's safety?

June 1985 was a watershed. Stalker thought it advisable to mark it with a formal letter to the Chief Constable outlining the situation as he saw it – even without access to the tape material. He informed Sir John, in advance of writing the incomplete report, that his team had accumulated a considerable amount of *fresh evidence* which, at the very least, would be available to the inquests still to be held on the six dead men. All the evidence, of course, would have to be assessed by the DPP. Prophetically, at the end of June 1985, Stalker informed Sir John that he suspected that in the months ahead his inquiry would come under very close scrutiny and said he wanted to make his position clear to protect himself and his team. He was anxious that Sir

John did not underestimate the possible damage the contents of his report might do to the RUC; as far as he and his team were concerned, there were now far more serious issues at stake than that of senior officers fabricating cover stories to protect informers. Stalker and Thorburn both felt that the full impact of their findings – even without the tape – might not be fully appreciated in Northern Ireland. Stalker considered writing to Douglas Hurd (who had succeeded James Prior as Northern Ireland Secretary, and with whom the Chief Constable had had discussions earlier that month) but in the end decided against it. By the early summer of 1985 the authorities could have had little doubt where the Stalker report was leading.

In July 1985 Stalker was back in Manchester writing his report. He wrote longhand and then had it transferred to a word processor. Meanwhile, he arranged for the mountain of back-up documents to be specially bound. Normally such operations were done 'in house' on a special binding machine, but Stalker sent the work outside for security reasons and had them bound in such a way that they could not be interfered with; no one could take out a leaf – unlike a spiral binding – without destroying the whole book. Stalker's team supervised the operation and never left it. Six full sets of the report were produced with each section (the Hayshed, Tullygally, Mullacreevie and Kinnego) bound in a different colour. Each full set ran to around fifteen volumes. The accompanying 'interim' report took Stalker about a fortnight to write on the basis of the material provided by Thorburn and the team. It was – bar the Hayshed – 95 per cent complete. It was always his intention to submit the full report, once the DPP had ordered Sir John to release the tape material. The interim report, about fifty to sixty typed pages, also outlined the areas to be examined in connection with the Hayshed when Stalker returned to Northern Ireland at some future date, after the agreed mechanism finally produced the missing material. Stalker also made a dozen recommendations about the general running of the RUC in the light of the observations he and his team had made over the preceding thirteen months.

1. The Special Branch had too much power and there was a feeling amongst senior officers that its covert operations should not be open to question.

2. The use of informers and agents should be placed on a proper legal and practical footing: a central record should be kept – a *bound* document – of all payments made; the Home Office guidelines on their use had been breached and should be firmly adhered to.

3. The CID was not told of the Special Branch operations: there appeared to be a tacit and disturbing acceptance by CID investigating detectives that the Special Branch dictated the point at which their inquiries should begin.

4. The Special Branch should cease to use the form which restricted what officers could say under the Official Secrets Act and could prevent them from telling the truth.

5. New ways of submitting classified and secret material to the DPP's office should be discussed so the director could be in possession of *all* the evidence in a case and maintain the full confidence of those who submitted it. (There was a feeling that some Special Branch officers did not trust the DPP's office.)

6. Special Branch, which seemed to have operated as a force within a force, should be opened up so it ceased to be a self-perpetuating élite.

7. When the word 'wanted' was used in connection with an individual, there should be a clear distinction made between what was *evidence* and what was *intelligence*.

8. Following an incident, officers should *not* be debriefed by the Special Branch *before* they were interviewed by the CID.

9. Special Branch surveillance officers working for E4A and other units *must* give evidence to the CID if they are witnesses to incidents.

10. Special anti-terrorist units like the HMSUs had a vital role, given the situation in Northern Ireland, but there was a case for their *operational* control being taken away from the Special Branch.

11. There should be *written* guidelines for officers who crossed the border in the course of their duties.

12. Investigations into any future incidents (such as those Stalker had conducted) should be carried out by an RUC team which was seen to be 'independent', or by an RUC team under the direction of a mainland officer, or by a team of officers from an outside force.

Crucially too, for the RUC and the government, Stalker concluded that there was *no evidence that there had been any 'shoot-to-kill' policy.* By September 1985 the interim report was finished. It was loaded into an unmarked van and escorted by two of the team to a military airfield in the south of England. The RAF flew it to Aldergrove Airport, Belfast. Stalker and Thorburn were waiting to convey it to RUC headquarters at Knock. On 18 September one of the team carried a succession of boxes up the stairs and officially delivered the report to Deputy Chief Constable Michael McAtamney, who was asked to sign for it. There were four sets; Stalker had retained two. McAtamney was said to be surprised by the size of it. The team was surprised that the Chief Constable was not there personally to receive it.

Stalker kept his team together for about a fortnight, discussing strategy and the course of action they would pursue in the final stage, when the DPP directed Sir John Hermon to make the tape material available. Days and then weeks went by and there was no news from RUC headquarters. Stalker, after all this time, had expected Sir John to read the report and forward it to the DPP so there could be a quick decision on the tape and Stalker's work could be completed. But he'd underestimated the time it would take for the RUC to digest it; understandably, after all the time it had taken from the RUC's point of view, a cursory reading was out of the question. Discreet inquiries were made about how long the report was going to stay in the RUC's hands; word came back that the RUC would have it until Christmas. There was nothing Stalker could do so he dispersed his team back to their normal jobs within Greater Manchester Police. Then he waited. The new year dawned and there was still no news; he'd heard that Sir John had appointed a high-powered team under ACC David Mellor to dissect the report. This was true. The Chief Constable had appointed ACC Mellor and two of his best superintendents to take the report apart. To put it mildly, they are said not to have been impressed. The picture of these events in 1985 as seen from RUC headquarters was, not surprisingly, very different. The 'mess talk' was that Stalker and his team were 'boy scouts turned cowboys'. The knife went in because the RUC's high command felt Stalker had no understanding of, or sensitivity to, the carefully protected, vital intelligence systems which he proceeded to take apart. There was no love lost between Belfast and Manchester.

As the weeks went by, John Stalker grew increasingly impatient and let Sir Philip Myers know of his annoyance. Around the end of February 1986 word finally came that the DPP's office had received the report. On 4 March, the DPP ordered Sir John Hermon to release every scrap of material connected with the tape and the surveillance of the Hayshed. The Attorney-General had ruled that, although protection of the information was required in the public interest, the protection should be waived so that Stalker could complete his inquiry in full accordance with the DPP's initial directive of April 1984. There was jubilation in Manchester; it had taken the DPP about twelve days to do what the RUC had failed to deliver in twelve months. Sir Barry's direction to Sir John was an 'open sesame': every tape, transcript, log and record was to be handed over to Stalker; the names of every person, RUC or otherwise, involved in the monitoring of the device were to be supplied; if material did *not* exist because it had been destroyed, full details were to be given; and if any of the material had been passed on to others, full details were to be revealed.

It was the middle of March 1986 before Stalker heard officially from Sir John that the Director had instructed him to make all the material available. But Sir John told Stalker he would like to discuss certain things with him first, and suggested a meeting in Belfast after he (Sir John) had returned from leave. He indicated that he was as keen as Stalker to tie things up once and for all and complete the inquiry. (It's important to remember that throughout this period – the first few months of 1986 – the RUC was again under great pressure as it contained Unionist protests, often violent, against the Anglo-Irish agreement. The Stalker report was not at the top of the Chief Constable's agenda.) An appointment was made for Stalker to visit RUC headquarters in Belfast on 30 April 1986. The Chief Constable was absent. Stalker had assumed he'd be there. ACC Trevor Forbes was left to look after him. Stalker said he wasn't going to kick his heels in Belfast until the late afternoon flight back to Manchester; he had the DPP's authorization and intended to use it to start getting what he wanted. Forbes apparently suggested that for him to go ahead without first seeing the Chief Constable would not be in order. Stalker was in no mood to be argued with – and he now had the DPP's authority to obtain the tape material. A Special Branch Chief Inspector reluctantly started to go through Stalker's shopping list, first providing details of how and where and by whom the tapes had been transcribed, the names of those who'd installed the device and then, crucially, the identities of the other non-RUC intelligence officers who were monitoring the device in the Portakabin alongside the RUC constable. Half-way through the afternoon, it appears, another senior officer came in and told Stalker that what he was doing was quite improper; that the instructions from the Chief Constable were that the material was only to be handed over with his personal authorization. Stalker said he'd had enough and was tired of being messed around. But he was left in no doubt that there'd be hell to pay. He ignored the warning and carried on digging out the information. Stalker asked about the existence of the tape and the transcripts and was told they were more difficult to get. He said he could wait and come back for them later. Stalker and Thorburn left RUC headquarters elated, convinced they'd made the breakthrough for which they'd been fighting for nearly eighteen months. The day's haul of documents was in Thorburn's brief-case. They didn't include the 'Crown Jewels' on the tape, but they (Stalker and Thorburn thought) were only another flight away. Stalker planned to call back his team from the four winds and get ready for the final stage of the inquiry.

The chronology is now crucial. Stalker left Belfast with the first set of documents on Wednesday, 30 April 1986. On 12 May the Chief Constable contacted him, apologized for his absence during his last visit, and said he was still anxious to meet Stalker before he recommenced the final leg of his investigation. Stalker immediately arranged to go over the following week. On 14 May Sir Philip Myers called Stalker and asked him to postpone his visit. He was very guarded. Stalker thought he was calling from Belfast, hence the caution over the telephone; he thought that the reason for the postponement was likely to be security problems caused by the Anglo-Irish agreement. At the beginning of the following week, Monday, 19 May, it was agreed that the team should go over to Belfast. On Friday, 23 May, Sir Philip Myers phoned Stalker again and, still guarded over the phone, asked the team *not* to go to Belfast the following week. Stalker had had enough. He told Thorburn to make arrangements for them both to go to Belfast on Monday, 2 June; come hell or high water, they were going.

Stalker had arranged to take off Tuesday and Wednesday, 27 and 28 May, to read himself back into the material. On the Tuesday evening John Stalker and Chief Constable James Anderton had dinner with me and Colin Cameron, the Executive Producer of BBC 2's (Manchester-based) *Brass Tacks* programme, at the Moss Nook Restaurant in Manchester; the purpose was to discuss the problems of policing the inner cities and relations with the media (Anderton's had not always been good). The date had been fixed about two months earlier – the Chief Constable has a very full diary. Anderton and John Stalker were both relaxed. As well as discussing the matters in hand, Anderton also treated us to an informed dissertation on his favourite wines. John Stalker's Northern Ireland inquiry was never discussed. At Greater Manchester Police Headquarters, that dinner became known as 'the Last Supper'. On leaving the restaurant, the Chief Constable gave his Deputy a file for a meeting he'd asked him to attend at the Home Office in London the following Friday. It became known as the 'poisoned chalice'.

The following day, Wednesday, 28 May, Stalker's day off, he was out in the garden when, about teatime, the telephone rang. Stella picked it up and told her husband it was Roger Rees, the Clerk to the Police Authority. Stalker was puzzled; he was on leave and he wondered how Rees had got his home number. The call was very formal: allegations had been made that could constitute a disciplinary offence; Colin Sampson, the Chief Constable of West Yorkshire, would be investigating them; could Stalker be in his office to meet him at 10 a.m. the following day? Stalker said he'd be there anyway. Rees corrected him; he was to be there only at 10 a.m.; his leave was being extended. Stalker asked what it was all about. Rees said that was a matter for Mr Sampson. Stalker was flattened. He picked up the phone and tried to reach James Anderton. The Chief Constable was not around. He asked his secretary to get him to ring as soon as he returned. About 5.30 p.m. James Anderton rang. He was very formal. Stalker asked him what on earth was going on. Anderton said he couldn't discuss it; that was for Sampson. John Stalker was on his own. The hunter was being hunted.

Chapter 8

The Quality Street Gang

What Stalker did not know, although his suspicions may have been aroused in those final few months, was that while he was carrying out his investigation in Northern Ireland, he was under investigation himself. All the circumstantial evidence seemed to point to a conspiracy and the hand of MI5. If there were a conspiracy, there seemed good political reasons for it: MI5 would never allow Stalker to succeed because it stood to lose too much if he finally unlocked the secrets of the Hayshed; the Security Service could not risk the scandal any more than the government and the RUC could stand the shock if Stalker's findings were publicly aired through the courts; and the RUC's morale had to be preserved at all costs as its officers were the fragile glue that held the Anglo-Irish agreement together. For these reasons the conclusion that Stalker was a victim of political expediency seemed on the face of it inevitable; in the teeth of opposition he was about to return to Northern Ireland and finally gain access to what he'd spent eighteen months fighting for, when he was stopped dead in his tracks.

To understand what really happened, one has to recognize that there were two largely unconnected chains of events developing between May 1984, when Stalker began his inquiry, and May 1986, when he was removed from it. The common denominator was John Stalker. We've seen what happened in Northern Ireland; we now have to examine what was happening in Manchester and elsewhere. In doing so, it's important to bear in mind what was going on at the same time across the Irish Sea. Telling this parallel story is not easy for two reasons. The first is operational: at the time of writing, investigations into Kevin Taylor (and perhaps certain other individuals) are still being conducted. The second is legal: much of the Manchester side of the story concerns individuals whom senior officers in the Greater Manchester Police suspected, among other things, of drug running; to date, these suspicions have been based entirely on intelligence and no evidence has been produced to bring any charges. To understand the mechanisms behind what happened to John Stalker, it is necessary to detail these suspicions and in a general way to identify those concerned. It is not my intention to suggest that these people are or may have been at any time involved in these activities. The same observation applies equally to Kevin Taylor. He has no criminal record and has never been charged with any criminal offence. He has been the subject of a GMP investigation for almost three years (inquiries first began around June 1984): he has repeatedly offered himself for interview and been prepared to facilitate the police in their inquiries. His home and office have been searched, the receivers have been called into his company, Rangelark Ltd., and he has been forced to put his house on the market. Kevin Taylor and his business are now in ruins. He denies in the strongest possible terms all the allegations that have been made against him, saying he's convinced that they have been made to discredit his friend John Stalker and destroy his Northern Ireland inquiry. To understand how Kevin Taylor's life and fortunes were turned upside down, it is necessary to go into some detail about the allegations that were being made against him, and how they came about, without wishing to suggest in any way that there was, or is, any substance to them.

It is also necessary to pursue the same course, for the same reasons, with the Manchester side of John Stalker's story. Without doing so, the impetus behind the events that led to his removal cannot be fully appreciated. Again, in order to stand back and see the complete picture (although sections of it inevitably remain blurred), it is necessary to detail the allegations that were being fed into GMP and the way they were handled by the Chief Constable and his senior colleagues – as well as by senior officials at the Home Office. These allegations were both extremely serious and monumentally trivial. Not one of them – beyond the existence of his friendship with Kevin Taylor, which was never a secret – was ever substantiated. It also has to be remembered that all John Stalker was ever charged with were *disciplinary* offences against police regulations which were subsequently disregarded by his Police Authority. And yet this witches' brew of allegations, which started to bubble away almost from the moment he commenced his Northern Ireland inquiry (May 1984), destroyed the career of one of the country's most senior police officers. Again, as with Kevin Taylor, for an understanding of what was happening within GMP whilst John Stalker was involved in the Northern Ireland inquiry, it's necessary to outline the allegations made against the Deputy Chief Constable of the country's largest provincial police force. In doing so, it must be borne in mind that these allegations invariably emanated from criminals (who have a vested interest in undermining the police) and that *there was never any shred of evidence to substantiate them*. So how did it happen? How were Kevin Taylor and John Stalker destroyed?

The origins of John Stalker's problems in Manchester lie in his friendship with Kevin Taylor and Taylor's friendship with a group of people known as the Quality Street Gang (referred to by detectives who know them as the 'QS' and to others as the 'QSG'). The QSG – most of them Damon Runyonesque figures with smart suits and shades, gold bracelets and chains – took their name from a television commercial for Quality Street chocolates which ran many years ago. A limousine rolls up to a bank; men with long coats, fedoras and dark glasses march in and the frightened cashier holds up his hands; a man with a fat cigar slips his hand inside his overcoat and pulls out . . . a box of Quality Street chocolates. The name originated when several members of the 'gang' walked into a pub one evening, looking incredibly dapper and smart, and someone shouted out 'Here's the Quality Street Gang'. The name stuck. The gang gained, and still enjoys, a notoriety among the public and police in Manchester, and many an unsolved crime has been laid at its door. Like many criminal fraternities, however, its precise membership is impossible to discover. Many friends and associates of the principal figures would not be involved in crime. For the police, looking in from the outside, it would have been easy to mistake a social friendship for a criminal conspiracy. Over the years, its membership has fluctuated but half a dozen individuals have long been considered its leading figures. They are mainly from the motor trade, the world of boxing and Manchester's pub and clubland. All of them have criminal records going back over the years, mainly for relatively minor offences. But senior detectives in Manchester have long regarded them as the figures behind most of the organized crime in the city – although little evidence had been produced to back up their suspicions. Most of them are regular visitors to Spain's Costa del Sol and in particular to the jet-set resort of Puerto Banus – a few miles down the coast from Marbella – where they used a yacht called the *Sherama*. For legal reasons it is not possible to name members of the 'gang', although their identities are known. There is no evidence to suggest that Kevin Taylor ever was – or is – a member.

Kevin Taylor first met members of the QSG in the late 1960s when some of them were selling used cars next door to Taylor's Vanland in Manchester's Great Ancoats Street. Taylor bought a pitch from one of their number. He took the fence down, removed the caravan from which they'd done business and increased the acreage of Vanland. He says he never did any business with them as they were in cars and he was in vans, but they would do each other favours from time to time. 'My neighbours were some local boys, from poor backgrounds, who tried to make money the best way they could,' he told me. 'All the people on that pitch always behaved like gentlemen towards me. I've never had any problems with them. They've always treated me with a lot of respect and I've given them the same kind of respect. They're the sort of people who give their word on something and keep to it. For instance, if they were doing a deal on a car, they'd shake hands and never, ever, go back on it. That's the sort of integrity those people have.' I asked Kevin Taylor if John Stalker knew that some of them were his friends. 'Yes, he did,' he replied, after hesitating over the definition of the word 'friend'. 'He was aware that they were my neighbours initially and he was aware that I would bump into them in the town from time to time; and he's aware that some of them I have quite a high regard for.'

Stalker, too, knew of the Quality Street Gang from his days as a detective sergeant (1964–68) attached to 'A' Division which covered the city centre and the old fruit and vegetable market which was at the heart of it. It was here that the QSG had its origins, long before it got its name. Many of the people later associated with it started life as market porters. The market was part of an area which in the early 1960s had one of the biggest concentrations of clubs and pubs in Europe. Here you could drink all day – legally – starting at 9 a.m. in the pubs around the market and ending up at five the following morning in the clubs around the town; there were only three or four hours in twenty-four when drinking was illegal. The market porters were strong, powerful men whom the police could find difficult to handle. They appreciated those who spoke their language. Stalker did: they shared the same Manchester working-class background, although his was considerably less harsh than theirs. They fought with their fists and their heads. One of them, a former boxer of great popularity, would have been considered the 'Rambo' of his day. He's said once to have bitten a man's ear off in a fight which, even in those circles, was considered un-ethical. The porters had a certain code: fights were fair, and policemen were fair game – although on a one-to-one basis. The notion of a wild pack setting on a policeman was unthinkable at that time. Firearms were seldom used; during his four years in 'A' Divison, Stalker came across them only twice. The Greater Manchester Police now deals with a firearms incident a day. These people never caused Stalker any aggravation and he never had any real problems with them. They had no particular love for the police but recognized that they had a job to do; they were there to be outwitted, not attacked. Most of the detective work around the markets involved break-ins; goods would dis-appear overnight and be dispersed with lightning speed. Traders would also buy protection to keep even harder men out.

The richer and the more successful the gang became from its activities in the motor trade and elsewhere,the more it attracted the increasing attention of the police. By the 1970s its premises were under surveillance. Detectives grew suspicious when their cover was blown on more than one occasion. Once, when a particular car pitch was being watched from the top floor of an old mill that overlooked the site, men were said to have come out with air rifles and blown the windows out of the observation point. One senior detective, who came to know the Quality Street Gang well, described its style. 'If we were watching them from a room across the road, they wouldn't make themselves scarce; they'd walk right across and put a brick through the window. They'd let us know they knew. There were lots of stories about how they got the information out, but nobody could put their finger on it.' By the early 1980s, credit card fraud was rife. A card would be stolen in the Home Counties one evening and be in circulation in Manchester by 10 a.m. the following day, before the banks could put a 'stop' on it. The frauds were international too: American Express travellers' cheques and credit cards stolen in England were soon in use along the Mediterranean coast. Drug trafficking, too, was on the increase. As more and more couriers were arrested – whether dealing in drugs or credit card fraud – the police found fingers pointing to the QSG. This perhaps wasn't surprising; just as criminals would boast of their association with it to boost their reputation, so any small courier could dump his crime at its collective feet. One courier who was caught on a credit card fraud was unlucky; he, uncommonly, never said a word to the police and ended up in Salford Royal Infirmary, 'bottled', with thirty stitches in his face.

In the early 1980s, Superintendent Bernard McGourlay, who became the Deputy Co-ordinator of the No.1 Regional Crime Squad, suggested efforts should be made to crack the QSG. The head of the CID, ACC Charles Horam, agreed; it was time somebody had a go. McGourlay organized a surveillance operation with the maximum secrecy possible. Apparently telephones weren't tapped, but more sophisticated methods of surveillance (shades of the Hayshed?) may have been used.

'Any decent villain will claim his telephone's being tapped,' McGourlay told me. 'It's part of getting his Duke of Edinburgh Award.' But whatever the techniques employed, the message to the surveillance team was clear: their targets seemed to know something was afoot by the way they talked and acted. 'They were doubly careful about what they would say,' McGourlay observed. 'They were very, very cagey.' Within a few weeks, McGourlay reported back to his superior and told him he thought his team had been 'blown out'. 'We knew they hadn't been blown out *in situ*, because they hadn't taken any counter-action [like a brick through the window].' There were continuing suspicions of a leak from within the Greater Manchester Police.

This is the beginning of a chain of events that climaxed in 1986. One of those responsible for setting them in motion was a police informer and petty criminal called David Burton (alias Bertelstein). Burton died of natural causes in Preston Prison in March 1985. Burton had been giving information to GMP since the late 1970s. Superintendent McGourlay first met him on a couple of occasions after joining the Regional Crime Squad in 1978, when he supervised handing over reward money – one amount in a car park – for information Burton had given which had led to the recovery of stolen property. McGourlay hadn't 'handled' Burton; he'd just overseen the delivery of the reward money in his capacity as senior officer. The next time he came across him was when one of his inspectors said there was information from Burton that a Liverpool criminal was coming to Manchester with jewellery stolen in burglaries. The man materialized and was arrested in possession of the property. Both McGourlay and his inspector were suspicious; they sensed that Burton had set the man up, having agreed to fence the jewellery himself. Consequently they didn't push the prosecution hard and the criminal ended up with a six-month sentence from a magistrates' court. A short time later Burton was on the phone, saying the man had been released, had a gun and was after him. 'He became a damned nuisance,' said McGourlay. 'He was always on the phone to my inspector. He couldn't get any work done.' Burton was unreliable. 'I wouldn't have told

Burton I was crossing the road, because he would have told somebody else I was committing suicide in front of a taxi.' But Burton wasn't discarded because, as McGourlay admits, 'he did come up with very good information from time to time. The problem was that he could not admit to not knowing something about anything, or anything about something. He became a bit of a joke. He had a very good memory. He could quote names, times, dates and places. He almost sounded as if he was reading them from a script. He appeared to have instant recall.' Burton was also a compulsive liar. 'He'd been known to pass on a dud cheque to a person one week – who'd complain – and then a few weeks later he'd do the same again and get away with it.'

Around the beginning of March 1983 Burton was arrested for cheque fraud. He told a superintendent in 'B' Division that he was working for McGourlay who'd given him *carte blanche* to go around passing dud cheques, but warned him not to overdo it. The incredulous superintendent rang McGourlay. McGourlay was furious; not only that Burton had said it, but that the superintendent had been moved to ring him, in case it were true. Burton was put on the phone and apologized profusely. He said it was a try-on to get off. According to one report, when Burton was arrested for cheque fraud he obtained bail because he said he had information about corrupt police officers.[1] If this was the case, getting bail over the cheque fraud did *not* involve Superintendent McGourlay. McGourlay insists that he never made any deal with Burton on this basis or any other. Burton did, however, give some information about officers he suspected to McGourlay and his inspector at a meeting in the Regional Crime Squad office. But this was not part of any deal. Burton talked about an inspector (named) who'd recently left the force who was, according to Burton, 'too friendly' with the QSG and used to visit its car pitches. He also mentioned another serving officer, a superintendent, whom he said he didn't like and didn't trust. McGourlay says Burton never mentioned, or ever talked about, John Stalker. Although Burton may have mentioned Stalker's name to others in GMP – using different channels and playing one off against the other would be in his nature – it seems surprising that, if he did he said

nothing to McGourlay, given that McGourlay was his con-
fidant. Neither did Burton ever mention Kevin Taylor to
McGourlay: at this stage (around 1983) the name meant
nothing to him.

There were reports that Burton was also an RUC informer[2]
who assisted its investigation into racketeering when, in the
1970s, certain individuals paid the IRA to bomb their premises
and then claimed the compensation. The RUC denies that
Burton ever worked for or helped it. One of the men charged
with making false insurance claims (although there was no
evidence of any IRA connection) was a Manchester discount
trader called Mark Klapish. In the mid-1970s Klapish had a
shop in Belfast's North Street called Pricerite, which sold food
and fancy goods. On 3 October 1975 the premises were
destroyed by fire. (Pricerite hadn't taken Belfast by storm. The
stock was out of date and didn't sell. 'It was a flop,' said one of
the assistants. 'It closed down after about a month.') Klapish
was charged with conspiracy to defraud the Northern Ireland
Office by falsely claiming £38,500 as part of the value of the
goods destroyed in the fire. A preliminary inquiry was held in
Belfast in 1983 and Klapish was granted bail on two sureties of
£5,000 each. He returned to Manchester and was arrested and
charged with conspiracy to obtain property by deception
(obtaining goods from companies on credit). His co-defendants
were David Burton and a leading member of the QSG. Burton
was known to have 'run' with Klapish, as well as being a 'gofer'
for the QSG. This is the time when Burton again got in touch
with McGourlay, who'd now become Deputy Co-ordinator of
the Regional Crime Squad, and asked to see him urgently.
McGourlay agreed. Burton was very anxious that he should
come to court and tell the judge, in mitigation, of all the help
he'd given GMP over the years. He begged McGourlay not to
let him down; he said he couldn't face the 'porridge' and his old
mother was ill. McGourlay pointed out to Burton (and to his
solicitor) the risks of what might happen if it became known
that he'd 'grassed'. Superior officers were consulted and
McGourlay agreed to speak on Burton's behalf. McGourlay
visited the judge in chambers and gave him a list of half a dozen

occasions when Burton's information had led to an arrest and the recovery of property. (It's significant that despite his reputation for unreliability, Burton did deliver the goods on at least half a dozen occasions.) For these six 'jobs', Burton had received around £2,000 in reward money from police funds and insurance companies. The judge accepted the list and McGourlay's assurance without question. He acted accordingly. On 4 September 1984 Burton was sentenced to two years. Klapish got four. The charges against the prominent member of the QSG were not pursued.

It wasn't until Saturday, 9 June 1984, that McGourlay first heard Kevin Taylor's name. It came up during a round of golf. McGourlay, a 'weekend' golfer, had seen a vacancy on the clubhouse list for an early morning game. He put his name down alongside one man he knew, Desmond Lawlor (a building contractor), and one man he didn't, Gerry Wareing (a contract painter). Wareing was a friend of Kevin Taylor and had just come back from a holiday in Spain on Taylor's yacht, *Diogenes*. (Taylor had brought *Diogenes* from Miami, via Salford, to Puerto Banus in August 1982, which is where it stayed, serving as a floating caravan, until the end of 1984.) Lawlor asked Wareing how he'd enjoyed his holiday and started pulling his leg about the 'Costa del Crime'. At this stage McGourlay seems not to have taken part in this conversation; he thinks he may have been off chasing golf balls. It was only after the game that the conversation developed. The round was finished before the clubhouse bar opened, so they adjourned to a nearby pub for a pre-lunch pint. By this time, Wareing and Lawlor had established that McGourlay was a policeman. Over the first round, Wareing asked how he was getting on with the miners' strike. McGourlay said it didn't affect him, as he was CID. Wareing remarked, then, that he must be familiar with the QSG. McGourlay said he was, although he didn't mention he'd done close surveillance on it. Wareing started to talk about some of the 'gang' who were known around Puerto Banus, and mentioned several by their nicknames. Wareing said that one particular 'gang' member wanted to come home to Manchester; Puerto Banus was killing him. (The man had faced charges of handling stolen goods, jumped bail, and taken refuge on the Costa del Sol.)* The conversation then came back to Kevin Taylor. McGourlay asked more about him, on the grounds that anybody with a yacht in Puerto Banus might be interesting. Wareing said Taylor had a big house at Summerseat, where he gave lavish parties. He mentioned that three leading members of the 'gang' had been to them. 'One of your bosses goes to them too,' he added, 'they're great dos.' McGourlay was taken aback. He had no idea to whom Wareing was referring and wondered whether it might be the superintendent Burton had mentioned. McGourlay also suspected that the 'boss' might be anything from a sergeant upwards, as people outside the force seldom understood the ranks within it. Not wanting any name to come out in public – and in a pub – McGourlay switched the conversation back to Puerto Banus. He knew he was treading on sensitive ground. As they were leaving the pub, the question still spinning round his head, McGourlay went up to Wareing in the car park and asked 'By the way, who's my boss who goes to these parties?' 'John Stalker,' Wareing replied without hesitation. McGourlay just laughed and said 'I was just curious to know who gets to all the good parties.'

McGourlay went home a worried man. Wareing had mentioned the names of three 'members' of the QSG going to parties at Kevin Taylor's and, in almost the same breath, the name of the Deputy Chief Constable, John Stalker. 'If John Stalker is involved with somebody who's involved with these people,' McGourlay thought to himself, 'or if he's at the same parties these people are at, then he ought to be advised about it.' It hardly seemed proper to McGourlay that 'people we had been doing surveillance on – and may do again – were people that John Stalker, unwittingly perhaps, was hobnobbing with'.

---

*Kevin Taylor (and possibly others) mentioned the man's desire to return to Manchester to John Stalker. Stalker said he wouldn't get involved personally, but there were other experienced detectives below him who could be put in touch and who might be able to help. The man returned to England and stood trial. On 17 October 1985 he was found guilty of handling a stolen Ford Escort XR3 and given a nine-month sentence suspended for two years. On 15 November 1985 he was sentenced to nine months for a passport offence and six months for failing to surrender to bail.

(In reality only one of the three named 'gang' members attended a party at Kevin Taylor's house when John Stalker was a guest and Stalker had no recollection of meeting the man there.)

McGourlay mulled over the disturbing conversation and, on the Sunday, made a detailed résumé of it. He made a note that Wareing had *not* suggested that Stalker had done anything wrong or secretive. When he went into his office on Monday morning, 11 June 1984, he rang Chief Superintendent Peter Topping, head of 'Y' Department, which dealt with complaints and discipline, and asked to see him urgently on a confidential matter. McGourlay saw Topping just before lunch. He told him of his conversation on the Saturday. Topping left the office, presumably to consult, came back and asked McGourlay to 'put it on paper' but it was to be very confidential. McGourlay wrote one and a half pages longhand and gave it to Topping. Topping then asked McGourlay to use one of his Regional Crime Squad teams to carry out surveillance on Kevin Taylor. McGourlay was introduced to an inspector in 'Y' Department and asked to report back to Topping through him. It was all to be done in the strictest confidence. McGourlay selected a sergeant and a constable and set them to work. They hadn't been involved in the previous surveillance of the QSG, but had been tested in other operations. According to McGourlay, 'wild horses wouldn't drag out of them what they were doing'. It wasn't intended to be a full-time job; McGourlay just asked his officers to keep an eye on Taylor. He told them that he appeared to be an associate of the QSG and he wanted to know more about him. The two detectives reported back, said it was going to be difficult to mount surveillance on his house, and suggested that McGourlay might come and see for himself. McGourlay went out and took a look. Through the trees from the railway embankment across the river they watched Taylor's house and saw 'a large man' (probably Taylor's handyman and family chauffeur) who came out and looked around 'as if checking for prowlers'. McGourlay agreed that surveillance would be risky and probably unproductive. As a matter of routine, the detectives checked Kevin Taylor's two cars on the police national computer. They were shown as belonging to one of his companies. McGourlay's men then received a follow-up inquiry from their colleagues in the Greater Manchester Drugs Squad, asking about their interest in Talor's BMW. Unknown to McGourlay, the Drug Squad was watching Taylor too. The BMW was 'flagged' (specially marked) on the computer so that a unit with a particular curiosity in it would automatically be notified of anyone else's interest. McGourlay went back to Topping and told him he was calling his surveillance team off, as the Drugs Squad was clearly doing the same thing and there were risks involved if two separate teams were operating against the same target.

What McGourlay didn't know in June 1984 was that Chief Superintendent Topping had already begun an investigation into allegations of corruption at a high level within GMP. The allegations had come from a number of sources, including McGourlay's informant, David Burton. The allegations were that Kevin Taylor was involved with the QSG and that, according to one source, he was a financier for drug trafficking. The same source also alleged that there was a corrupt relationship existing between John Stalker, a leading member of the 'gang' (the onetime 'Rambo' figure) and Kevin Taylor. (Despite the gravity of these allegations and the seriousness with which they seem to have been taken, no evidence has ever been brought forward to substantiate them.) The fact that the person also referred to another police officer (retired at the time) suggests that the source may have been Burton. If indeed it was, it seems surprising that Burton had not mentioned either Stalker or Taylor to Chief Superintendent McGourlay – who had, after all, got him off with a lighter sentence. Whatever the sources, the intelligence existed and appeared sufficient for Topping to write a highly confidential four-page report on the information received. It should be said, however, that Chief Superintendent Topping did have reservations about the quality of some of the information – reservations which, one assumes, he would have made known as an experienced and professional senior officer. On 17 July 1984 Topping delivered the report to his superior, ACC Ralph Lees, who then passed it up to the Chief Constable, James Anderton. The gist of it was that allegations had been made that Kevin Taylor was linked with the QSG and suspected drug dealers. Links were also alleged with criminals in Spain, although it's unclear whether this particular connection was made in Chief Superintendent Topping's original report of 17 July, or at a later stage in the inquiries.

It should be said at this point that the precise mechanism and detail of events between June 1984 (McGourlay's conversation on the golf course) and March 1985 (Burton's death in gaol) have been extremely difficult to establish. It was the crucial period in which the seeds of John Stalker's downfall were sown. The main difficulty has been to tie down the precise nature of the intelligence, the channels through which it came – and whether there was any corroboration of it, without which Chief Constable James Anderton ought not to have taken such an extraordinary course of action, which led to the investigation of the Deputy Chief Constable by his own men. The timing of these events is also critical. The first allegations of links, however tenuous, between Stalker, Taylor and the QSG were made in June 1984 by Chief Superintendent McGourlay, and possibly others. Stalker had only been appointed to the Northern Ireland inquiry on 24 May 1984 and had scarcely had the chance to find out where the Falls Road was. At that stage, there would hardly have been a motive to undermine Stalker, as he'd not started asking any awkward questions. Neither was there at that time, whatever the internal politics of GMP, any tension between the 'old' CID (with which Stalker was associated) and the 'new' CID, which later came under the control of ACC Ralph Lees and Chief Superintendent Peter Topping. (It's been alleged that John Stalker might have been the victim of an *internal* conspiracy.) The tensions arose because there were senior officers in the force who felt that Lees and Topping had insufficient detective experience to run the CID. Although at this period (June 1984 to March 1985) there was no investigation into John Stalker, James Anderton saw fit *not* to warn him about his friendship with Kevin Taylor, which Chief Superintendent McGourlay clearly thought should have happened. One can only assume that the Chief Constable did not trust his Deputy and was not prepared to take the risk of information getting back to Kevin Taylor and his friends, thus alerting them to the investigation. Anderton's suspicion of Stalker could not have existed *before* June 1984, as it is inconceivable that he would have been appointed to the Northern Ireland inquiry in May or been appointed Deputy Chief Constable in March had there been any suggestion of a failing. Whatever his idiosyncrasies, Anderton would be unlikely to countenance any action which would be contrary to his own deeply held Christian ethics and professional code as a policeman. The fact that James Anderton decided to act in this way must have been a measure of his deep concern.

After the Chief Constable had received Chief Superintendent Topping's confidential four-page report in July 1984, he authorized further inquiries. These were to be carried out under the direction of ACC Lees (and CS Topping) after ACC Lees had become operational head of the CID on 1 October 1984. Drugs, and in particular those involved in the financing, supply and distribution of them, were one of the Chief Constable's stated priorities for the following year, 1985. The size of the Drugs Squad was increased, and in January–February 1985 a Drugs Intelligence Unit (DIU) was set up to target the traffickers. The DIU was under the direct control of Chief Superintendent Topping, who was then head of CID Operations. One of its main tasks was to investigate the QSG, which the Chief Constable and ACC Lees believed to be closely linked with drugs, and Kevin Taylor's connections with them. Although the DIU was *not* tasked to investigate John Stalker or his relationship with Kevin Taylor, all information about Taylor and the QSG was to be channelled directly to the Chief Constable through Topping and Lees, thus by-passing the Deputy Chief Constable. Early on, detectives from the new DIU visited David Burton, who was now in Preston Prison serving his two-and-a-half-year sentence. He was interviewed on tape by two detective inspectors on four occasions prior to his death in gaol in March 1985. Among the totally unsubstantiated allegations Burton made to them were that John Stalker was 'on a pension' from Kevin Taylor or the Quality Street Gang; and that one member of the gang had told him (Burton) that Kevin Taylor and another member could get things 'straightened' through John Stalker. There has never been a shred of evidence to suggest that there were any grounds for thinking that such remarkable allegations might be true. Nevertheless, at this stage (March 1985) James Anderton passed on his concern for the first time to HM Inspector of Constabulary, Sir Philip Myers, that allegations had been made against John Stalker and that they were being investigated. It appears that Sir Philip subsequently, and informally, notified Sir Lawrence Byford, HM Chief Inspector of Constabulary at the Home Office, that there might be a problem in Manchester but that it was being taken care of. There is no evidence that Sir John Hermon, who in March 1985 was refusing to give John Stalker access to the tape, was told of what was happening in Manchester or heard any rumours on the grapevine. The RUC insists that Sir John knew nothing of the allegations against Stalker until over a year later, in early May 1986, a very short time before Stalker was removed.

As the allegations against John Stalker mounted, based to a considerable extent but not entirely on the allegations of David Burton, James Anderton decided *not* to do what he did a year later – pull the lever on his Deputy. He could at this stage have called in an outside force to investigate the allegations, either openly or covertly, which would have jeopardized the Northern Ireland inquiry at its most sensitive stage. Instead, the Chief Constable decided to keep the investigation in house. The fuse continued to burn away.

Chapter 9

Diogenes and the 'Octopus'

Kevin Taylor's yacht, *Diogenes*, is central to the story and yet leads to a detour involving the 'Octopus', the codename of a gang of criminals smuggling drugs from the Costa del Sol. I have decided to pursue it because, at the time of writing, the end of the detour – and perhaps even the whole story of the *Diogenes* – remains unknown.

Diogenes is central because it figured prominently in the high-level discussions between Manchester, London and Belfast in the fortnight prior to John Stalker's removal. John Stalker had spent a holiday with Kevin Taylor on board his yacht and that had aroused suspicions. One informant suggested that the holiday had been at Kevin Taylor's expense. Stalker insisted he always paid his way. That holiday – in November–December 1981, when Stalker was seasick and Taylor scalded his hand (see Chapter 2) – was, like their friendship, no secret. But Stalker wasn't the only visitor from Manchester to go sailing in Florida on board *Diogenes*. The leaders of the QSG were no strangers to Kevin Taylor's yacht. Several of them had been on board in Florida a few months before John Stalker. The first visit was made in March 1981 by a senior figure in the 'gang' in the company of another man who was a good friend of Kevin Taylor's but not thought to be connected with the QSG. Both men were with their wives and visiting friends in the Miami area. It appears they only stopped by to see Kevin Taylor for the day. The second visit of members of the QSG to *Diogenes* was on 15 June 1981 and involved four of its alleged leaders. Taylor said it was a way of saying thank you to those who'd helped him in his early days in the motor trade. Taylor remembered his friends and *Diogenes* took them cruising round the Bahamas. There is no reason to believe that it was anything other than a purely social occasion.

On 2 January 1982, three weeks after John Stalker and Kevin Taylor returned from their eventful Bahamian cruise, Kevin Taylor held his lavish fiftieth birthday party. There were around a hundred guests. Among them were John and Stella Stalker and two members of the QSG who'd been on *Diogenes* in Miami a few months before the Deputy Chief Constable. One of them had his photograph taken with Mrs Stalker. Taylor denies that the man was an officially invited guest (he maintains otherwise) and says he came as a guest of another friend. The man alleges that Kevin Taylor introduced him to (then ACC) Stalker, who, after a short, polite conversation, said he'd call into his premises next time he was in the vicinity. John Stalker says he has no recollection of meeting the person concerned. The Stalkers didn't stay long at the party and left before midnight, as Mrs Stalker had a migraine and an upset stomach. The hundred guests came from all walks of Kevin Taylor's life. Thirteen of them had criminal records, although many went back years. Among them was a former detective, who'd once been a colleague of John Stalker's in the Drugs Squad, who'd resigned from the force in 1975. On 15 September 1980 he was convicted of trying to bribe a former colleague, and on 22 May 1981 of demanding money with menaces. There is no evidence that they spoke to each other at the party. Among the other dozen guests with criminal records were a professional confidence trickster and fraudsman; a man on bail for a £4 million fraud (who'd already been convicted for false accounting); a man convicted for criminal deception; a man convicted for dishonesty and disorderly conduct; a man convicted for handling stolen goods, and for receiving stolen goods; a man convicted for shop-breaking and wounding with intent; and a man convicted of burglary and theft in 1944. These dozen people with criminal records (whose names are known) represented only a fraction of the guests; they are mentioned not with the intention of impugning the reputations of others present – like

Conservative MP Cecil Franks – but merely to illustrate that Kevin Taylor had a wide range of friends from a wide range of backgrounds. Socializing with Kevin Taylor, it was inevitable that Stalker brushed shoulders with some of them.

Later that year, 1982, Kevin Taylor decided it was time to move *Diogenes* away from Miami. It seemed a long way to go for pleasure trips. The yacht was moored in Salford Docks for a while, and then sailed to Puerto Banus in Spain. It arrived there on 6 August 1982 and stayed put, apart from the odd excursion, serving largely as a holiday base for the Taylor family and friends, until Taylor decided to sell it at the end of 1984. How much of the following sequence of events was known to the new Drugs Intelligence Unit at the time is unclear: they certainly may have had their suspicions but no hard evidence they could use. Again, the story is difficult to tell in full for legal reasons. Police and Customs rely on informers just as much as the Special Branch in Northern Ireland. In the case of the *Diogenes*, the authorities subsequently had at least one source of information. The information supplied concerned certain cargoes. These are the bones of what the authorities believed happened on the voyages *Diogenes* made in 1985.

Taylor decided to sell *Diogenes* because cruising off the coast of Spain wasn't like sailing around the Bahamas, and the boat had developed a creeping disease of the hull called osmosis, which is common to fibre-glass boats. The marina at Puerto Banus, lined with some of the most expensive boutiques and restaurants in Europe, is littered with yachts displaying 'For Sale' signs. At the end of 1984 *Diogenes* joined the parade. Whilst playing Kalooki in a waterfront bar called Stripes, Kevin Taylor met an American called Bill Whittaker whom he thought might help with the sale of the boat. Whittaker was a freelance yacht captain who'd been looking after a boat for an Arab whom he'd met in Gibraltar. Whittaker said he'd take customers out for 'test drives' and try to sell her locally, or sail her to Fort Lauderdale in Florida, where repairs could be done more cheaply, and *Diogenes* would would fetch a better price. Whittaker found a prospective buyer in Puerto Banus, a motor trader from Blackpool called John Alan Brooks. Brooks had been involved in car fraud; on 3 February 1983 he'd passed a dud cheque for £16,342 to buy a Mercedes and a Range Rover from British Car Auctions at Brighouse near Leeds; the following day he'd defrauded the company again by passing another bouncing cheque for £7,420 to buy a Jaguar. Bill Whittaker introduced Alan Brooks to Kevin Taylor. Taylor knew of him – he'd met him on one of the quays in the marina with his wife and a large BMW motorcycle; most of the *habitués* of Puerto Banus would know Alan Brooks for his rich lifestyle and expensive taste in cars (he later developed a penchant for Ferraris). Brooks told Whittaker he was interested in buying *Diogenes* and Whittaker contacted Taylor to tell him he might have a customer. *Diogenes* had been out of the water for a month undergoing repairs. She was refloated on 26 December 1984. The repair bill was £2,472. Whittaker told Castlemain, the company which had carried out the work, that there was some problem with funds and the ownership of the boat given Alan Brooks's declared interest in buying it.

At 10 p.m. on 6 January 1985 Whittaker sailed *Diogenes* past the Martello tower that guards the entrance to the harbour and headed for Gibraltar. Whittaker arrived at the helm of *Diogenes* the following day. He then flew to Manchester to see Kevin Taylor. Taylor gave him the boat's papers and authorization for Alan Brooks to test drive *Diogenes* for a fortnight in Portuguese–Spanish waters. By the following week, Whittaker was back in Puerto Banus with the authorization. By this time Castlemain was getting worried about the payment of the bill, as they feared Whittaker might be getting ready to take *Diogenes* back to America. When no money was forthcoming from Kevin Taylor, despite several inquiries, on 21 January 1985, Castlemain arranged for *Diogenes* to be arrested and immobilized at her mooring in Gibraltar. A vital piece of the engine was removed. Within two days the money was paid and *Diogenes* was ready to put to sea again. On 26 January 1985 a person who, for legal reasons, I shall call Mr X sailed her out of Gibraltar. According to intelligence the authorities later received, *Diogenes* headed for Morocco, picked up a Mr Y and a cargo, and made for England. The cargo, it is alleged, was

landed at Brixham in Devon. On 3 February 1985 Mr X sailed
Diogenes into Dartmouth. The crossing had not been easy and
the yacht was in need of repairs to the engine and rigging. Mr Y
paid a local yacht-delivery skipper called Geoff Worsfold
(whose part in these affairs was totally innocent) about £700 as
a down-payment in cash to oversee the repairs and then take
Diogenes back to Spain. Mr Y then disappeared with a man
whom Worsfold thought had brought the money from London.
Customs were suspicious because *Diogenes* had not informed
them of her arrival. They searched the boat and found nothing.
Having heard that ownership was in the process of being
changed, they were also concerned about the payment of the
VAT. The first Kevin Taylor heard of his boat's final destination was when he received a phone call from a Customs
officer in Dartmouth. Taylor says he was suspicious and angry
at the news: Dartmouth wasn't in Portuguese–Spanish waters.
He told Customs to search the boat. *Diogenes* stayed in the
boatyard in Dartmouth for a couple of months before Geoff
Worsfold delivered it, towards the end of April 1985, to Portugal, from where it was to be taken on to Spain by others. Mr X
and Mr Y were waiting when Worsfold arrived. He was paid
over £1,000 in cash for his work.

Taylor was anxious to finalize the sale of the boat to Alan
Brooks. He flew out and met Whittaker to close the deal. The
sale was arranged through the office of a Gibraltar lawyer called
David Faria, and the transfer of ownership was made from
Kevin Taylor's company, Gantry, to Alan Brooks's company,
Malindi. The bill of sale was dated 1 April 1985. Brooks paid
Taylor around £80,000 for the boat and Whittaker received
nearly £6,000 in commission. Taylor says he wasn't happy with
what had happened to *Diogenes* and spoke of his concern to
John Stalker and Chief Constable James Anderton.

Mr X had been involved with Mr Y *before* the voyage of the
Diogenes. In 1984 Mr Y was talking to a couple from London,
Peter and Sue Atkins-Jones, in a bar called Da Paulo's in
Puerto Banus. They were about to return to England. He asked
if they were interested in chartering their yacht, the *Olympus
Nova*, while they were away. He said a client was interested in

sailing around the Canaries. The Atkins-Joneses agreed and told him to pick up the key from their agent in the port. But *Olympus Nova* apparently ran into problems and ended up, half underwater, in Portugal. Mr Y asked Mr X to have a look at the crippled yacht in the harbour where it was immobilized prior to having it brought back to Spain. *Olympus Nova* was made seaworthy again and sailed back to the Costa del Sol. At the end of February 1985, after he'd returned to Spain from Dartmouth, Mr X got ready to make another trip with Mr Y – same route, same cargo, same destination – but now on a different boat. This time Mr X put to sea in the *Olympus Nova*. On 14 March 1985 Mr X was towed into Dartmouth on board the *Olympus Nova*. (There was subsequently intelligence that the cargo had been landed near Brixham.) Mr X had got into difficulties a few miles out off Blackpool Sands, and was towed in by the harbourmaster around 8 p.m. The *Olympus Nova* was in a dreadful condition: the engine was full of water; the batteries were flat; the genoa was tangled up in the forestay; the rigging was a mess; and the Zodiac rubber dinghy and outboard motor were missing. Customs in Dartmouth impounded the boat. They found nothing on board. A Customs intelligence officer from London had been down earlier that day and told them to watch the *Olympus Nova*. The Atkins-Joneses were informed of the location and condition of their yacht. They too had not expected their boat to end up in Dartmouth; they too were deeply suspicious. Peter Atkins-Jones subsequently met Mr Y in London. Mr Y told him they'd encountered foul weather off Portugal, couldn't make it back to Spain and, as the client who chartered the boat needed to be back in England for business, they'd decided to head north and ended up in Dartmouth. Peter Atkins-Jones didn't believe the story. He says Mr Y paid him £1,000 for the charter and £2,000 for the damage – in cash produced from a plastic bag.

In April 1985 Mr X was back in Spain again, ready to pick up *Diogenes*, which was due to be returned to the Costa del Sol after Geoff Worsfold had delivered it to Portugal. Preparations were made for a third voyage with Mr Y. Again, according to later intelligence, the same route, the same cargo, and the same destination were involved. This time there was also another passenger on board, a former car dealer from the North West of England whom I shall refer to as Mr Z. He was due to appear at Preston Crown Court towards the end of the month, on 23 April 1985, to face charges of burglary and handling stolen goods. He didn't turn up. A Bench warrant was issued for his arrest. Mr X, Mr Y and Mr Z, the authorities believe, sailed *Diogenes* from Morocco to the Dartmouth area and then, having landed the cargo, put into Guernsey for repairs around 16 May 1985. (A third repair job in Dartmouth, to say the least, might have seemed a bit suspicious.) Two delivery skippers were hired to sail *Diogenes* back home again from Guernsey. On 1 June 1985 Mr X flew off to America (where, at the time of writing, he's still thought to be).

On 3 June Alan Brooks, the man who'd bought *Diogenes* from Kevin Taylor, was arrested; he was stopped in Plymouth as he was driving a brand-new Ferrari on board the ferry bound for Spain. He was travelling under different Christian names on a British Visitor's passport, which he'd obtained illegally on 23 May. He was carrying around £50,000[1] in cash and five jewelled watches worth over £20,000 which had been stolen in an armed robbery at a Mayfair jeweller's in London on 15 May 1984. Brooks was taken to Manchester and questioned by GMP detectives. He stood trial on 31 October 1985 at Manchester Crown Court and was sentenced to two and a half years in gaol. He received twelve months for the cheque frauds involving British Car Auctions, six months for dishonestly receiving the five stolen watches, and twelve months for making a false statement to obtain the British Visitor's passport.

Brooks served over six months of his sentence in gaol and was released on parole on 26 May 1986. He returned to Puerto Banus. Six months later, on 2 February 1987, the Spanish police arrested Alan Brooks and three other Britons on a beach by the hotel Rincon Andaluz just outside Puerto Banus. On the beach with them were 500 kg of Moroccan cannabis resin and 323 kg of hashish oil. The street value of the drugs was said to be over £2 million. All the consignment, the Spanish authorities believed, was bound for Britain. The police claimed they'd smashed *'una organizacion internacional'*, one of the biggest drug-smuggling rings they'd ever encountered in Spain. They called it *'el Pulpo'*[2] – the 'Octopus'. The organization, they said, had been running drugs from Morocco through Spain to the rest of Europe. The Spanish coup made headlines in Britain: 'Jet set Britons held after £2 million Costa drugs raid';[3] 'the heat is on for the barons along the Costa del Coke';[4] '£3 million swoop on Octopus gang'.[5] The gang was known as the 'Octopus' because its tentacles reached into so many places. One of those at the centre, according to the police, was Alan Brooks. They said they'd been watching him and others for nearly two years and had been waiting for the right moment to make the arrests. The police also seized Brooks's girlfriend, Sarah Dawn Labram, who was subsequently released and pursued by half Fleet Street. The *Daily Express* won and ran 'My drug arrest ordeal by freed model Dawn'.[6] During their raid on the beach the police also seized radio transmitters, a Zodiac inflatable dinghy, two Range Rovers, one with British and one with German plates, and a Ford caravanette. In the follow-up operation, they confiscated a Rolls-Royce, a Porsche, a Jeep, a Ford Mustang and several other vehicles. They also uncovered a garage where they said the cars were stripped down, packed with drugs and then driven across Europe.[7] The 'Octopus's' tentacles, they said, travelled over land and sea. They also seized four boats. Two of them belonged to Alan Brooks: the *Masai* a – red speedboat with three powerful outboard motors; and the *Diogenes*. Drug intelligence officers from GMP and Customs and Excise flew to Marbella for discussions with their Spanish counterparts. At the time of writing, Alan Brooks is in Spain awaiting trial.

Mr Z, who was on board *Diogenes* with Mr X and Mr Y during their third trip to the Dartmouth area, also ran into trouble with the law. Shortly after *Diogenes* had put into Guernsey in May 1985, he was arrested, on 10 June 1985. He appeared at Preston Crown Court on 25 June 1985 and pleaded guilty to handling stolen goods. He was sentenced to 150 hours of community service. The following year he was back in Spain; and heading for the beach. On 7 September 1986 he was arrested by the Civil Guard, rowing a Zodiac inflatable dinghy ashore off Marbella. He'd been spotted dropping things overboard. He said he'd been fishing. The following day scuba divers recovered 210 kg of hashish with a street value of around £1 million from the spot where he had been.[8] He gave his address as *Diogenes*, Puerto Banus. The Spanish court granted him £10,000 bail and he returned to England. In 11 March 1987 he was arrested again, attempting to enter the country with 5 kg of cannabis. He was charged the following day at Uxbridge Magistrates' Court with 'being ... concerned in an attempt to avoid the prohibition on the importation of a quantity of cannabis'. At the time of writing, he is out on bail. The day after his arrest, coincidentally, Customs officers made another find. They raided premises in London where they seized a large quantity of cannabis and a six-figure sum in cash. Four more arrests were made as a result of which Customs officers believed they had cut off one of the 'Octopus's' main arms in Britain.

Despite all the political assurances about the close co-operation between the police and Customs in the war against drug traffickers – and the much-heralded improved co-operation between international agencies – there was little co-operation between police and Customs in the two-year saga involving *Diogenes*. That was partly because both agencies had different objects: GMP was interested in Kevin Taylor and John Stalker; Customs and Excise were after drug runners. GMP were surprised they found out that a man they were hoping to use as an informant (before most of the gang were arrested) had already been supplying information to his Customs 'handler' for some considerable time. The rivalries between the two agencies die hard. Neither, surprisingly, was there any co-operation between the Spanish police and the British authorities. The arrest of Alan Brooks and his colleagues came as a complete surprise to police and Customs officers in England. There was no joint operation. Detectives from GMP and officers from Customs Intelligence went to Marbella in the wake of the arrests to pick up what they could. The officers from GMP were obviously anxious to see if any connections existed between Alan Brooks and *Diogenes* and

Kevin Taylor and the members of the Quality Street Gang who frequented Puerto Banus. There is no evidence at the time of writing that they have succeeded in making any such connection. Kevin Taylor has always insisted that he has never been involved in *any* criminal offence, let alone drugs. Customs and Excise would not dispute the latter, which is the area that concerns them. GMP officers also now accept that Kevin Taylor had no prior knowledge of what happened to his yacht on its voyages to the West Country. Furthermore, in 1985 when *Diogenes* made its trips, Kevin Taylor actually informed both John Stalker and the Chief Constable about his suspicions. Not only that but on 16 May 1985, around the time *Diogenes* put into Guernsey, Taylor named several people to James Anderton whom he said were involved in drugs; he added that he was putting together a dossier for Mr Stalker to give to Interpol. At that period, the first half of 1985, Kevin Taylor had no idea he was under surveillance and that he'd been targeted by the Drugs Intelligence Unit. He found out only in August, when he received a telephone call from his sister.

Chapter 10

Downfall

In the corner of Kevin Taylor's lounge, by the television with the huge back-projector, there's a board game called 'Downfall'. For Taylor and Stalker, 1985 was the year the fall began. Stalker was in Northern Ireland, fighting to get access to the material on the tape, and Taylor was involved in his biggest property deal to date. He wasn't quite sure who was responsible for the change in his fortunes. 'It's chicken and egg,' he told me shortly after he'd seen Stalker suspended and the receivers called into his company. 'I don't know whether he's in trouble because of me or I'm in trouble because of his Northern Ireland thing.'

For Kevin Taylor, 1985 had all the makings of a prosperous new year. The previous year he'd sold what had become his Asian trading estate near Strangeways Prison to a company within the Virani Group for several million pounds. He looked around for another project to absorb his energies, create some work and make him some money. As chairman of the Manchester Conservative Association, job creation was also an important consideration. His eyes fell on Trafford Park, the derelict area of land between Manchester United's football ground and the now dormant docks. The area had once been the economic hub of Manchester and, as Taylor recalled, 'the birthplace of the industrial revolution and the manufacturing base of the world'. The days when factories there (like Metro Vickers where John Stalker's father had worked) employed 20,000 people were gone. The only advantage to a developer was that land was relatively cheap, there were signs of economic regeneration and the council was ready to help developers with job-creating projects in mind. Taylor lighted upon a ten-acre site he thought he could package and sell. Several stages were involved in any such project: find the site, envisage its use, get planning permission and then sell it to another company, which would rent or lease it to another party who would use the site for the purpose intended. Taylor found the land down by the docks and consulted the council. He'd been thinking of a leisure centre, given the proximity of Old Trafford football ground. The council suggested a DIY shopping complex which would generate about 600 jobs, a healthy rateable income, and business as well. The DIY boom was well under way and megastores were mushrooming all over the country – many on the fringe of conurbations, under the banners of B & Q, W. H. Smith, Texas and others. Taylor liked the idea. He went to the Co-op Bank in Manchester, borrowed £240,000 and put the package together for his company, Rangelark. 'Of course it was a gamble. It's venture capital, the risk business,' he said. 'You take a gamble from the moment you are born. There are only two things certain in life: birth and death. Everything else is a gamble.' Taylor had no problems in borrowing the money; his bankers saw him as 'a winner'.

By the summer of 1985 it seemed that Kevin Taylor was still on a winning streak. On 7 August the Taylors threw a party to celebrate their twentieth wedding anniversary at the Mason's Arms near their Summerseat home. There were fifty-one guests, among them John and Stella Stalker (Stalker was now back in Manchester writing up his report); again, they were from the same varied background as the guests at Taylor's fiftieth birthday party three and a half years earlier. Seven of the guests had criminal records; six of them had been present at the previous party. Three of them were last convicted of offences in 1966, 1962 and 1944. The seventh guest had not been at the previous party. If he had, he'd have been noticed. He was six foot three, weighed twenty-three stone, had a scarred face and fourteen convictions including burglary, theft, robbery with violence, handling and assault. This prominent figure was a former bouncer at Manchester's nightclubs and casinos and had got to know Kevin Taylor on his gambling rounds. He was also known to be Taylor's minder when he was carrying large sums of money around the casinos and card schools. John Stalker was pointed out to the man, but they were never introduced.

Having returned to Manchester to write up his report, Stalker had dispersed his team back to their normal duties. Chief Superintendent John Thorburn had become head of the CID's Policy Administration – which some felt inappropriate, given his vast experience as a working detective – and the team's number three, Superintendent John Simons, had become head of the Fraud Squad. What neither Taylor nor Stalker knew at the time of the twentieth-anniversary dinner was that Taylor had been under surveillance by a special investigation team from GMP's Operational Support Group. He'd been watched for several months, perhaps since March or April 1985. The nucleus of the team was made up of officers from the Drugs Intelligence Unit supplemented by Fraud Squad officers (both bodies come under the Operational Support Group). The first that Taylor heard of the operation against him was when he received a phone call from his sister that August. She said two policemen had been making inquiries and had been asking about Vanland. Immediately Taylor's solicitor wrote to the Chief Constable, asking what the investigation was about, and offering his client for interview. The offer was refused and no information was given. Taylor says the police denied there was any investigation. The next Taylor heard was from his bankers in London, who'd also been approached by GMP. In October 1985 Taylor mentioned these inquiries to John Stalker. The bank had given Taylor the name of the detective who was making the inquiries and he passed it on to the Deputy Chief Constable.

John Stalker had met Kevin Taylor earlier, on 12 October 1985, at a fund-raising event for Swinton Rugby League Club at Belle Vue. He was the guest of one of Taylor's business associates, Derek Britton, not Taylor himself. The meal wasn't very good and the party moved on to a Greek restaurant called the Bazouki Club. With the Stalkers and the Taylors in the party were Taylor's massive friend with the fourteen convictions, and the former GMP detective with the criminal record.

On 23 November 1985 John Stalker was Kevin Taylor's top-table guest at the Manchester Conservative Association's autumn ball at the Piccadilly Hotel. It was a purely fund-raising event, with tickets at £50 each. Guest of honour was David Trippier MP, who the following year became a junior minister at the Department of Employment. Stalker said grace. As he knew his friend was under investigation, he checked with James Anderton before he accepted. The Chief Constable did not advise him against it. It appears he told his Deputy that he too had been invited but had declined. It seems that at this stage, surprisingly in the light of Stalker's inquiry, there was no mention made by him or by the Chief Constable of the investigation into Kevin Taylor.

On 12 December 1985, John Stalker took up the matter of the investigation into his friend with Superintendent John Simons, the head of the Fraud Squad and the superior officer of the detective who'd been making inquiries of Kevin Taylor's London bankers. Simons had been – and still was at the time – one of Stalker's senior officers on the Northern Ireland team. He told Simons that he was thinking of asking Kevin Taylor to be his guest at a forthcoming senior officers' mess function and wanted to know what the investigation was all about. Superintendent Simons said he couldn't help, and suggested he speak to Chief Superintendent Peter Topping who was in overall charge of the investigation. Stalker did not approach Topping or make any further inquiries – or check with the Criminal Intelligence Unit. But he did decide not to invite Taylor to the mess function. Clearly, by Christmas 1985 John Stalker knew there were problems but he probably had little idea of how potentially serious they were. He was deliberately being kept in the dark by the Chief Constable above him and the handful of senior officers below. The secrecy bordered on paranoia – perhaps understandably. Just before Christmas 1985, officers from the Drugs Intelligence Unit were told, yet again, that Kevin Taylor had a 'top man' in the Greater Manchester Police.

At the beginning of December 1985, Kevin Taylor's solicitors had also contacted Superintendent Simons. A meeting was held on 6 January 1986. Taylor's solicitor at the time, Guy Robson, offered his client for interview, should the police wish it. They said they did not want to interview him and made it clear they had no wish to discuss the matter generally with Taylor present in the room. Robson asked his client to leave. Taylor left his briefcase behind – in it a tape recorder left running to record what was said.[1]

Taylor says that he also offered the police full access to all the documentation they might require. Again, he says, the offer was refused. Superintendent Simons said he couldn't enlighten them as to the nature of the investigation as it was being conducted independently of the Fraud Squad office.

After that meeting, it seems that Taylor's solicitor tried to contact the Chief Constable directly. James Anderton was away and John Stalker was in charge. On 14 January 1986, the Chief Constable's staff officer informed John Stalker that Kevin Taylor's solicitor had phoned and insisted on speaking personally to the Chief Constable. He told the solicitor that Anderton was away and the solicitor had said he would send a letter. When the letter arrived, on the same day, addressed to Anderton and marked 'Strictly private, personal and confidential', John Stalker opened it. When Anderton returned the following day, John Stalker handed him the open letter. He said he wasn't mentioned and, for the first time, told the Chief Constable that Kevin Taylor had told him about the police investigation. As a result he said he had decided to keep his distance from his friend. John Stalker never saw Kevin Taylor again – apart from a chance encounter one day in the city centre. When Taylor met James Anderton the following month at another function at the Piccadilly Hotel, on 28 February, he complained of the disastrous effect the investigation was having on his business since the inquiries had been made at his bank. He also said that John Stalker had stopped speaking to him.

That same month, February 1986 – as the RUC delivered Stalker's report to the DPP – Kevin Taylor suspected there had been a break-in at his office. His colleague, Derek Britton, was going through the files in one of the cabinet drawers and noticed that they were all out of order. He asked Kevin if he'd been looking through them. Taylor said he hadn't touched them; neither had anyone else in the office. They were files containing details of two of his off-shore companies, La Certa Investments and Crumlin Investments, both registered in the Isle of Man. (The companies were subsequently mentioned in one of the search warrants obtained by the police and served on his solicitors, A. J. Adler of Oldham.) In March 1986 – the month Sir Barry Shaw directed Sir John Hermon to give John Stalker the 'open sesame' on the tape – the police gained access to Kevin Taylor's personal and business bank accounts under the Police and Criminal Evidence Act 1984. His American Express records revealed that he had purchased tickets for himself and John Stalker for a flight from London to Miami on 29 November 1981. The police had already received 'information' that Stalker had been on holiday at Taylor's expense. (Stalker has always insisted he paid his way and that he reimbursed Taylor for the air fare.) The American Express records seemed to confirm the allegation. By the end of March 1986 there were strong suspicions within a very tight circle of officers within GMP that John Stalker's relationship with Kevin Taylor was suspect. Although the investigation was cloaked in secrecy, rumours inevitably grew. Chief Superintendent Thorburn, alarmed at what he heard on the grapevine, wrote to the Chief Constable requesting a meeting. It appears there were several matters he wanted to discuss, but in particular he was anxious to establish whether there was an elephant trap lurking as the Northern Ireland team got ready to return to Belfast. It seems John Thorburn never had his meeting. It's almost inconceivable that, as May approached and rumours amongst senior officers were rife, John Stalker had no idea what was going on. The rumours, as one of them told me, were about senior officers and drugs, and a scandal whose implications were unclear: a man called Taylor (of whom few had heard) was mentioned, as was John Stalker. There were rumours of 'a whole heap of shit on the way' and talk of suspensions. This was the atmosphere as May 1986 approached. In Belfast John Stalker was about to get final access to the tape material, while in Manchester gossip among his own colleagues was linking his name to Kevin Taylor and the Quality Street Gang.

Again, for legal reasons, this is an extremely sensitive matter to report, and again I emphasize that I do so only to indicate what senior officers within GMP *suspected* and not what I believe to have been the case. To understand the extraordinary events that followed, it's crucial to have at least some intimation of the view from the Chief Constable's office – a view conditioned by information fed through a very narrow and tightly controlled channel. The following account of the crucial twenty days in May 1986, the countdown to John Stalker's removal, is based on a precise and hitherto not fully disclosed chronology of events. They clearly indicate that the impetus and the mechanism for John Stalker's removal came from Manchester and Whitehall, not from Northern Ireland. What happened to John Stalker on 30 May 1986 – when he was sent home on leave – has since remained a puzzle to all, including, as he has always insisted, John Stalker himself. I offer, given the legal constraints, the most likely explanation of it.

On Wednesday, 7 May 1986, Detective Inspector Anthony Stephenson from the Taylor investigation team applied for search warrants in connection with an alleged 'conspiracy to obtain dishonestly from the Co-operative Bank PLC £240,000 by deception'. The warrants sought access to 'ledger accounts, accounting documents and correspondence, namely minutes and business records'; they applied not only to Taylor's home and office, but to the premises of one of his solicitors, A. J. Adler of Oldham. The warrant on Kevin Taylor's home was executed at 8.18 a.m. on Friday, 9 May. Kevin Taylor had just emerged from the jacuzzi when there was a knock on the door. His wife Beryl was frightened and worried. About half a dozen police officers were standing there. She asked to see the authority on which they were entering her home. 'Grudgingly' they passed the warrant to her husband. The officers in the search party 'weren't hostile generally; they just got on with what they were doing'. Kevin Taylor was furious at the intrusion and admits he made some remark like 'Heads are going to roll after this'. He was doubly angry, he recalls, because he says the Chief Constable had assured him that if an approach was necessary, it would be made through his lawyers.

Beryl Taylor say she was puzzled by the way the search was conducted. 'It seemed to me that whenever they came across a photograph, they looked at it very closely.' Kevin Taylor too was suspicious. 'They spent more time looking at photographs than they did at documentation – which is what they were supposed to have come into the house for. How could photographs have any relevance to defrauding the Co-op Bank – the purpose of the warrant?' The search concluded shortly after a discovery was made under the stairs by a detective constable. That's where the Taylors kept their old photograph albums, which went back to the time when their daughters were children. Among the memorabilia were two albums of Kevin Taylor's fiftieth birthday party in January 1982. One had been presented as a souvenir by one of the guests. In them were photographs of John and Stella Stalker. 'Once the photographs were found,' says Beryl, 'the whole thing went cold.' Whether the albums were a bonus or not, their discovery precipitated events. One of the officers in charge of the search, Detective Inspector Rodney Murray who had conducted the crucial interviews with the informer David Burton in Preston Prison in February and March 1985, indicated that Taylor's remarks were stronger than 'heads will roll'. According to him, Taylor said 'This has been going on for years and I'm going to find out who keeps pushing this. When I find out, I'll have someone out of Chester House for this.'

Certainly Kevin Taylor was not cowed by the search and the seizures. Two days later, on Sunday, 11 May, he was talking quite openly about drugs to the police – on a purely informal basis. He met a GMP Chief Inspector at a social function – the opening of a Danish restaurant. He told the officer that he knew the Chief Constable and was a great friend of his deputy; he mentioned that John Stalker had made it clear that he would never allow himself to be compromised in any way. Taylor also spoke of knowing many high-class criminals and mentioned an occasion when an approach had been made to use *Diogenes* for drug smuggling. According to Taylor, this was not a reference to her sojourn in Spain but to a time when she was in Miami and someone in the boatyard asked him if he'd like to make a million dollars by hollowing out *Diogenes*' keel to carry drugs. Taylor says the offer was refused. The conversation worried the Chief Inspector, who feared that Taylor might be tempted to smear John Stalker as a way of extricating himself from his problems. (Taylor, on the other hand, claims that his problems are a direct result of the Stalker investigation and not the other way round.) The Chief Inspector reported his conversation back to Chief Superintendent Topping. Anxiety grew as John Stalker began to make arrangements to go back to Belfast. The first arrangement to return was probably made around Tuesday, 13 May, after Stalker had received word from Sir John Hermon that he should make an appointment to come over so matters could be sorted out as quickly as possible, and the final report completed. A date was probably fixed without delay as, on the following day, Wednesday, 14 May, Sir Philip Myers appears to have made his guarded phone call to John Stalker asking him to cancel his visit. This leads one to assume that James Anderton had contacted Sir Philip shortly before, alerting him to the discoveries made during the search of Taylor's house and, possibly, the disturbing conversation about Stalker, *Diogenes* and drugs the Chief Inspector had been party to at the Danish restaurant. But Sir Philip's delaying phone call seems only to have been a holding operation. What finally appears to have triggered the meeting at which Stalker's fate was sealed was another conversation that was reported back to Chief Superintendent Topping on Thursday, 15 May. It involved Chief Superintendent Arthur Roberts, a friend and colleague of John Stalker, and Ian Burton, the solicitor who was acting for Kevin Taylor at the time.

Roberts and Burton had grown up together and were professional as well as personal friends. Most weeks they played squash together. While they were getting changed for a game around the middle of May at the Mere Golf and Country Club, Burton mentioned the speculation that was going around GMP. Roberts knew what he was talking about. Burton said he was representing Kevin Taylor and the matter involved a senior officer within the force; in case his partner felt embarrassed and was concerned that his position as a police officer might be compromised, he was happy to call off the game. Roberts told him not to be silly; if he called off a game every time a client was mentioned, they'd never play squash. Roberts said he didn't know Kevin Taylor personally and knew his name only from the rumours; he certainly didn't feel compromised. The game was played. Roberts won.

On Thursday, 15 May, Chief Superintendent Topping came to see Chief Superintendent Roberts about a sensitive inquiry that was being conducted into a CID officer. It was the setting for a remarkable conversation that was to prove one of the two main elements that finally triggered James Anderton's decision to take action against his Deputy. (The discovery of the photographs during the search of Kevin Taylor's house was the other.) What is extraordinary, given the crucial importance of this conversation in the light of subsequent events, is that both senior officers have conflicting recollections of it. Chief Superintendent Roberts believes it was reported inaccurately. Chief Superintendent Topping stands by the minute he made of it. The discrepancy has never been satisfactorily resolved.

Not knowing that Topping was heading an inquiry into Kevin Taylor, Roberts mentioned the rumours that were flying around the force – and the fact that the 'dep's' name was mentioned. One rumour, he said, was that a senior officer had been on holiday abroad with a villain – a real 'toe-rag' – that a boat was involved and there was some talk of drugs. (It should be stressed that these were rumours run riot.) Roberts then told Topping about his pre-squash exchange with Taylor's solicitor, Ian Burton, and soon realized that Topping knew something about the situation. Topping went away, and made a minuted note of the conversation. He listed three points:

1. That Taylor was saying John Stalker had been to his parties, and to America at his expense.

2. That if nothing were done to put paid to the investigation, then Taylor would 'blow out John Stalker and associates'.

3. That Taylor was always talking about his friendship with John Stalker.

When Roberts subsequently found out about the minute he was furious and denied that Topping could ever have drawn the first and second inferences from their conversation. He later appears to have confronted Topping for not checking a minuted conversation between professional colleagues, feeling he had been sucked into a web without knowing what was happening; if Topping had bothered to check, Roberts seems to have pointed out, he'd have been told he'd got it 'arse about face'. Furthermore, Roberts was a friend of John Stalker and, on the face of Topping's minute, seemed to be dropping him in it. I asked Chief Superintendent Topping about the discrepancy. He said, with considerable emphasis, that all his actions would withstand the most careful scrutiny.

The minuted note went straight up to the Chief Constable. James Anderton decided it was time to sound the alarm. Probably on Friday, 16 May (the day after Robert's conversation with Topping) Anderton contacted Sir Philip Myers and, presumably, furnished him with the dossier on his Deputy. The matter now appeared so serious, because of its Northern Ireland implications, that it had to be referred to the level of Sir Philip's superior, Sir Lawrence Byford, HM Chief Inspector of Constabulary at the Home Office. By the time options and details had been discussed between Sir Philip and James Anderton, Sir Lawrence Byford would have left the Home Office for the weekend at his family home 150 miles away. (Sir Lawrence is the former Chief Constable of Lincolnshire.) Sir Philip would have called him there on Friday night or the Saturday and told him how serious and urgent things were. It wouldn't have come as bolt from the blue; Sir Lawrence had been advised a year earlier about 'a problem' in Manchester, but it must still have come as a shock. Conversation over the telephone would have been guarded and Sir Lawrence would have asked to see a summary of the dossier. Such a sensitive document would not have been entrusted to the post in Colwyn Bay, north Wales (Sir Philip's headquarters) and dispatched to the other side of the country where Sir Lawrence Byford lived. Because time was of the essence, it would have been sent with a trusted police courier. By Saturday night or Sunday morning, 18 May, it would have been in Sir Lawrence's hands. He would have read with alarm a general intelligence report on two or three pages in a foolscap envelope about the QSG, Kevin Taylor and John Stalker. His first reaction would have been to consider the effect of such allegations on John Stalker's Northern Ireland inquiry: it might only be a matter of time before the allegations broke out, sinking John Stalker and the inquiry; all the progress he and his team had made over two hard years would be sent to the bottom with him. Sir Lawrence probably also feared leaks at ACPO (the Association of Chief Police Officers) as well as GMP, which might find their way back to the RUC with incalculable consequences. No doubt Sir Philip would have agreed with such an assessment. Sir Lawrence's paramount concern would have been to protect the integrity of the Northern Ireland inquiry. John Stalker could be sacrificed; his inquiry could not. Over the telephone that weekend the real 'conspiracy' was born. John Stalker was to be removed before the damage could be done.

The other powerful consideration was what would have happened had the allegations lain dormant and exploded when the inquiry was finished. That, it was anticipated, would have been the end of the inquiry. Would not the Home Office have been blamed for not taking any action when it knew about it earlier and the inquiry could still be saved? It was, in effect, a benign 'conspiracy', but it wasn't kind to John Stalker. The move had to be made swiftly and in the utmost secrecy. If word leaked out before the axe fell, the blow might be impossible to deliver amidst the clamour. Sir Lawrence would have decided on the course of action that Sunday: an investigating officer would be needed to examine the complaint James Anderton was now ready to make; several names would have been considered, although the country's most senior police officer would have known that technically he had no power to make any such appointment; such a political consideration – the appointment could be made only by the Greater Manchester Police Authority – would not have prevented Sir Lawrence and Sir Philip approaching a suitable candidate. On Sunday, 18 May, it was decided that the Chief Constable of West Yorkshire, Colin

Sampson, was the man. Sir Lawrence knew Colin Sampson and had the highest possible regard for him, and was convinced that his conduct and reputation were beyond reproach. Sir John Hermon also had to be informed as a matter of priority. A telephone call was made to him that Sunday. He was warned that there was a problem with John Stalker, but was given few details at that stage. Despite all the speculation and assumptions made, the RUC insists on the highest authority that that telephone call was the first indication that the Chief Constable had had of John Stalker's problems in Manchester. By the Sunday evening the plan of campaign had been worked out. Four of the country's most senior police officers were to meet the following day at Scarborough where Sir Lawrence was attending the Police Federation conference which the Home Secretary was due to address later in the week. They were to be Sir Lawrence Byford, Sir Philip Myers, James Anderton and Colin Sampson. It was here at Scarborough, on Monday, 19 May, that James Anderton formally lodged his complaint, based on the internal investigation of his Deputy. The charge was the *disciplinary* offence that

> between 1 January 1971 and 31 December 1985 John Stalker, an officer in the Greater Manchester Police, associated with Kevin Taylor and known criminals in a manner likely to bring discredit upon the Greater Manchester Police.

The four officers met over lunch at the Royal Hotel but didn't get down to business in a dining room full of Police Federation delegates. Sir Lawrence asked the manager for a private room for the afternoon. Colin Sampson had been taken completely by surprise. He wasn't even aware that there was an inquiry going on in Northern Ireland. He'd just arrived from Wakefield and had been driven straight to the Royal Hotel. There, in the private room, he was asked if he would consider taking on the inquiry into John Stalker, and if he would assume responsibility for the Northern Ireland investigation as well. The decision to combine the two inquiries in the hands of one man was not made on the spot. It was only reached shortly afterwards, following long and agonizing discussions. Those who made it knew the decision was bound to excite controversy and there would inevitably be allegations of a 'fix'. But they firmly believed it was the right course of action. Colin Sampson agreed because he felt it was his duty. Checks also needed to be made on the other members of Stalker's team to make sure they were 'sound' – which is a measure of their suspicions about John Stalker – and it was felt that one man heading both teams was best placed to do this. No doubt concern was also expressed that the RUC was not 'up to dirty tricks': Sir Philip Myers knew at first hand the problems John Stalker had faced in trying to obtain the evidence he needed; Sir Lawrence Byford, his policeman's nose twitching, was anxious that Colin Sampson should establish whether or not John Stalker had been a victim of any plot to discredit him. It was also suggested that the Greater Manchester Police Authority should be encouraged to have the new Police Complaints Authority supervise the investigation. They believed that the independent body would give it credibility. (The PCA wasn't bound to do so, as the offence did not involve death or serious injury.)

It was agreed that Sir Philip Myers should go to Northern Ireland to see the DPP, Sir Barry Shaw; technically, Stalker could be taken off the inquiry only by those who put him on it. James Anderton was to see Roger Rees, the Clerk to the Greater Manchester Police Authority, and hold a secret meeting with Norman Briggs, its chairman. The Authority was to be presented with a *fait accompli*. A discussion as to whether John Stalker should be removed would have resulted in mayhem on the Labour-controlled Authority. There was meticulous planning behind the surgical removal of John Stalker.

That Monday, while the mechanisms for his removal were being plotted in Scarborough, John Stalker had telephoned Sir John Hermon to rearrange the meeting that Sir Philip Myers had asked him to postpone the week before. A new date, Monday, 2 June, was fixed. The same evening, the deliberations in Scarborough complete, Sir John received another phone call – one assumes from Sir Philip Myers – informing him that John Stalker would *not* be coming. The Chief Constable was by then away from Northern Ireland attending a conference; he'd spoken to Stalker on the phone just before he left.

Stalker was kept in the dark, although his suspicions must have been aroused when Sir Philip Myers rang him again on Friday, 23 May, and said that the team was not to go. Either before then, or shortly afterwards, Sir Philip flew to Northern Ireland to consult with the DPP, Sir Barry Shaw, about taking Stalker off the inquiry. Sir Barry consulted with Sir John Hermon who was technically the man who'd brought Stalker in. Sir John, therefore, had to agree to his removal. The Chief Constable and the DPP gave their mutual consent and Sir Philip Myers returned to England with Belfast squared. Sir John, presumably to distance himself from events, was apparently of the view that it was Sir Philip who'd appointed Stalker, so it had to be Sir Philip who took him off. Sir John was also shown the Stalker intelligence report and then handed it back, saying it was no concern of his. Sir John Hermon was said to be furious because of what it would do to the inquiry and because it would look as if the RUC had set Stalker up. Sir John Hermon had no sympathy for John Stalker.

It was left to James Anderton to square the Greater Manchester Police Authority. Again John Stalker was kept completely in the dark. If he did have any suspicions, they did not show when Colin Cameron and I had dinner with him and James Anderton on Tuesday, 27 May (see Chapter 7). Neither was there the slightest indication from the Chief Constable either in manner or word that anything was amiss. It was a brilliant piece of theatre, given the real drama off-stage. The key figure whose co-operation had to be enlisted and silence ensured was Norman Briggs, the chairman of the Police Authority which paid for and oversaw the running of the Greater Manchester Police. The Authority was Labour-controlled and was still finding its feet after the local government reorganization and abolition of the Metropolitan boroughs. There were tensions, too, on the controlling Labour group due to the split between right and left. Norman Briggs, a close friend of the former Labour minister, Stan Orme, was a right-winger and determined to stop a take-over of the Authority by what he saw as the hard left, led by Tony McCardell, the leader of the five Labour members from Manchester

City Council. Relations between the Authority and the Chief Constable had not been good and there had been several public clashes over issues like the use of plastic bullets and the policing of Leon Brittan's visit to Manchester (when he was Home Secretary) which had led to considerable violence. But despite the differences between the Chief Constable and the Authority, it was felt that Norman Briggs could be trusted. I met him on 15 July 1986, shortly before he died of a heart attack. In between heated phone calls in which he tried to out-manoeuvre the left, he told me what happened. He said he had 'greatness thrust upon him'. He'd received a call from Roger Rees, the Clerk to the Authority, saying that there was a problem. He went to Swinton Town Hall (where the Police Authority meets) and saw Rees and the Chief Constable who was with him. The date was probably Wednesday, 28 May, the day after the 'Last Supper'. Councillor Briggs told me that the Chief Constable said they'd been investigating a local businessman (whose name he didn't mention) and while they were doing so, one name kept cropping up – John Stalker; the businessman's solicitor had made it known that if the matter were pursued, he would call John Stalker in evidence; Stalker had been on holiday in Miami on the businessman's yacht, called *Diogenes*, and there was information from US law enforcement agencies that the boat was being watched;* there also appeared to be some question about who paid for the holiday. Councillor Briggs was also shown five photographs from Kevin Taylor's fiftieth birthday party; John Stalker was in one, and Stella Stalker in the other four. The prima facie evidence was sufficient to persuade the chairman of the Police Authority that John Stalker should be sent home on extended leave, pending an inquiry into the alleged disciplinary offence. He agreed that Colin Sampson should head the inquiry and that it should be supervised by the Deputy Chairman of the Police Complaints Authority, Roland Moyle. Moyle was telephoned in London and he agreed to take on the inquiry. At the time, he had no idea that Colin Sampson was also to take over John Stalker's Northern Ireland investigation. If he had, he

*This has never been substantiated.

might well have had second thoughts. Councillor Briggs agreed to everything that was put to him. He acted unilaterally, as he was empowered to do, without consulting any of his colleagues on the Labour group. Everything that had been discussed in Scarborough ten days earlier was now in place. Roger Rees telephoned John Stalker, who was at home in his garden on a day's leave. He told him to be in his office at 10 a.m. the following day – not the usual 8 a.m. – to meet Colin Sampson. Stalker was stunned. He said he'd no idea what had happened.

Chapter 11

Back to the Future

At Scarborough Colin Sampson had been told the broad outline
of the allegations against John Stalker forming the basis of the
disciplinary charge of 'discreditable conduct' he'd been asked to
investigate. He'd been told about John Stalker, Kevin Taylor
and the Quality Street Gang, but so far as he was concerned
they were simply allegations which he now had to translate into
evidence by taking witness statements. Once he'd been given
the job by Sir Lawrence Byford and Sir Philip Myers at Scarborough, he was left to get on with it. They knew better than to
tell Sampson how to do it. For forty-eight hours he agonized
over the best way to proceed. He had three options: to conduct
a covert investigation; to suspend the Deputy Chief Constable;
or to send him home. He knew how sensitive his task was, not
just because of the Northern Ireland dimension but because he
was investigating allegations of a disciplinary offence against
the officer who was himself responsible for discipline within
GMP. Sampson rejected a covert operation, presumably
because he felt it inappropriate and risky. He also rejected
suspension on the grounds that he himself would not like to be
suspended on the basis of the unsubstantiated allegations he
had before him. He therefore chose the last course: to send
John Stalker home on leave while he started his inquiries.
Sampson was said to feel great sympathy for the predicament of
a fellow senior officer. On Thursday, 29 May, Colin Sampson
and the officer who was to be his John Thorburn, ACC Donald
Shaw LL.B., drove to Manchester from their headquarters in
Wakefield. They first saw James Anderton and Norman Briggs,

chairman of the Police Authority, then went straight to the 10 a.m. meeting in John Stalker's office. The meeting was amicable and informal. None of the participants wore uniform. Sampson said he didn't have to see Stalker, but was doing so out of courtesy. No minutes were taken. He said he had wanted to be the person who told Stalker what it was all about (which may have explained the lack of detail given to Stalker over the telephone the previous evening in his calls from the Clerk to the Authority and the Chief Constable). Sampson told Stalker he was investigating innuendo, rumour and gossip about his associations in Manchester. Stalker asked who the people were. Sampson said he was unable to tell him. Strangely – and for whatever reason – no names were mentioned. There was no reference to Kevin Taylor or the Quality Street Gang. Sampson suggested that Stalker go home on leave of absence with full pay until things were clearer. Stalker declined and said he would extend his holiday (he was already taking a couple of days off) by bringing forward his annual leave. He asked how long the inquiries would take and was told about a month. Sampson then asked about his engagements over the next few days. Stalker said he was due to go to London the following day to stand in for the Chief Constable at a Home Office meeting and to Northern Ireland the following Monday, 2 June, to see Sir John Hermon. Sampson said he wouldn't be going to Northern Ireland as he was now off the inquiry. Stalker asked for how long: a week? a month? forever? 'Forever,' Sampson replied. He said he was now taking it over. There was apparently no animosity and Stalker thanked Sampson for handling things the way he had.

Stalker packed his briefcase and left the office. He went to his parents' house and walked into the kitchen as he'd done as a child. 'You're not at work, John?' asked his father. 'What's the matter?' His parents could see that all was not well. 'They've something against me,' said Stalker. His parents were stunned. 'He just sat there and we just couldn't believe it,' they told me. 'That was the awful thing: he just didn't know. He was trying to fathom out what he could have done. He hadn't a clue. He was upset. All he knew was that he was going to Ireland on the Monday to finish off that report.' His parents were bitter about the way the Chief Constable – known to their grandchildren as 'Uncle Jim' – had treated their son. They heard about the dinner on the Tuesday night and of John being given the papers to stand in for him at the Home Office meeting on Friday. 'That was the poisoned chalice,' said his father with great bitterness. 'That was cruel; that was diabolical.' His mother added 'I think it could only have been one of two things: either they wanted him off the Northern Ireland thing or they had something against him. If he'd done something wrong, it could have been resolved by hauling him over the coals and charging him with whatever he's supposed to have done.' Later, when more details came out, his mother reflected, 'The friends that Kevin has aren't the friends that John should have on the job that's John's. But if there aren't any criminal charges against Kevin, how the devil are you to know his friends are dodgy?'

He left his parents and went home to his family. They were shattered. No one knew what to do or whom to trust. There was turmoil and no family solicitor to turn to. Stalker then thought of a friend who was a solicitor in the Midlands whom he'd met when he was Detective Chief Superintendent in Warwickshire. On Thursday night he rang him and was told to be at his office at 11 a.m. the next day. On Friday, 30 May, Stalker made a statement to the solicitor which was then locked in a safe. The solicitor was said to be frightened by what he heard and to have felt he was out of his depth.

At 1 p.m. that day the controlling Labour group on the Greater Manchester Police Authority met as usual for half an hour before the full Authority meeting. The chairman, Councillor Norman Briggs, told his colleagues that there was an item he wanted to raise, but he'd leave it until the end and carry on with the agenda. According to the Deputy Chairman of the Authority, Councillor David Moffat, 'we discussed CS gas, plastic bullets and the odd Sherman tank. Norman never said a word during the meeting about John Stalker.' At 2.27 p.m., just as briefcases were being packed and the members were getting ready to leave for the full Authority meeting, Councillor Briggs dropped his bombshell. 'I have suspended John Stalker,' he said. 'Members were aghast,' Councillor Moffat recalls. 'They just couldn't believe it. It was incredible that he'd taken the power to do that – suspend the Deputy Chief Constable. He'd deliberately left it to the last minute, I suspect, because he had so little information. He'd just taken the Chief Constable's and Rees's recommendation. That's the biggest clanger he ever dropped in his political career.' Councillor Briggs adopted the same tactic at the full Authority meeting. At the end, under 'Private agenda', he repeated what he'd told the Labour group. The Authority was prepared to sanction what its chairman had done. 'He had validity,' said Councillor Moffat. 'People tended to believe him. He was a very experienced politician and if he had decided to act in that way on the basis of the information laid before him, they were prepared to accept his decision.' Inevitable questions followed. Councillor Briggs said he couldn't discuss the matter any further as it was confidential and he didn't have all the details. He then disappeared. The Authority then issued a statement which had been prepared by its Clerk the day before:

1. Information has been received in relation to the conduct of a senior police officer which discloses the possibility of a disciplinary offence.
2. To maintain public confidence, the Chairman of the Police Authority, Councillor Norman Briggs, JP, has requested the Chief Constable of West Yorkshire, C. Sampson, Esq., QPM, to investigate this matter under the appropriate statutory provisions and the Police Complaints Authority, an independent statutory body, has agreed to supervise the investigation through its Deputy Chairman, Roland Moyle, Esq., who has approved the appointment of Mr Sampson.
3. The Deputy Chief Constable is on temporary leave of absence whilst the matter is being investigated.[1]

Two other terse statements were issued. One by James Anderton:

I find it very regrettable indeed that this situation has arisen, and I am obviously upset by what has happened. It is my hope that this matter will be cleared up as quickly as possible.[2]

The other was from the RUC:

The Chief Constable, in consultation with Her Majesty's Inspector of Constabulary [Sir Philip Myers] is considering the implications of this development.[3]

It wasn't surprising that rumour and speculation had a field day, given the total lack of information. There was pressure from some quarters in the Home Office for a much fuller statement to be made, explaining that the overriding concern had been the integrity of the Northern Ireland inquiry, and that the decision to remove John Stalker had been made by Sir John Hermon in consultation with the DPP. Such a statement could have come only from the Attorney-General's office. The proposition was discussed and found favour in Northern Ireland too, but it was decided – to the regret of those who wanted a statement – that the authorities should remain silent. With all lips sealed, the conspiracy theory flourished. It seemed to be given even more credence when on Monday, 16 June 1986, BBC TV's *Panorama* revealed that MI5 had bugged the Hayshed and that John Stalker was about to return to Belfast to get (it was assumed) the tape of the shooting.[4] I interviewed Sir John Hermon live in the studio in Belfast after the film. He was adamant that the RUC was not involved in any way in what had happened to John Stalker. He evaded questions about the tape. Allegations were also made in the press that Stalker was the victim of a Masonic plot involving freemasons in the RUC and the Greater Manchester Police. Such was the anxiety that the chairman of the East Lancs Province of Freemasons, Colin Gregory, held a press conference – the first to be held in the Manchester Temple's fifty-seven-year history – to quash the speculation.[5] Councillor Norman Briggs was said to have been particularly upset by these allegations, to which his name was linked, and went away on holiday to escape from the spotlight. On 1 August 1986 he died of a heart attack. His friends blamed it on the pressure.[6]

By this time, Stalker was being advised by one of the best-known solicitors in Manchester, Rodger Pannone. Pannone had sprung to national prominence by the skilful and successful way he'd handled compensation claims resulting from the crash of the British Airtours Boeing 737 at Manchester Airport on 22 August 1985. Fifty-five of the 137 passengers and crew died in the tragedy. John Stalker had supervised the rescue services. (Pannone – 'the Right Stuff', the *Sunday Times* called him,[7] – since setting up this aspect of his practice, has taken on six major disasters including the North Sea helicopter crash and the Zeebrugge ferry disaster.) Stalker had decided to employ a solicitor the week after his first meeting with Colin Sampson when he'd been told that the *Daily Mail* was running a story about his friendship and holiday with Kevin Taylor. Rodger Pannone advised him to hold a press conference, break his silence and deny the allegations and rumours that were flying around. Stalker, through Pannone, seized the initiative and publicly never lost it, until he walked out of GMP headquarters for the last time on Friday, 13 March 1987. At the press conference, held on 6 June, John Stalker, obviously under great strain, insisted he was innocent of any disciplinary offence and that there had been nothing improper about his friendship with Kevin Taylor. He said he still didn't know the details of the allegations that had been made against him. The same day it was announced that Colin Sampson was also taking over John Stalker's Northern Ireland inquiry. Sir John Hermon issued a statement:

> In view of the leave of absence of Deputy Chief Constable Stalker, the same inquiry team consisting of the same officers is now, after consultation with Her Majesty's Inspector of Constabulary, and on his recommendation, to be headed by the Chief Constable of West Yorkshire, Mr Colin Sampson, whom I have asked to do so, and who will report to me. I am anxious that this extended investigation be completed quickly and professionally, so that I may receive directions from the DPP.[8]

The Police Complaints Authority was not happy at the news. It kept its silence.

On Monday, 9 June, John Stalker was first seen officially by Colin Sampson. After consultation with his solicitor, he agreed to give the investigating team access to all his bank accounts and credit card statements going back to June 1980 – two months after he'd returned to Manchester from Warwickshire as Deputy Chief Constable. The meeting was described as 'useful'. No details emerged. 'Stalker Stays Silent. Probe Veil of Secrecy,' headlined the *Manchester Evening News*.[9] Rodger Pannone said there would be no statement from his client for fourteen days unless Sampson had concluded his inquiries by then. Before the two weeks were up Stalker was seen again, this time at Colin Sampson's headquarters in Wakefield on 23 June. He was asked about his trip to Miami and who had paid for it. He said he'd paid his share of the cost in cash to Kevin Taylor, from the £300 he'd withdrawn from his bank the week before his holiday. The rest of the money, he added, came from a loan of US dollars (which he subsequently said was around $600) supplied by his brother. He was then shown five photographs from Kevin Taylor's fiftieth birthday party. He was on one; Stella was on four. He identified one man on the photograph with his wife, but denied any knowledge of the prominent QSG figure, who was also on the photograph. He was also questioned about others who were at the party, including his former colleague from the Drugs Squad with a criminal record. He was then asked about three other functions he'd attended and the people who were present: the greyhound racing at Belle Vue and the adjournment of the party to the Bazouki restaurant; his attendance at the Conservative autumn ball; and Kevin Taylor's twentieth wedding anniversary dinner. On 27 June two of Colin Sampson's team visited Stalker again at his solicitor's office in Manchester. They showed him the criminal records of the individuals they'd mentioned who had been present at the four functions, and of members of the Quality Street Gang. When Stalker was shown the convictions of one leading member of the 'gang', he remarked, 'I probably locked him up for that offence in 1962. He bit off someone's ear.' On 7 July Kevin Taylor was interviewed at the office of his solicitor, Ian Burton (who'd played squash with Chief Superintendent Arthur Roberts).

Taylor made a sixteen-page statement about his long friendship with John Stalker and made reference to his (Taylor's) various friends and associates. Taylor said he had only a vague knowledge of what the QSG was and of who might be its members. He accepted that three of his guests on board *Diogenes* for its cruise around the Bahamas in 1981 (before John Stalker's holiday) were believed to be members of it and had been there at his invitation. Ian Burton advised him not to comment on the circumstances of the invitation. He said he didn't know whether John Stalker knew they had visited the yacht. He agreed he'd bought the tickets to Miami and said that they'd settled up after buying groceries on the first day of the holiday; John Stalker had given him around $470 in cash to cover his share. Stalker, he said, always paid his way and wasn't a 'freeloader'. Questioned about named persons with criminal records, he said he'd met many of them over his many years as a gambler; it was inevitable, given his visits to casinos and clubs, that he came into contact with members of the criminal fraternity. But he insisted that he would never cause John Stalker any embarrassment, and there had been occasions when his friend had declined invitations because of the persons he'd been advised would be there.

By this time Kevin Taylor was in deep trouble, which he publicly laid at the door of John Stalker's Northern Ireland inquiry. He said his business was in ruins, the receivers had been called in to his company Rangelark Limited (which was involved in the land deal at Old Trafford), and he was going to have to sell his house. He traced the turn in his fortunes to an anonymous phone call he said he'd received well over a year earlier. 'The caller warned me that some people were doing a character assassination job on me, and that I should be careful,' he told me in the summer of 1986. 'I ignored it. I thought it was just one of these political fantasy-land things. But it seems to have worked out. Through the whole of last year and the whole of this year, I've had instances of business people coming in to see me saying "Kevin, what's happened to you?" And I say "Why, what have you heard?" It's gone from drugs to armed robbery. I think the only thing I've not been accused of is rape.

But these stories [Kevin Taylor alleged] have come out from GMP and spread throughout the business section of the city.' Around the middle of June 1986 Detective Inspector Stephenson submitted a preliminary report of GMP's investigation into Kevin Taylor to the office of the DPP in London, Sir Thomas Hetherington. In his report, Detective Inspector Stephenson concluded that there was – or would be – evidence available to sustain a successful prosecution of conspiracy to defraud. On 19 June 1986 he had a meeting with a representative of the Director's office and was instructed to proceed with his inquiry and obtain full statements of evidence.[10] I'm assured that the fact that the file on Kevin Taylor was about to go to the DPP was *not* a consideration in the decision to remove John Stalker. Throughout the summer Kevin Taylor continued to profess his innocence. 'I wish they were going to prosecute me for drug-running and armed robberies,' he said, 'I wish they would come and arrest me. I'd be so overjoyed.' His wish wasn't granted.

Colin Sampson did not just investigate the allegation of the disciplinary offence. In the course of his inquiries he came across other issues he felt needed attention. One of them was John Stalker's attendance at Conservative political functions; the other was his alleged misuse of police cars. The latter came up as a result of a chance remark made by one of Kevin Taylor's business associates, Derek Britton. When Taylor's office was being searched on 9 May 1986, Derek Britton remarked that he'd been in a police car with John Stalker. Sampson investigated and found that the DCC had made five journeys which suggested 'improper use of official police vehicles'. The reason he felt the matter merited investigation was that John Stalker had laid down strict rules in 1984 governing the use of police cars and was himself in receipt of a car allowance of nearly £3,000 a year. Although Colin Sampson would probably deny it, this was a side issue that diverted attention from the main question of John Stalker's relationship with Kevin Taylor and his friends. It was a diversion that was also to undermine the burden of the Sampson report. Many thought it an issue of monumental insignificance set alongside the danger John

174

Stalker was running not only in Northern Ireland but also back home in Manchester. Special Branch had told him he was under threat from the IRA and he had installed an alarm system at his home. The five journeys identified were: 18 April 1985, when John Stalker collected Kevin Taylor and his business associates, Vincent McCann and Derek Britton, to take them to a lunch at Manchester City football ground; the evening of the same day, when a police car took him from his home to Swinton rugby club; 31 August 1985, when he attended an inspector's retirement party at Dukinfield Masonic Hall; 21 March 1986, when he was driven to a senior officers' mess Ladies Night at Old Trafford; and 23 April 1986, when he went to a senior officers' mess St George's Day function at Chester House.

John Stalker was interviewed on two more occasions before Colin Sampson finally completed his inquiries. At those meetings Stalker again denied having any knowledge of Taylor's relationship with known criminals and asked why, if some of his friend's associates were undesirable, he had not been warned. He also denied any improper use of police vehicles drawing attention to IRA threats, and that his attendance at the Conservative autumn ball implied any political support for the cause. Over the nine weeks of the inquiry (which cost over £200,000) Colin Sampson and his team took 154 witness statements and obtained 64 photographs, 156 documents and 50 exhibits. The whole report and supporting documentation ran to around 1,500 pages.[11] It was delivered to the Police Complaints Authority on 6 August 1986. The Deputy Chairman of the PCA, Roland Moyle, who supervised the inquiry, said 'I am satisfied that it has been as thorough as possible and has been completed to our satisfaction.[12] The report concluded that there was no RUC or Security Services involvement in the instigation of the allegations against John Stalker. It listed ten counts on which he was considered to have committed a disciplinary offence. Eight of the counts, remarkably, were in relation to the unauthorized use of police vehicles; one concerned his attendance at Conservative party functions which 'was likely to give rise to the impression amongst members of the public that he may not be impartial in the discharge of his duties'; and one

– the original allegation – that he'd associated with Kevin Taylor and known criminals in a manner likely to bring discredit upon the Greater Manchester Police. On this last count, which was undoubtedly the most important, the report concluded that there was no evidence that Stalker had had dealings with the Quality Street Gang and noted that there was 'remarkably little corroboration' of what the informer David Burton had alleged. On the subject of the holiday in Miami on *Diogenes*, it said:

> Despite some misgivings about this explanation [of how John Stalker said he'd paid] there is no evidence to prove that Deputy Chief Constable Stalker accepted a gift or undue hospitality from Mr Taylor. Nor has any evidence been found to show their relationship was corrupt or could be the basis of a criminal charge.

Before drawing his conclusions in the last paragraph of his report, Colin Sampson asked the members of the Greater Manchester Police Authority, to whom the report was addressed, to bear one most important matter in mind – which he again emphasized:

> . . . there is *no allegation made of any criminal offence* being committed by Deputy Chief Constable Stalker. Indeed, if that were so, the papers would be submitted to an entirely different authority [the DPP]. *What is alleged is a series of disciplinary offences clearly demonstrating a less than excellent standard of professional performance.* This standard of excellence is that which is set by the service itself and expected of it by the public. In consequence, therefore, I have given the most careful consideration to the whole of the circumstances of this case, and *having regard to the considerable amount of public speculation and interest* it has generated, I am of the opinion that the *evidence supports, indeed demands, that it be ventilated before an independent tribunal.* *

*Under new police regulations governing the discipline of senior officers (based on the 1984 Police and Criminal Evidence Act), a charge against a senior officer of the rank of Chief Constable, Deputy Chief Constable

The first person to see a copy of the Sampson Report was the Acting Chairman of the Police Authority, Councillor David Moffat. A special meeting of the Authority had been scheduled for Friday, 22 August, at which the report would be discussed and John Stalker's fate decided. It had been agreed that the forty-five members of the Authority (twenty-four Labour, three Conservatives and three Liberals, and fifteen *appointed* magistrates) should receive copies of the 144-page summary of the report by special Securicor courier on the Wednesday morning. Councillor Moffat and his family, like several other members, planned to be away on holiday that week, but would return in time for the crucial meeting. Since he would not be back in Manchester until the day of the meeting, he needed an advance copy to study during his break in Brittany. With some difficulty he prised the first advance copy out of a reluctant Police Authority official (Roger Rees was on holiday) the day he left for France. He made it clear he wasn't leaving the country without one. He also suggested that someone should get hold of John Stalker's phone number because, whatever the decision, John Stalker would have to be spoken to. A photocopy of the report was made and sent round to Moffat's house. The family drove to France, so there was little chance to read the report until they reached their rented house near Lorient. Councillor Moffat looked through it quickly over the weekend and, on first impression, was convinced that the report was very damning and John Stalker was 'sunk beyond recognition'. He considered the references made were to 'genuine criminals' and that if

---

and Assistant Chief Constable should be heard 'by a tribunal consisting of a single person selected and appointed by the appropriate authority [i.e. the Police Authority] from a list of persons nominated by the Lord Chancellor'. That person would be assisted by 'one or more assessors selected by the Authority with the approval of the tribunal'. One of the assessors would be a serving or former Chief Constable – from outside the force to which the accused belonged. The tribunal would sit in private, witnesses would be cross-examined, and a transcript would be made and sent to the Authority. If the tribunal reached the conclusion that the case was proven, it could recommend a punishment of dismissal, enforced resignation or a reprimand. The Police Authority would make the final decision. The accused's legal costs would be defrayed out of the police fund.[13]

Stalker had at any time associated with them, at either a party or a celebration, then he was not acting as a Deputy Chief Constable should.

On the Tuesday Moffat sat down to read the report again in far greater detail; he began to see the 'holes'. 'I just couldn't see that the Deputy Chief Constable would be so foolish as to actively associate with the criminal classes,' he told me. 'It was just beyond me. At the end of the day, when I'd gone through it, the only link was Kevin Taylor. Stalker didn't seem to have been anywhere near associating with the Quality Street Gang or any member of it.' Moffat's interpretation was correct. He made the crucial distinction – that the Sampson Report failed to spell out – that the only occasion on which John Stalker was *physically* in the presence of members of the QSG was at Kevin Taylor's fiftieth birthday party. Even on that occasion, there were only two of them present, one whom Stalker said he never saw and the other whom he said he'd never met. All the other individuals who were present at the various functions – whose criminal records had been so meticulously investigated by the Sampson team – were *not* members of the QSG. That would not, of course, necessarily absolve John Stalker of the charge of being in criminal company. But in terms of the investigation into John Stalker, the distinction between 'ordinary' criminals and the QSG was of crucial importance. Councillor Moffat also regarded the concentration on the alleged misuse of police cars as 'petty' – and that was eight of the ten charges. Neither was he impressed by the suggestion that Stalker's attendance at Conservative functions indicated a political bias. 'Nine of the ten items were peripheral and pettifogging. It was not the concerted, co-ordinated report I'd expected from a man in such a high position,' he said. 'It rambled on from one set of circumstances to the next. I wasn't pleased with the report at all.' Giving himself the finest of margins, David Moffat left his holiday home on Friday morning, 22 August, drove at French *vitesse* up the motorway to Nantes, caught the flight to Heathrow, connected with the shuttle to Manchester, was met by two policemen and escorted at top speed to Swinton Town Hall where he avoided the press by sneaking up the back stairs.

Despite his strong reservations, as a politician and acting chairman of the Police Authority he was anxious to see which way the rest of the Labour group would jump.

The second most important figure on the Labour group was Councillor Tony McCardell, the leader of the left-wing faction. McCardell had flown back from Crete on the Wednesday morning. He arrived at Manchester Airport at 7 a.m. and went straight to Swinton Town Hall to pick up his copy of the report. He took it home and went to bed. From noon onwards the press laid siege to his house. McCardell obliged with a general statement, permitted a few shots of the report's cover, and went back inside hoping to get some peace to read it. The peace was denied. At 4 p.m. he went across the road to his father's house and took refuge in the back kitchen so the press, when the next wave arrived, couldn't see him through the front-room window. His father plied him with tea whilst McCardell got stuck into the report. '"Rubbish" was my reaction when I'd finished reading,' he told me. 'I just couldn't believe it – that he'd been suspended for three months because of this. My first impression was "well, OK, he might have been naïve in some ways", but all the hullabaloo made me absolutely convinced there was something else to it. The more it's gone on, the more I'm absolutely convinced it's a conspiracy – involving the political and police establishments – probably initiated by MI5. I can't say who did it, but I think Anderton was used.' The fact that Colin Sampson had categorically rejected any such involvement did not convince him. All good plots have to have a villain. As far as McCardell and most of the press were concerned, the finger clearly pointed elsewhere. When McCardell held his pre-Authority caucus at Manchester Town Hall on the Thursday afternoon with his Labour colleagues from the city council, all agreed it was a 'carve-up'. They decided to 'pull him off the roof', even though not all of them were fans of John Stalker.

By that Thursday, John Stalker had broken his silence – on the advice of Rodger Pannone. It was a brilliant tactical move. He gave several interviews to the press, including myself, in which he and his wife eloquently and movingly described the agonies the family had gone through during the preceding three months. But, most important from the tactical point of view, he made a plea to be heard at the Friday meeting of the Police Authority before it decided his fate. He feared that the Sampson Report did not adequately reflect his side of the story. There was no doubt where public sympathy lay, as it had done from the moment of his removal. By Thursday evening it began to look as if John Stalker was to be saved. Mrs Audrey Walsh, chairman of the fifteen appointed magistrates on the Authority, said 'I want to see this settled tomorrow, with the Authority sending John Stalker back to work as quickly as possible. This has gone on for long enough. The man has already learned the hardest lesson of his life. He and his family have suffered enough. I don't believe he has been devious in any way. At the very most he has been a bit naïve. The criminals named in the report say they have not even spoken to John Stalker. He went to five or six functions where people with criminal records attended. I bet I have been to functions where people with criminal records have been present. But despite all this, I have known John Stalker for many years and he is a fine policeman. He should be back in his old seat. I rate him very highly.'[14] Councillor Eric Kime, one of the three Liberals, said that an impartial tribunal was the only answer. 'I don't see how Stalker could pick up the reins as Deputy Chief Constable again,' he said, 'I don't see how any other force would employ him either, because this must have left some stain on his character.'[15]

On Friday morning, the Stalker family sat round the breakfast table opening still more of the hundreds of letters of support they had received over the preceding three months. 'On the negative side,' he reflected philosophically, 'it's wasted three months of my life. On the positive side, it's brought us closer together as a family.' Colette brought in her father's dark suit, and he put on two odd socks. The family also made sure that he had the talisman with him he'd kept in the corner of his wallet all through the Northern Ireland inquiry: it was a tiny heart-shaped stone, found on the beach at Morecambe Bay when Francine was six or seven; she'd painted 'Dad' and a heart on one side and 'Love' and a heart on the other. John Stalker was ready for the most important day in his professional life. As the family gathered round the television to watch 'Granada Reports' to see the Stalker-watchers examine the omens, there were two telephone calls – both bringing bad news. First, that the Police Authority had refused his request to address them, and second that the Chief Constable had refused his Deputy permission to park his car that afternoon in Bootle Street Police Station, round the corner from his solicitor's office in the busy city centre. That news caused more pain than the other. For the Stalkers, that single act summed up the way they felt they'd been treated by the Chief Constable: abandoned out on a limb and left to swing in the wind. Stella took the call. 'The bastard,' snapped Stalker, his face unusually hard with anger. The family spent the afternoon at Rodger Pannone's office, awaiting the call that would indicate whether the Police Authority had put thumbs up or down. They lunched on meat pies, sandwiches and soft drinks from Kendals' Delicatessen across the road.

At Swinton Town Hall, the Labour group was in session as David Moffat arrived hot-foot from Brittany. There was no unanimous view. One Labour member said they shouldn't even bother with a tribunal; Stalker should be sacked outright. At the other extreme, another argued that Stalker should be given a medal for his work in Northern Ireland and sent back to work with the bands playing. The Clerk to the Authority, Roger Rees, said they had three options: to return him to work, send him to a tribunal, or sack him. 'We wanted to send him back,' said Tony McCardell, 'but we didn't want to send him back with the bands playing, because there were some things he should have been more careful about – although we didn't see it amounting to a disciplinary offence.' Councillor McCardell reflected the consensus. David Moffat agreed. 'I didn't believe, quite Christianly and honestly, that Stalker was in those terms "guilty". He was a bit stupid and naïve but I didn't think he was guilty of a disciplinary offence.' After much discussion they decided to hear Colin Sampson, whom Councillor Moffat had insisted be present, adjourn for tea and then reach a decision.

The meeting started at 3.30 p.m. Colin Sampson, dressed in a suit, went through his report and faced questioning on it for over two hours. He produced the photographs and gave 'validity' to the points he'd made. 'He was very guarded and professional,' said Councillor Moffat. 'He presented the evidence but left the decision to us. He kept his decorum all the way along the line.' Not all his audience was friendly. One of the Manchester City councillors, Ken Strath, accused Colin Sampson of producing a 'Mickey Mouse' report. Sampson appeared angry. He asked Councillor Strath what he meant. He was told it was like a report with a mouse in, running all over the place – up alleyways and back again. Sampson said that was the intention: the aim had been to present the full facts as they were known; if there were 'ups and downs' and 'ins and outs', that's the way it was. Sampson was impressed by the way the Authority conducted itself; not the way, he thought, many might have expected a 'left-wing' Police Authority to act. The members then adjourned for a late tea of salmon and cucumber sandwiches rushed in by the chief executive's staff. The mood was sombre. Chief Constable James Anderton – in uniform – was then questioned for an hour. He told the Authority he had no alternative other than to act the way he had. He refused to answer questions about how much he'd been involved in the preliminaries, such as the Scarborough meeting. 'He was uncomfortable,' observed one of the members. 'He's never liked being questioned about his part in anything.'

The meeting adjourned again at about 7.30 p.m. to consider what action to take. The Labour group still couldn't make up its mind; it wasn't happy about sending John Stalker to a tribunal whose composition was out of its hands. 'Politicians wanted to see it kept within the Authority,' said Councillor Moffat. 'They didn't want to see Stalker judged by people – barristers and judges – in London.' Councillor McCardell put it more strongly. 'One of the things our group [from Manchester City Council] played on was that the members of the tribunal weren't our choice. We could only pick from a select list [supplied by the Lord Chancellor]. This upset a lot of Labour members, whether they were for or against Stalker. The establishment, which may be involved in the conspiracy, tells you who you can pick. They select the judge and the jury.' So, for political reasons, a tribunal was ruled out. After discussion, the

Labour group felt it wasn't appropriate anyway. Another powerful consideration for acting chairman Moffat was the battered morale of the police force: to go to a tribunal meant not only further agony and uncertainty for John Stalker and his family, but continuing turmoil within the Greater Manchester Police. The Labour group felt that Stalker should be sent back to work, but not without a reprimand. 'There was definitely a feeling that there should be some form of condemnation,' said Moffat. 'He wasn't perfectly white or clean. A compromise was reached.' A resolution was put that John Stalker should return to work, but should be 'more circumspect in his political and criminal associations in future in view of his high office'.[16] (The Authority also decided to scrutinize the use of police cars by senior officers.) The members went back into the council chamber and the Clerk called out the members' names for a 'Yes' or 'No' vote. James Anderton, according to one of them, looked 'as sick as a chip'. He'd looked 'more and more annoyed as the debate went on'. At around 9.45 p.m. the Police Authority voted to send the Deputy Chief Constable back to his desk. All twenty-three Labour members (one was absent) supported the resolution, as did eleven magistrates and two Tories. The three Liberals, two magistrates (two were absent) and one Tory voted against.

David Moffat had insisted that John Stalker should hear the news, whichever way it went, through the Authority and not through the press who'd been excluded from the meeting. The members agreed to remain in the council chamber while the acting chairman went off to a telephone. He asked for Stalker's number. The Clerk hadn't got it, neither had his deputy, neither had the Chief Constable. Moffat wasn't going to ask the press. He left the chamber with one of the Chief Constable's aides, who said he'd phone the control room at police head-quarters from the members' lounge. When he got the number, Moffat rang Stalker's home. Francine's boyfriend answered and said John Stalker wasn't there. What did he want to talk about? He was at Mr Pannone's office. Another member, a solicitor, came in and supplied the number. There was no reply. (The switchboard was closed down and Rodger Pannone's direct line was the only one available.) 'Absolute, rampant chaos' developed in the members' lounge as people rushed in to ring their families and friends to let them know where they were, as it was now so late. Eventually Tony McCardell appeared with what he thought was Pannone's home number; fortunately it wasn't, it was the direct line to his office. Rodger Pannone answered. Moffat said it was the acting chairman of the Police Authority calling and could he speak to John Stalker. Stalker came on the line. 'I recognized his voice,' recalls Moffat. 'I said "The conclusion of the Police Authority meeting is that you are to go back on duty, but that you are to be more circumspect in your friends and contacts as Deputy Chief Constable of Manchester. Good luck."' The line went dead for about ten seconds. Moffat felt he could hear the relief down the phone. 'Dust your uniform and polish your shoes,' he continued, 'I expect you to be back on duty tomorrow morning.' 'Yes, I'll be there,' said Stalker.

There were pandemonium, kisses and tears in Rodger Pannone's office as he organized the press for the photo opportunity they'd been waiting for all afternoon – and for three months. I asked Mr Pannone if there was any qualification to the reinstatement. 'No,' he said. The champagne flowed. John Stalker told the press he thought his reputation had been enhanced rather than damaged by the affair. 'I have been exonerated completely,' he said. 'I think that's the important thing. I always said that my good name was all that mattered to me. My life has been ripped apart, dissected and put together again. The Police Authority has decided that I am a suitable person to be their Deputy Chief Constable.'[17]

The press were there too for breakfast the following morning. But they were denied the picture they wanted. John Stalker's uniform was still in the office. But they caught something better. Jack and Theresa Stalker arrived, unexpectedly, to watch their son go back to work. His mother threw her arms round his neck and sobbed through her tears, 'John, John, how could they do this to you?'

John Stalker returned to work on Saturday, 23 August 1986. He'd assured the press that he would continue to work with the Chief Constable, as one professional with another. On Monday morning, 25 August, the beginning of John Stalker's first full week back at his desk, the Chief Constable said:

> It may be thought that personal relationships at senior command level in the Greater Manchester police force could be affected by the traumas of the past few months, but John Stalker and I have always worked very well together in the public interest and to the good of the force, and there is no reason why we cannot do so again. A police force without a Deputy Chief Constable is certainly not fully effective, and I am glad to have John Stalker back on duty.[18]

The two men did work together but the relationship was cold and formal. Stalker felt increasingly unhappy and frozen out. Having to work with those who'd just investigated him wasn't easy – for either party. It was only a matter of time before the final break came. In December 1986 Chief Superintendent Peter Topping reopened the search for the bodies of Keith Bennett and Pauline Reade on Saddleworth Moor, two more of the victims of Myra Hindley. (She confessed to their murder on 3 April 1987.) The expedition followed Myra Hindley's decision to talk following a plea she received from Keith Bennett's mother on 31 October 1986. Stalker, who'd been involved in the original Moors investigations, wasn't happy at the decision. He thought the time of year was wrong, nothing would be found, and the result would be only more upset for the parents. He was right. The digging was called off when the snow came down and the earth froze. But for Stalker, the final blow came when Myra Hindley was flown to the Moor and he wasn't consulted or informed. The writing seemed to be on the wall. John Stalker wasn't wanted. (Some of his senior colleagues, however, took a different view and denied that he had been 'frozen out' of the decision-making process. In a long letter to *Police Review*, published after he'd left the force – see Appendix 5 – they regretted that he'd parted on such a bitter note.) But John Stalker had had enough. He talked it over with his family and decided to go. They were also deeply upset by the Police Authority's refusal to help with his legal bill of over £20,000. The public was outraged too, and donations poured in to help him out. Over £16,000 was raised. A charity concert added another £6,000 to the legal fund. When Stalker broke the news to James Anderton, the Chief Constable is reported to have said 'Oh no, not that.' He said he was going for 'personal and family reasons'. He told the press, 'I am not a broken man. It is simply that my family don't want me to be a policeman any more. It was killing me to come home and see my wife Stella so upset. And I have seen my mother turn from a sprightly lady into an old woman.'[19] Although the return to work was painful and the scars of the summer were slow to heal, John Stalker had come to the conclusion that, whatever happened, his police career was finished. He'd always intended to soldier on for a decent interval – say until the spring of 1987 – while looking around for another career. When John Stalker resigned, he already had another future in view – in television. He'd been approached by Mersey Television's Phil Redmond, the founder of *Grange Hill* and *Brookside*, to be General Manager of the company.

Kevin Taylor had toasted John Stalker's reinstatement with Taittinger champagne, but there was to be no silver lining to his cloud. Cornered, still uninterviewed and uncharged, he embarked on a guerrilla war through the courts as the investigation into the fraud allegation continued, now under the aegis of the DPP. On 23 September 1986, his solicitors issued an originating summons in the Chancery Division against the Chief Constable, James Anderton, and the Greater Manchester Police Authority, for an order that they should disclose all the confidential documents GMP had used in the application for the warrants to search his home and business premises on 9 May 1986. The action was heard before Mr Justice Scott on 15 October 1986 and lasted two days. In court Kevin Taylor's counsel said that his client had been the subject of police inquiries for nearly two and a half years, yet he had never been charged with any criminal offence. In a sworn statement read out during the proceedings, Taylor said 'No bank would touch me. All have refused to deal with me for no commercial reasons. Professional people avoid me. The mental distress and suffering of the last few months cannot be adequately described. Apart from my own feelings, the pressure on my wife and children has been horrific. I have

begun to feel I am being persecuted.'[20] Counsel for the Chief
Constable said that the court had no power to order production
of the documents and they were covered by public interest
immunity: they were part of the allegations against Taylor now
being considered by the DPP; they might contain material
which risked jeopardizing the case and revealing the identity of
informants who had given evidence to the police. Mr Justice
Scott concluded that the documents *were* covered by public
interest immunity and therefore dismissed the action. But
Taylor had got his retaliation in first. On 14 October 1986 – the
day before Mr Justice Scott's hearing began – his wife Beryl,
acting as a director of Rangelark Limited, obtained three summonses from the Bury magistrate against the Chief Constable,
Chief Superintendent Peter Topping and Detective Inspector
Anthony Stephenson, alleging conspiracy to pervert the course
of public justice in obtaining the search warrants.

The police responded by applying for a judicial review to
quash the summonses on the grounds that they were impeding
the continuing investigation into Kevin Taylor's alleged fraud of
the Co-op Bank. The application for review was granted on 24
November 1986. The case was heard in the High Court on 27
February 1987. Counsel for Mr Anderton said that the summons had created 'an enormous impediment' which had been
used as a device to hinder police investigations and embarrass
officers. Kevin Taylor's counsel argued that his client and his
solicitor had several times unsuccessfully asked the police for a
meeting to clear up any suspicions: instead of which, he argued,
the police had applied to a judge in chambers for an order
giving them direct access to Taylor's bank accounts. He maintained that the police must have lied to the judge to obtain such
an order because there was no evidence of wrongdoing to
justify it.[21] Judgment was reserved and finally delivered on 3
April 1987. The Judge said:

> I am driven to the conclusion that obtaining the issue of the
> summonses was oppressive and an abuse of the process of the
> court. The fact that the application was made a day before
> the Chancery Court hearing is in my view significant. It is

quite clear that neither Rangelark Limited, Mrs Taylor nor their legal advisers had any idea what had been placed before . . . the Stipendiary Magistrate [i.e. the documents on which the summonses had been granted].

The Judge concluded:

Finally, I think that the initiation of the criminal proceedings against the present applicants had, as its principal aims, the discovery of the documents which [Mr Justice Scott] refused to order the police to disclose two days later, to try to find out, directly or indirectly, to what point the police investigations into Mr Taylor and his companies had reached, and to hamper any further investigation and, if it were to come to it, any criminal proceedings against them.[22]

The Judge agreed to the application to quash the summonses, although he gave Kevin Taylor the right to appeal.

His legal battles with Kevin Taylor apart, James Anderton had other problems too. They were largely self-inflicted. He has been Britain's most controversial Chief Constable since he took over GMP in 1976. His moral fervour and straight talking ensured his place in the headlines long before he shared them with John Stalker. His first crusade was against pornography and prostitution and his special squads raided 264 premises during his first year in office. Seizures included the *Sun Page Three Girl Annual*.[23] Subsequent missions included plain-clothes patrols charged with hunting down gays in public lavatories.[24] Such forays against the over-permissive society may have brought protest and ridicule from the libertarians, but they were supported by the majority of his men and perhaps by the majority of the public. In December 1986 he marked his tenth anniversary in true, and undoubtedly sincere, Anderton style. In a speech at a police seminar in Manchester, he blamed the spreads of AIDS on homosexuals and prostitutes, whom he described as 'swirling around in a cesspool of their own making'.[25] He later said that the spirit of God had moved him to make such a remark; and in a BBC radio programme he elaborated on this by saying that in view of his religious beliefs, he had to accept that God might be using him as a prophet.[26] Fleet Street had a field day. *Today* excelled itself by plastering London with huge hoardings, showing James Anderton surrounded by heavenly clouds and the caption 'Halo, Halo, Halo, Have our police got ideas above their station?' Councillor Tony McCardell, never one of the Chief Constable's fans, said 'If he was the chief executive of a local authority or a company, we would be advising him to seek medical help.'[27] One of his senior officers, who *is* one of his admirers, told me 'What he said on AIDS needed to be said. Everybody accepted it. But his fervour borders on paranoia. On the "prophet of God", he's lost his marbles!' The Chief Constable, a recent convert to Roman Catholicism, was unrepentant. 'The way I'm being treated by some critics raises the assumption that they would like to persecute me for my honestly held beliefs,' he said. 'As a Christian I was taught from childhood, in church, school and at home to seek help and guidance through prayer. I shall continue to do that.'[28] The Home Office intervened. The Chief Constable and leaders of his Police Authority were summoned to London on 22 January 1987 and an enforced truce was declared. After AIDS and prophets and body-hunting on the moors – not to mention six months of John Stalker – the Home Office was ready for Greater Manchester Police to lower its profile.

John Stalker was relieved to be out of the spotlight. With the heat now off, he was able to reconsider and reorganize his life. The future could hardly have seemed brighter. He signed up with Mersey Television, prepared articles for the *Observer* and the *Evening Standard*, discussed a television series with BBC Manchester about 'The Police We Deserve', and a Hollywood movie with the impresario David Puttnam, and director Ken Loach. He also planned to write a book, and there were talks with publishers, who were reported to be offering appetizing sums. One Fleet Street newspaper was said to be dangling six figures for a series of articles along the lines of 'My Life with Jim'. Stalker declined.

On Friday 13 March 1987 John Stalker left the police force that had been his life since that day he ran into a police station in Manchester to get out of the rain. In a valedictory piece in the *Observer*, he wrote:

I have resigned from the job I have done for almost thirty years, primarily because my family asked me to – but also because I felt no longer truly a part of it. It was also made quietly clear to me that my next and final promotion, to Chief Constable, was never going to happen.[29]

Stalker also reflected on his Northern Ireland inquiry and said that he left the police force with only one real regret – that he had never been allowed to finish the job. He was also hurt by the fact that Colin Sampson had never once sought his views on the inquiry he had taken over. 'He has not been in touch,' he wrote, 'and I must suppose that he believes my views have no value.' He concluded enigmatically, 'No convincing explanation has ever been given for my removal from the investigation, or for why Mr Sampson was asked to take it on. I believe I know the truth, but the picture is still too diffuse and strangled with legal issues for me publicly to discuss it. I *can* however say that there are people in Manchester and *elsewhere* [my emphasis] who privately admit that events last May were stupendously mishandled and I know enough to realize that some of those responsible are ashamed and embarrassed by their part in it all.'

On Wednesday, 18 March, John Stalker was the star guest on the 'Wogan' TV chat show. Terry Wogan remarked that it looked as if someone had been out to get him. 'I look at the facts,' replied Stalker. 'If you ask me as a policeman, I'm not sure. If you ask me as a man, I am.' John Stalker, the civilian, now let the conspiracy balloon float off in the air. But, those twenty days in May apart, the final indication that there was no conspiracy – at least involving Northern Ireland – lies in the outcome of the RUC inquiry that Colin Sampson took over from John Stalker. It is to this that we must finally turn.

Chapter 12

Last Tape at the Hayshed

On 23 March 1987 the final section of Colin Sampson's Northern Ireland report went to Sir John Hermon and the DPP, Sir Barry Shaw. The Home Office was well pleased with Colin Sampson's work, and with John Stalker's old team. 'What happened to the Northern Ireland inquiry was a godsend,' one highly placed official told me. 'Our concern was that no stone should be left unturned and we should finally get to the bottom of what happened. The right decisions were taken at Scarborough and its objects were achieved. There were no regrets. No one has taken Colin Sampson for a ride.' From the beginning to the end of Colin Sampson's stewardship of the Northern Ireland inquiry, he never consulted John Stalker. He never felt the need to as John Thorburn, who'd covered the fine detail from the beginning, carried on doing so under Colin Sampson and could tell him anything he wanted to know. There was probably another unspoken consideration too. John Stalker was perhaps still not trusted by key policemen in high places, even after he'd returned to work. There were strong feelings that his case should have gone to a tribunal. 'I've no sympathy for Stalker,' said one, 'none at all. We're no nearer knowing the truth of the allegations against him.'

When he officially took over the inquiry from John Stalker, Colin Sampson was hurt by any suggestion that he'd been 'nobbled', was a tool of the Conservative government or had been brought in to whitewash or cover up. To him, his own integrity was at stake, as much as that of the investigation. He was determined to see that neither was compromised. It may seem unnatural for a Chief Constable to be 'hurt', but Sampson always insisted he didn't have – or want – a thick skin; he valued his sensitivity.

John Stalker's team needed some convincing that their new leader would carry on where their old one had so abruptly left off. There was a lot of straight talking to start with. There were press reports that John Thorburn had been demoted and the team had been forced to move their quarters. Then there was a story that John Thorburn had resigned. All helped fuel the notion of a conspiracy. None of the stories was true. Any doubts the team may have had were removed when Colin Sampson, after a month at the helm, again asked Sir John Hermon to suspend two senior officers. John Stalker had made the same request fifteen months earlier and the Chief Constable had declined, although he had removed the men from operational duty. On 12 July 1986, the most important day in the Protestant marching season, a message from Sir John Hermon appeared on the force information bulletin:

1. The Force will be aware that arising out of the inquiry by Mr Stalker and his subsequent enforced leave and suspension, much ill-founded, distorted and seemingly malicious material has been published in the news media. Information has been selectively and insidiously leaked in such a way that the reputation of the RUC has been unjustly maligned and security in Northern Ireland damaged to the extent of endangering life. In order to prevent further deliberate distortion, I wish to make the force aware of the present situation.

2. In April 1985 the Deputy Chief Constable of Greater Manchester wrote to me recommending that two officers of the RUC should either be suspended from duty, or removed from operational duty. The latter course was followed. Recently, on 7 July, Mr Colin Sampson, who has assumed responsibility for this inquiry, advised me that he felt the two officers should be suspended from duty. The two officers have accordingly been suspended

after consultation with Her Majesty's Inspector of Constabulary, who is over-viewing the investigation. The same consultation procedure with Her Majesty's Inspector of Constabulary was followed in respect of the action taken by the RUC on Mr Stalker's recommendation.

3. The inquiry headed by Mr Sampson continues. For this reason and more particularly for obvious security reasons, the RUC is not divulging the names of the officers or their ranks. The news media are earnestly asked to bear this security consideration in mind.

John Thorburn was not demoted. Colin Sampson brought in ACC Donald Shaw to act as his liaison officer, as he had done on his Stalker inquiry. Thorburn carried on – not to the RUC's delight – as the cutting edge of the inquiry as he had been under John Stalker. Neither did he resign. After initial suspicions, which were not surprising given the circumstances in which the changeover was made, he recognized that Colin Sampson would finish the job that he and the team had started. Thorburn gave Sampson his loyalty, which was fully reciprocated as it was to all the team. John Thorburn retired, as he'd always intended, in November 1986 and took up a job in security. He left with no bitterness, but with anticipated satisfaction that the job had finally been well done. It was thought that Thorburn's hand drafted the detail for Sampson's report, as it had provided the detail for John Stalker's interim submission. As for the change in the team's accommodation, that was done at their request to enable them to avoid the spotlight and get on with the job.

John Stalker never learned at first hand how the riddle of the Hayshed was resolved. When he left Belfast on 30 April 1986 the relevant papers on the Hayshed were in John Thorburn's briefcase. The 'Crown Jewels' – or what there was of them – never included an actual tape. That had been destroyed shortly after the shooting. Its destruction was ordered, it appears, not because it might – or might not – contain incriminating evidence, but because it was *policy* to destroy these intelligence tapes. What Stalker perhaps had not realized (possibly because nobody had told him) was that such operations were routine: there may have been as many as a dozen of them in place in that area around Lurgan at that particular time; it may have been saturated not just with undercover policemen and soldiers following the IRA's and INLA's killing spree in 1982, but with covert surveillance operations similar to the one at the Hayshed. These and the maintenance of informants were the most crucial and secretive aspects of the government's anti-terrorist counter-offensive. 'Our intelligence is protected in deadly earnest,' one of those closely involved told me, 'because that's how we succeed. That's our life's bread. We're not just protecting a source, but our systems that have been refined and protected over many years.' The use of electronic surveillance and the rules and procedures governing what it produced were sanctioned at the highest possible level – perhaps by the Cabinet Joint Intelligence Committee which reports directly to the Prime Minister. Under these strict and top secret rules, all surveillance tapes are physically destroyed, not just wiped, once transcripts have been made of them to harvest material of intelligence value. This, I understand, is what happened to the Hayshed tape. What was also perhaps not known at the time was that there was not just *one* tape from the Hayshed but between three and four dozen, presumably covering the six-week period during which it had been under surveillance. The monitoring and recording of these tapes were also part of an elaborate and fail-safe system. The electronic device in the Hayshed which was being monitored in the Portakabin a few miles away was not just being listened to by a Special Branch constable with headphones; several army intelligence officers were there too, each with a specific role, to make sure that no scrap of intelligence was lost. The Special Branch officer had a direct line to his superior at the Tactical Co-ordinating Group at Gough Barracks. The constable was the vital operational link in the deployment of the HMSUs, while the soldiers monitored and noted what was coming over from the 'bug' and being recorded on the tape. Some wore headphones; each had a specific task. One would write a handwritten log of individual words he could make out; another would make sure that at the appropriate point the machine was automatically switched over to a new tape so there was no possibility of losing vital intelligence; and another would just listen. Other intelligence officers present had other tasks, too. It seems that the original plan formulated at the TCG was for the HMSU tasked for the operation to stop Tighe and McCauley at a VCP, once they'd left the Hayshed – presumably if they left with the guns. This is the way the 'system' normally worked, as it had with the seizure of the explosives on the hay lorry at the end of August 1982. This is why there was, under normal circumstances, never any concern about the material on the tapes because the 'evidence' required for the court was automatically supplied when the HMSUs – seemingly 'normal' policemen – just happened to intercept their quarries at a VCP. When the sound of clicks came from the Hayshed, the RUC constable is said to have put the receiver – or headphones – to his secure link to the TCG at Gough Barracks so the senior officer could hear what was going on. That was when, it seems, the order was given to go in. The HMSU apparently knew the Hayshed was under surveillance, although the extent of their knowledge is unclear.

The crucial tape was the one with the shooting recorded on it. When the incident was over, again following strict procedures, that tape was handed over with the others and signed for by a senior officer at the TCG. They were then sent in a sealed package by army courier to Belfast, where their contents, or 'product', were transcribed. The tapes would then be destroyed. I understand that the tape with the shooting on it may have been destroyed soon after the incident. When the DPP finally gave Sir John Hermon authority to release all the material related to the tapes – the transcripts, the logs, the notes and the names of the personnel involved – the team could begin to piece together what had happened. It appears there were transcripts of more than three dozen tapes which had been made during the period of surveillance. There were tapes, too, of Tighe and McCauley in the Hayshed. There were, according to the transcripts, the sound of rifle clicks and words – some of them unintelligible. That tape, which was timed from the transcript, lasted nearly ten minutes. The transcript ended with a note to the effect that there was nothing more of security interest. That tape ended a few minutes before the shooting started. The shooting itself was on the next reel but its 'product' (the transcript) may have been missing – if ever one had been made. In its absence, the crucial question of whether a warning was given *before* the shooting, as the police officers involved had insisted at the McCauley trial, could not be answered. But now with the names of the intelligence officers and the authority to interview them with all restrictions lifted, the team could take witness statements as to the sequence and nature of events. At least four of the intelligence officers in the Portakabin heard what happened in the Hayshed. The team interviewed them all. It seems some said there was a warning; others said there was not.

Remarkably, in the most dramatic twist of all, the team had other witnesses to interview who had also heard the tape. It appears that the most sensitive regulations of all had been breached. A clandestine copy of the tape seems to have been made, by whom and when was unclear. I understand it was not the Special Branch officer. The intelligence agencies had never captured an actual shooting before. The 'missing' tape was a collector's item some clearly thought worth preserving – a unique piece of memorabilia from one of the most sensitive operations in Northern Ireland. It may be that the authorities learned of the existence of this dramatic bootleg tape on which a man is shot dead from a senior MI5 training officer who was doing the rounds of 'stations' in Northern Ireland to collect material for a field course in England. If that was the case, he was certain to be horrified at what he heard and incredulous that those who had it in their possession had so little appreciation of its implications. That tape too, I understand, was subsequently destroyed. Again, at what stage is unclear. It seems that about half a dozen MI5 officers may have heard the tape. Most of them appear to have said there was no warning.

At the time of writing, what recommendations Colin Sampson has made to the DPP are not known. Neither would it be proper in the light of possible court proceedings to speculate on their *precise* nature or on the identities and ranks of the officers who may, or may not, be involved. Whatever the recommendations may be, whether covering conspiracy to pervert the course of justice, or charges involving murder, Sir Barry Shaw will first consult the Attorney-General, as was made clear in a written answer in the House of Commons on 28 January 1987:

> When the DPP (NI) receives the completed report, he will consider the question of prosecution. I have asked him to inform me fully with regard to the facts reported to him, and to consult me before any directions are given.

It may be that even if the DPP decides that the evidence does warrant a prosecution or prosecutions, after consultation with the Attorney-General, he will not proceed. Having already unsuccessfully prosecuted four police officers in relation to the shootings of Grew and Carroll, and Toman, Burns and McKerr, Sir Barry Shaw has to be as sure as he can that he will not lose again. He may also decide that the evidence is not strong enough to prosecute senior officers and that, in their absence, it would be unfair and improper to put junior ranks through the courts. In addition it may also be that officers who were prepared to give evidence to the Stalker–Sampson inquiry might be reluctant to do so for criminal proceedings against their colleagues.

But there is another overriding consideration which could apply and prevent prosecutions, however strong the evidence. The Attorney-General could rule that prosecutions would not be in the public interest. This is not a statutory power he has at his disposal but a discretionary authority rooted in custom and practice. Under the tradition of English criminal law, the Attorney-General and the Director of Public Prosecutions intervene to direct a prosecution only when they consider it in the public interest. Clearly in 99.9 per cent of cases, the public interest *is* best served by bringing criminal wrongdoers to justice. But there may be rare exceptions when the public interest is best served by prosecutions being waived. The principle was most clearly and fully elucidated by Labour's Attorney-General, Sir Hartley Shawcross, when he addressed the House of Commons in 1951. He prefaced his remarks by making it clear that 'there is only one consideration which is altogether excluded, and that is the repercussion of a given decision upon my personal or my party's or the government's political fortunes; that is a consideration which never enters into account.' He then defined what the 'public interest' was and the extent to which Cabinet colleagues would be consulted. (All these procedures would be germane to matters arising from the Stalker and Sampson inquiries.)

I think the true doctrine is that it is the duty of an Attorney-General in deciding whether or not to authorize the prosecution to acquaint himself with all the relevant facts, including, for instance, the effect which the prosecution, successful or unsuccessful as the case may be, would have upon *public morale and order, and with any other consideration affecting public policy.* In order so to inform himself, he may, although I do not think he is obliged to, consult with any of his colleagues in the government and indeed . . . he would in some cases be a fool if he did not. On the other hand, the assistance of his colleagues is confined to informing him of particular considerations which might affect his own decision, and does not consist, and must not consist, in telling him what that decision ought to be. The responsibility for the eventual decision rests with the Attorney-General, and he is not to be put, and is not put, under pressure by his colleagues in the matter . . . it is the Attorney-General, applying his judicial mind, who has to be the sole judge of those considerations.[1] [my emphasis]

It is possible, although by no means certain, that the Attorney-General, Sir Michael Havers, may decide in consultation with Mrs Thatcher and her Cabinet colleagues, and in particular with Tom King, the Northern Ireland Secretary, that the effects on 'public morale and order', with particular reference to Northern Ireland, would render prosecutions unwise in the public interest. The effect on the RUC, still holding the line on the Anglo-Irish agreement, would no doubt fall within this definition. But there are also other areas which may come under the wider heading of 'any other consideration affecting public policy' – not least the sensitivities involved in the use of informers, the 'national assets', and covert operations run by MI5 and other intelligence agencies. In the end, assuming the evidence exists, the Attorney-General and the DPP have to make a finely balanced judgement: whether the public interest is best served by directing prosecutions of police officers or by wiping the slate clean. To take the latter course, after all the traumas, controversies and drama of almost five years, would provoke a public outcry, although the sting may be drawn somewhat if a judicial (or similar) inquiry were to be announced. Neither is it likely that a great deal would come out at the inquests which have still to be held. The rules governing coroners' courts in Northern Ireland are very strict. Juries have no power to return a verdict. They are only allowed to make 'findings'. And they can no longer make a finding of 'unlawful killing', now being strictly confined to establishing 'who the deceased was, how, when and where he came by his death'.[2] No coroner's court could even begin to answer, for example, the crucial questions that arise from the Hayshed:

1. What was on the tape recorded at the moment of the shooting?

2. Who made the clandestine tape and who destroyed it?

3. What were the rifles doing in the Hayshed?

4. On what grounds was Home Office approval given for the surveillance?

5. At what political level was it approved?

6. How many similar operations were protected by cover stories?

Even if prosecutions are directed, some of these questions may never be answered.

But the overriding question, which was the genesis of my search for the truth and which lies at the heart of these extraordinary events, is whether justice will be seen to be done. If it is, however painful the process, our institutions, which have been severely tested by the violence in Northern Ireland, will be strengthened by it. The final chapter has still to be written.

Chronology

1956
John Stalker joins Manchester City Police Cadet Force

1958
Stalker appointed Constable

1961
Stalker joins CID

1964
Stalker becomes Detective Sergeant

Early 1960s
Kevin Taylor – professional gambler in London

1968
Stalker becomes Detective Inspector

Late 1960s
Taylor returns to Manchester and establishes Vanland

1971 (approx.)
Stalker meets Taylor at school fund-raiser

1972
Taylor develops land near Strangeways

1973
Stalker positively vetted

1974
Stalker becomes Detective Chief Inspector

1976
> Stalker becomes Detective Superintendent
> James Anderton becomes Chief Constable of GMP

1978
> Stalker becomes Detective Chief Superintendent and head of Warwickshire CID

Late 1970s
> Taylor converts mill into luxury home

1979
> Taylor stands as Conservative candidate in local elections

1980
> Stalker returns to GMP as Assistant Chief Constable

1981

February	Taylor buys *Diogenes* in Miami
June	Taylor entertains four members of QSG on board *Diogenes* in Miami
December	Taylor and Stalker holiday on *Diogenes* and cruise the Bahamas

1982

2 January	Taylor's fiftieth birthday party
6 August	*Diogenes* arrives in Puerto Banus
29 August	Hay lorry of IRA explosives discovered
27 October	Kinnego IRA landmine kills three RUC officers
11 November	Toman, Burns and McKerr shot dead by HMSU
24 November	Tighe killed and McCauley wounded at Hayshed by HMSU
12 December	Grew and Carroll shot dead by HMSU

1983
> Stalker on RCDS course

June	DPP (NI) directs reinvestigation of three incidents. DCC McAtamney in charge. Attorney-General waives Official Secrets Act

1984

1 March	Stalker appointed Deputy Chief Constable of GMP
3 April	Constable John Robinson acquitted of murder of Seamus Grew
24 May	Stalker appointed to head NI inquiry
4 June	Sergeant Montgomery and Constables Brannigan and Frederick Nigel Robinson acquitted of murder of Eugene Toman
11 June	CS McGourlay mentions golf course conversation to CS Topping
17 July	CS Topping submits confidential report on allegations. Report received by Anderton
22 August	Armagh coroner resigns
4 September	David Burton sentenced to two years for fraud
Autumn	Anderton targets drug traffickers for 1985
	Stalker and team discover existence of MI5 tape recordings made at the Hayshed

1985

January	Stalker meets with MI5 in London
2 February	*Diogenes* into Dartmouth
15 February	McCauley found guilty of possessing rifles in the Hayshed
February	Stalker requests access to the 'mole's' file
	GMP Drugs Intelligence Unit set up (DIU)
February–	DIU officers interview Burton in Preston
March	Prison
	Special Unit set up to investigate Taylor and his relationship with the QSG
14 March	*Olympus Nova* into Dartmouth
March	Burton dies in prison of natural causes
	Anderton informs Sir Philip Myers about allegations
	Stalker requests access to tape and transcripts
(approx.)	Stalker informed targeted by IRA

April	Stalker requests Sir John Hermon to suspend two officers
	Stalker requests personal access to the 'mole'
1 April	Bill of sale of *Diogenes*
16 May (approx.)	*Diogenes* in Guernsey
June	Stalker meets MI5 in London with Sir John Hermon
7 August	Taylor's twentieth wedding anniversary dinner
	Taylor hears he's being investigated
18 September	Stalker delivers interim report to Sir John Hermon
	Stalker learns Taylor under investigation
23 November	Stalker attends Conservative autumn ball
December	Taylor's solicitors contact GMP

1986

15 January	Stalker tells Anderton he's distancing himself from Taylor
13 February	Hermon submits Stalker interim report to DPP
4 March	DPP directs 'open sesame' on tape
12 March	GMP obtain orders of access to Taylor's bank accounts
30 April	Stalker visits Belfast
9 May	Taylor's home and office searched by GMP
15 May	CS Roberts reports conversation with Taylor's solicitor to CS Topping
17–18 May	Home Office weekend consultations
19 May	Scarborough meeting
27 May	'The Last Supper'
28 May	Stalker phoned by Clerk to Police Authority
29 May	Stalker sees Colin Sampson
30 May	Police Authority announces Stalker on extended leave pending investigation of alleged disciplinary offence

6 June	Stalker press conference
	Announcement that Sampson is to head NI inquiry
16 June	BBC TV *Panorama* reveals MI5 'bug' in Hayshed
30 June	Stalker suspended
12 July	Hermon agrees to suspend two officers at Sampson's request
6 August	Sampson completes Stalker investigation
22 August	Stalker reinstated by GMP
23 September	Taylor's solicitors issue summons for disclosure against Anderton
14 October	Beryl Taylor applies for summons against Anderton, Chief Superintendent Topping and Detective Inspector Stephenson
15 October	Application for disclosure heard by Mr Justice Scott. Application rejected
24 November	Anderton granted application for judicial review of summons brought by Beryl Taylor

1987

4 February	Spanish police announce breaking of 'Octopus' drug-smuggling ring
27 February	Hearing of judicial review
13 March	Stalker leaves GMP
16 March	Stalker joins Mersey Television
23 March	Sampson delivers final section of NI report to Sir John Hermon and DPP
3 April	Summons brought by Beryl Taylor quashed by judicial review

Appendix 1

Statement from the Bench of Lord Justice Gibson

Having regard to the widespread publicity which parts of my judgment in the recent trial of three police officers for murders have received and the observations which have been made upon it in the press and elsewhere, I have considered it desirable to clarify my views on two matters.

First, I would point out that my observations related to the particular circumstances of that occasion and ought not to be read out of context. I would wish most emphatically to repudiate any idea that I would approve or that the law would countenance what has been described as a shoot-to-kill policy on the part of the police.

Like every other member of the public they have no right, in any circumstances, to use more force than appears to be reasonably necessary having regard to all the circumstances as understood by them.

They stand in a different position from other citizens only in that they have greater duties imposed upon them in relation to the arrest of suspected criminals and often face greater dangers which may necessitate the use of correspondingly greater force in exercise of their right of self-defence and which may, in the last resort, require the degree of force used in this case.

Secondly, I understand that in some quarters certain further words of mine have been thought to mean that I was contemplating that the police force might be regarded as entitled to mete out summary justice by means of the bullet.

I do not believe that on any fair analysis my words were

capable of that interpretation. Indeed, nothing was further from my mind, nor would I or any other judge contemplate for a second that such a view was tenable.

The Yellow Card (British Army) 1980

RESTRICTED
Army Code No. 70771

Instructions for Opening Fire in Northern Ireland
General Rules
1. In all situations you are to use the minimum force necessary. FIREARMS MUST ONLY BE USED AS A LAST RESORT.
2. Your weapon must always be made safe: that is, NO live round is to be carried in the breech and in the case of automatic weapons the working parts are to be forward, unless you are ordered to carry a live round in the breech or you are about to fire.

Challenging
3. A challenge MUST be given before opening fire unless:
   (a) to do so would increase the risk of death or grave injury to you or any other person.
   (b) you or others in the immediate vicinity are being engaged by terrorists.
4. You are to challenge by shouting:
'ARMY: STOP OR I FIRE' or words to that effect.

Opening Fire
5. You may only open fire against a person:
   (a) if he* is committing or about to commit an act LIKELY TO ENDANGER LIFE AND THERE IS NO OTHER

* 'She' can be read instead of 'he' if applicable.

WAY TO PREVENT THE DANGER. The following are some examples of acts where life could be endangered, dependent always upon the circumstances:

(1) firing or being about to fire a weapon;
(2) planting, detonating or throwing an explosive device (including a petrol bomb);
(3) deliberately driving a vehicle at a person and there is no other way of stopping him;*

(b) if you know that he* has just killed or injured any person by such means and he* does not surrender if challenged and THERE IS NO OTHER WAY TO MAKE AN ARREST.

6. If you have to open fire you should:
  (a) fire only aimed shots;
  (b) fire no more rounds than are necessary;
  (c) take all reasonable precautions not to injure anyone other than your target.

* 'She' can be read instead of 'he' if applicable.

Appendix 3

Home Office Guidelines on the Use of Informers

INFORMANTS WHO TAKE PART IN CRIME

1.92 Informants, properly employed, are essential to criminal investigation and, within limits, they ought to be protected. The risks attached to their employment are obvious, however, and safeguards are needed before use is made of an informant taking part in crime. Circumstances vary so widely that it is difficult to establish rules of general application; but the following points have been agreed upon by the Central Conference of Chief Constables:

(a) No member of a police force, and no public informant, should counsel, incite or procure the commission of a crime.

(b) Where an informant gives the police information about the intention of others to commit a crime in which they intend that he shall play a part, his participation should be allowed to continue only where:
  (i) he does not actively engage in planning and committing the crime;
  (ii) he is intended to play a minor role; and
  (iii) his participation is essential to enable the police to frustrate the principal criminals and to arrest them (albeit for lesser offences such as attempt or conspiracy to commit the crime, or carrying offensive weapons) before injury is done to any person or serious damage to property.

210

The informant should always be instructed that he must on no account act as *agent provocateur*, whether by suggesting to others that they should commit offences or encouraging them to do so, and that if he is found to have done so he will himself be liable to prosecution.

(c) The police must never commit themselves to a course which, whether to protect an informant or otherwise, will constrain them to mislead a court in any subsequent proceedings. This must always be regarded as a prime consideration when deciding whether, and in what manner, an informant may be used and how far, if at all, he is to be allowed to take part in an offence. If his use in the way envisaged will, or is likely to, result in its being impossible to protect him without subsequently misleading the court, that must be regarded as a decisive reason for his not being so used or not being protected.

(d) The need to protect an informant does not justify granting him immunity from arrest or prosecution for the crime if he fully participates in it with the requisite intent (still less in respect of any other crime he has committed or may in future commit).

(e) The handling of informants calls for the judgement of an experienced officer. There must be complete confidence and frankness between supervising officers and subordinates; and a decision to use a participating informant should be taken at senior level.

(f) Payment to informants from public funds should be supervised by a senior officer.

(g) Where an informant has been used who has taken part in the commission of a crime for which others have been arrested, the prosecuting solicitor, counsel, and (where he is concerned) the Director of Public Prosecutions should be informed of the fact and of the part that the informant took in the commission of the offence, although, subject to (c) above, not necessarily of his identity.

IRA statement concerning the 'execution' of David McVeigh

The following is the text of a statement issued to our office from the Irish Republican Army.

'The Irish Republican Army claims responsibility for the execution last night of David McVeigh, of Victoria Street, Lurgan.

McVeigh was an IRA volunteer dismissed with ignominy for treachery.

The IRA have been aware for some time that information concerning IRA operations in the Lurgan area was being passed on to the Crown forces. After exhaustive inquiries, evidence was gathered which identified David McVeigh as the source of this information. He was arrested and when confronted with the evidence of his activities he admitted his role as an informer.

In his statement of admission McVeigh revealed that he first began working for the RUC following his arrest in connection with an explosion at Lurgan golf club in 1982.

From January 1983 he met the RUC on a three-weekly basis. These meetings took place at Tannaghmore School, Kinnego Marina and Lurgan golf club. Each meeting was held on a Wednesday night and McVeigh was instructed to ring 6585 between 8 p.m. and 9.30 p.m. on that night and ask for his handlers whose code names were 'George' and 'Jim'. He was told to use the name 'Davy' when telephoning. His last meeting was on 20 August and his next meeting was due for 17 September.

At each of these meetings he received a payment of £20. He was also helped financially to go on holidays and while in Dublin during 1984 he travelled home at weekends, made contact with his handlers and gave information concerning the movement of known Republicans in the Dublin area.

During the three years in which McVeigh worked for the RUC he was involved in six separate incidents in which he passed on information which led to the arrest of five Republicans and the seizure of explosives, weapons and ammunition. On these occasions he was given bonus payments of up to £200 each time.

To ingratiate himself even further with his RUC handlers McVeigh passed on information about two IRA operations, an ambush on an RUC patrol and a landmine, with the intention of wiping out those volunteers involved in the operation. This failed only because volunteers on the ground noticed unusual RUC/British Army activity and aborted the operations.'

Republican Press Centre
10 September 1986

Letter from GMP senior officers

The departure of John Stalker

During the whole of the 'John Stalker affair' there were many occasions when chief officers in the force felt a pressing need to respond to adverse public references and innuendo affecting them individually and collectively. We refrained from doing so for obvious reasons, not least of which was a genuine desire to channel our efforts and energies into serving the public of Greater Manchester (which they have every right to expect) at a particularly difficult time.

We have now decided that our silence on some issues cannot continue any longer in the light of recent television and press reports.

It has been suggested, more than once, that John Stalker was 'frozen out' of the decision-making process by chief officers adopting by-pass practices which channelled administrative and policy matters direct to the Chief Constable.

The facts are that John *was* involved in the decision-making process in exactly the same way as he had been before his suspension. There was great sympathy for him at chief officer level because of the stress and personal anguish which he and his family suffered, and special efforts were made to assist him with what was seen as a re-entry problem. Consultation was part of that process, as was the examination of correspondence and reports passed to him by assistant chief constables. Furthermore, his chairmanship of the chief officers policy committee continued as before. In short, the Deputy Chief Constable was

214

involved in the management of the force in a way that everybody would expect of the Deputy in any force.

One further point is worthy of comment.

In any healthy corporate management team there is room for different management styles, personalities and approaches to the realities of modern-day policing. The daily working environment at senior level should allow officers the freedom to express to the Chief Constable a firm and, if necessary, blunt point of view about his policies and public profile. That environment has always existed in this force and it is unfortunate, to say the least, that specific criticisms of the Chief Constable's personal style of management have been voiced by his former Deputy, *not within the management team*, but in retirement. It is sad that a senior officer who has distinguished himself in so many ways, and who has been such an amiable friend and colleague, should leave the force on such a bitter note.

For our part we do not relish having to write in this way, but we have been left with no alternative.

Glyn James, Paul Whitehouse, Ralph Lees, Dan Crompton, John Phillips, Bernard Divine, *Assistant Chief Constables, GMP*

From *Police Review*, 27 March 1987

References

Chapter One

1. *Panorama* 'Coincidence or Conspiracy?', BBC Television, 16 June 1986.
2. Annex to RCDA 11/04, 5 February 1987.
3. *Ibid.*
4. *Ibid.*

Chapter Three

1. Peter Taylor, *Beating the Terrorists? Interrogation in Omagh, Gough and Castlereagh.* Penguin Special 1980, p. 22.
2. *Ibid*, p. 328.
3. *Ibid*, p. 324.
4. Lieutenant Colonel Michael Dewar, RGJ, *The British Army in Northern Ireland*, Arms and Armour Press 1985, p. 232.
5. W. D. Flackes, *Northern Ireland, A Political Directory*, Gill and MacMillan, Dublin, 1980, p. 286.
6. Desmond Hamill, *Pig in the Middle, The Army In Northern Ireland 1969–1984.* Methuen, London, 1985, p. 269.
7. *The British Army in Northern Ireland*, *op. cit.*, p. 173.
8. *Belfast Telegraph*, 5 March 1983.
9. *Pig in the Middle*, *op. cit.*, p. 257
10. *Irish News*, 23 June 1984.
11. Kader Asmal, *Shoot to Kill?* International Lawyers' Inquiry into the Lethal Use of Firearms by the Security

Forces in Northern Ireland, Mercia Press, Dublin, 1985, pp. 75–6.

12. *Ibid*, p. 77.
13. Criminal Law Act (Northern Ireland) 1967, section 3(1).
14. *Regina* v. *William James Montgomery, David Brannigan and Frederick Nigel Robinson*. Judgment of the Right Hon. Lord Justice Gibson at Belfast Crown Court, 5 June 1984.
15. *Regina* v. *John Robinson*, Belfast Crown Court. Judgment of the Hon. Mr Justice MacDermott.
16. *Panorama*, 'Justice under Fire', BBC Television, 12 November 1984.
17. *Ibid*.
18. *Ibid*.
19. *Shoot to Kill?*, *op. cit.*, p. 83.
20. *Ibid*, p. 85.
21. Peter Taylor, 'The Semantics of Political Violence'. Essay in *Communicating Politics. Mass Communications and the Political Process*. Edited by Peter Golding, Graham Murdoch and Philip Schlesinger, Leicester University Press, 1986, p. 221.
22. Updated statistics supplied by Dr Stephen Greer, Lecturer in Law, University of Bristol.
23. RUC Press Statement, 21 November 1986.
24. Frank Doherty, *The Stalker Affair*, Mercia Press, 1986, p. 37.
25. From the court transcript *Regina* v. *John Robinson*, 26 March 1984.
26. *Panorama*, 'Justice under Fire', *op cit*.

Chapter Four

1. Frank Kitson, *Low-Intensity Operations. Subversion, Insurgency and Peace-Keeping*. Faber and Faber, 1971, p. 96.
2. Richard Deacon, *'C', A Biography of Sir Maurice Oldfield, Head of MI6*. MacDonald, 1985, p. 168.
3. *Ibid*.
4. *Ibid*.

5. *Regina* v. *Thomas Charles McCormick*, Belfast Crown Court, 9 March 1983 (take from court transcripts which also form the basis of the account).
6. Kevin Kelley, *The Longest War. Northern Ireland and the IRA*. Brandon, 1982, p. 155.
7. *Regina* v. *McCormick*, Judgment and sentence by the Hon. Mr Justice Murray at Belfast Crown Court, 2 April 1982.
8. *Pig in the Middle*, *op. cit.*, p. 214.
9. *Evening News*, 13 October 1977 and *The Times*, 5 November 1977.
10. *Pig in the Middle*, *op. cit.*, p. 216.
11. *Daily Telegraph*, 11 November 1978.
12. *Pig in the Middle*, *op cit.*, p. 220.
13. *Beating the Terrorists? op. cit.*, pp. 345–7.
14. *Pig in the Middle*, *op. cit.*, p 246.
15. *Ibid*, p. 247.
16. *Ibid*, p. 248.
17. *The British Army in Northern Ireland*, *op. cit.*, p. 160.
18. *Pig in the Middle*, *op. cit.*, p. 221.
19. David Charters, Dominick Graham and Maurice Tugwell, *Trends in Low Intensity Conflict*. Operational Research and Analysis Establishment (ORAE), Dept of National Defense, Ottawa, Canada. ORAE extra-mural paper No. 16, August 1981.

Chapter Five

1. Official Secrets Act 1920, section 9 (1) (a).
2. Home Office Consolidated Circular to the Police on Crime and Kindred Matters, 1.92 (c).
3. *Regina* v. *Montgomery*, *Brannigan and Robinson*, Judgment of the Right Hon. Lord Justice Gibson, *op. cit.*
4. *Ibid*.
5. Transcript of evidence of the trial of Martin McCauley before the Right Hon. Lord Justice Kelly on 15–18, 21 and 22 January 1985. (Note: all the other direct quotes in this chapter of the court proceedings in the McCauley case are taken from the transcript of the trial.)

6. *Regina* v. *John Robinson*, *op cit*. (The subsequent quotations are taken from the transcript of the trial.)
7. Government statement on alleged RUC activities in this state following meeting of the Taoiseach with the British Ambassador, 5 April 1984.
8. Statement by the Taoiseach, Dr Garret FitzGerald, TD in Dail Eireann on 10 April 1984, relating to the incursion in our jurisdiction by members of the RUC in December 1982.
9. *Daily Telegraph*, 'Coroner quits over "irregularities" in RUC files' (undated), DT No. 40180.

Chapter Six

1. The Prosecution of Offences (Northern Ireland) Order 1972, section 6 (3). Statutory Instrument 1972, No. 538 (M.I.1).
2. *Belfast Telegraph*, 7 May 1983. Other references for the death of Eric Dale are to be found in the *Irish Times*, 9 May 1983; *Irish News*, 9 May 1983.
3. *Irish News*, 9 May 1983.
4. Patsy McArdle, *The Secret War*. Mercia Press 1984, p. 49.
5. *Ibid*, p. 48.
6. *Irish News*, 9 April 1984.
7. Consolidated Circular to the Police on Crime and Kindred Matters, *op. cit.* 1.92. (b).

Chapter Seven

1. *Irish Times*, 30 August 1982. Also, *Guardian*, 30 August 1982; *Newsletter*, 30 August 1982.
2. Northern Ireland Prosecution of Offences Order, *op. cit.*, section 5 (1).

Chapter Eight

1. David Leigh, Paul Lashmar and Jonathan Foster, *Observer*, 28 September 1986.
2. *Ibid*.

Chapter Nine

1. *Blackpool Evening Gazette*, 1 November 1985.
2. *The Sunday Times*, 8 February 1987.
3. *Daily Telegraph*, 6 February 1987.
4. *Sunday Today*, 6 February 1987.
5. *Daily Star*, 6 February 1987.
6. *Daily Express*, 7 February 1987.
7. *Nota Informativa*, Comisaria de Policia, Marbella. 4 February 1987. Also for detailed Spanish accounts see: *La Tribuna*, 6–7 February 1987; *El Diario de la Costa del Sol*, 6 February 1987; *Sur*, 6 February 1987.
8. *El Diario de la Costa del Sol*, 26 September 1986.

Chapter Ten

1. Draft judgment, 'The Queen v. Bury Justices Ex Parte Anderton, C. J. and ORS', 3 April 1987.

Chapter Eleven

1. Greater Manchester Police Authority press statement, 29 May 1986
2. Press statement by James Anderton, Chief Constable of Greater Manchester Police relating to a matter affecting the Deputy Chief Constable, 30 May 1986.
3. *Manchester Evening News*, 31 May 1986.
4. *Panorama*, 'Coincidence or Conspiracy?', *op. cit.*
5. *Guardian*, 7 August 1986.
6. *The Times*, 1 August 1986.
7. *The Sunday Times Magazine*, 29 March 1987, p. 70.
8. *The Times*, 7 June 1986.
9. *Manchester Evening News*, 10 June 1986.
10. 'The Queen v. Bury Justices', *op. cit.*
11. Police Complaints Authority news release, 14 August 1986.
12. *Ibid.*
13. The Police (Discipline) (Senior Officers) Regulations 1985, regs. 12 and 13. Statutory Instrument 1985, No. 519. HMSO.

14. *Manchester Evening News*, 21 August 1986.
15. *Ibid.*
16. *Guardian*, 23 August 1986.
17. *Ibid.*
18. *Police*, 1 September 1986.
19. *Guardian*, 20 December 1986.
20. *Guardian*, 16 October 1986.
21. *Guardian*, 27 February 1987.
22. The Queen v. Bury Justices, *op cit.*
23. *Guardian*, 21 January 1987.
24. *Ibid.*
25. *Ibid.*
26. *Ibid.*
27. *Manchester Evening News*, 20 January 1987.
28. *Ibid.*
29. *Observer*, 15 March 1987.

Chapter Twelve

1. J. Ll. J. Edwards, LL.D. (Cantab), *The Law Officers of the Crown. A study of the offices of Attorney-General and Solicitor-General of England with an account of the office of the Director of Public Prosecutions of England.* Sweet and Maxwell, 1964, pp. 222–3.
2. *Shoot to Kill?*, *op. cit.*, p. 112.

Bibliography

Asmal, Kader, *Shoot to Kill?* International Lawyers' Inquiry into the Lethal use of Firearms by the Security Forces in Northern Ireland, Mercia Press, 1985

Bell, J. Bowyer, *The IRA, The Secret Army 1916–1979*, The Academy Press, Dublin, 1979

Boyle, K., Hadden, T. and Hillyard, P., *Law and the State, the Case of Northern Ireland*, Martin Robertson, London, 1975

Boyle, K., Hadden, T. and Hillyard P., *Ten Years On in Northern Ireland. The legal control of political violence*, The Cobden Trust, 1980

Coogan, Tim Pat, *The IRA*, Fontana, 1980

Deacon, Richard, *'C', A Biography of Sir Maurice Oldfield, Head of MI6*, MacDonald, 1985

Dewar, Lieutenant Colonel Michael, *The British Army in Northern Ireland*, Arms and Armour Press, 1985

Doherty, Frank, *The Stalker Affair*, Mercia Press, 1986

Evelegh, Robin, *Peace-Keeping in a Democratic Society. The Lessons of Northern Ireland*, C. Hurst & Co., 1978

Flackes, W. D., *Northern Ireland, A Political Directory, 1968–1979*, Gill and Macmillan, Dublin, 1980

Hamill, Desmond, *Pig in the Middle. The Army in Northern Ireland 1969–1979*, Methuen, 1985

Bibliography

Kelley, Kevin, *The Longest War. Northern Ireland and the IRA*, Brandon, 1982

Kitson, Frank, *Low-Intensity Operations. Subversion, Insurgency and Peace-Keeping*, Faber and Faber, 1971

McArdle, Patsy, *The Secret War*, Mercia Press, 1984

Moloney, E. and Pollack, A., *Paisley*, Poolbeg Press Ltd, 1986

Index